PERCEIVER

The Perceiver Trilogy Book One

E. C. FULLER

A WHIFF OF GASOLINE

A figure stood stretched and alien on a distant hill. As the car rounded a second hill, the figure vanished behind the waving switchgrass and wild rye.

"Did you see that?" Hattie asked her parents. Their trip was in its final stages. Her mom's head lolled on her shoulder and her dad drove in tired but pleasant expectation.

"See what?" asked her dad.

"Look. There!" The land fell back. Sure enough, there was someone on the hill, someone like an afternoon shadow, thin and elongated. Her mom craned her head and squinted.

"There's nobody there. Don't stare at the sun."

But Hattie wasn't staring at the sun; she was staring at the figure. Was she the only one who could see it? Maybe she had spots in her eyes from the strong afternoon sunlight, but were spots people-shaped?

"I dunno, that looks like somebody."

"Well, I don't see it." Her mom twisted in her seat to face her directly. Cassandra Flores was pretty, with pink cheeks, dark-brown hair curling over her shoulders, and the bright, sharp look of someone with something to say. But however she stood or sat, whatever her posture, she always gave the impression that she was about to fold her arms over her chest. Hattie's heart deflated. She recognized the beginnings of a *talk*. "Listen, Hattie. I wanted to talk to you about...Well, you know." Her mom smiled at her. "You. You've got to be more *out there*. Do you understand?" Hattie did understand but didn't like it. She was good enough at soccer that she would be welcomed in a game. What more did she need to do? "I want you to be more social now that we've moved to a new place. This is a new start. I want you to have more friends. And I want people to have a good impression of you. That's how you make friends and get ahead in life: by making good impressions."

Her dad cut in, "Personally, I think if you make one good friend, that's better than a passel of them." Plump, with a trimmed, black beard, combed black hair, and a green argyle sweater-vest, he had the attitude of someone taking a long pleasant stroll. His new position as a computer engineer made him shine with cheerfulness.

"I guess," said Hattie slowly. Her mom broke out in a relieved, genuine smile.

"Good! Well, you have all summer before school starts to make friends."

Hattie's plans for the move did not involve making friends. In their old neighborhood, Hattie had one friend, a tiny girl she had befriended in kindergarten. Their houses were close enough that Hattie could run out her door, hammer on her friend's door, and yell "Kate! I found a nest of ladybugs! Come see!"

She would later find the scientific name of the ladybugs in the library reference books. Her eyes would drift down the page, down the Latin names which looked like spell words. She could be lost in her world learning the names of ladybugs, grasses, and birds, not minding that she did this alone.

She had a goal to learn how to braid her dark-brown hair to keep it out of her penny-round face and penny-bright eyes. Her newest plan was to not be like her mom, who thought it was fine to ignore the uncanny.

* * *

They moved at the beginning of the summer, two weeks after school let out. Their car trundled along the bends in the road, heavy with their belongings. The prairie hills smoothed, and dogwoods dotted the grass, their branches hanging over the road so that mottled sun licked the car. Houses peeked through the trunks in flashes of painted siding and brick. Finally, the trees fell away and before them sat their new neighborhood with its green lawns shining from the water of whisking sprinklers. Hattie thought that this place might be okay but was too loyal to Kate to say it out loud.

Hattie's new house was blue as an elephant and two stories tall. Inside was wood floors and white walls with a narrow stair to the second floor.

"Your room is upstairs," said her dad, hoisting her backpack out of the trunk and handing it to her. "Go see. And tell me if anything needs to be fixed before I leave to meet my boss."

Her room was behind a small door on the left side of the hall. The seashell-blue walls were freshly painted; the chemical smell lingered. The large window on the wall directly across from the door—*her* new window, she told herself—framed a strand of birch in the backyard. The house ticked and creaked like a ship at sea in the raging wind.

She took out her notebooks and toys and arranged them on the dresser. They didn't look as good as they did on her old dresser in her old room. She didn't understand why they had to move when her dad's old job was perfectly fine. She didn't know what *higher salary* and *corporate benefits* meant and was angry enough not to care.

Her dad had soothed her by saying, "You can call Kate whenever you want!" But why not just stay so she could *see* her whenever she wanted? She did have other friends, but Kate was her best friend. Now, she didn't know when, or if, she would see her again.

Her mind drifted back to the person on the hill. What if she would never figure out if the ice cream man really lost his eye in a fight with a terrorist or if the seventh-grade biology teacher really did give donuts to kids who got As on tests? Maybe that person was still there. She thundered down the stairs—already a new pleasure, to thunder down stairs—and ventured outside.

It was one of those summer days where the heat simmered pleasantly, the grass breathed out a nice roasted smell, and clouds built up into castles. Behind the house, the backyard was hemmed by a toothy fence. Beyond the fence, apple trees. They stooped over fallen apples, which littered the ground and released their sickly-sweet odor. She had overheard her dad tell her mom that there was an old apple orchard nearby, but he hadn't said how close. She squeezed through the fence and walked under their branches to explore.

As she hiked on, the pale gold grass grew as high as her waist and buzzed with insects. Soon the trees stopped being neatly ordered and began to crowd out the sunlight.

"What are you doing here?"

Hattie jumped. A boy stood not far from her, where the light was dimmest. He had thick black hair parted to one side and black eyes. Every bit of him was thin and long, even his mouth and nose. He looked distinctly *wrong* in a way that she couldn't put her finger on.

"I'm just walking," she said. "What are you doing here?"

He took one step and covered two yards. His mouth cinched tight and one eyebrow arched in suspicion. He looked older than her, not by much, but old enough that an adult might listen to him if he decided to get her in trouble. "How did you get in?"

"I walked. I live over there." She pointed. "I'm Hattie. I just moved here." She could not help feeling slightly unsettled by him. Up close, she understood what unsettled her: his arms, legs, and fingers were longer than normal and they seemed to bend like rubber, rather than hinge at the joints. "What's your name?"

"Jack," he said in a clipped voice. "Hate to be rude, but you need to leave before my uncle finds out you crossed the boundary. He won't be happy."

"Boundary?" Hattie asked. "The fence?"

"Yeah...a fence. You really shouldn't be here," he added. "He doesn't like trespassers."

"Oh. I guess I'll see you around then?"

"Sure." He didn't move except to fold his arms, and she realized he wanted to watch her go.

"Well...nice to meet you." She intended to walk back up the road, but she was caught coming out of the orchard. Her mom's hands jumped to her hips, and Hattie instinctively tuned out the scolding. But she couldn't escape. Under her mom's eye, she trudged back inside to help unpack. She was left frustrated and aching to know who was on that hill and what Jack was doing in the orchard.

* * *

Sometime shortly after dinner, she heard the front door opening and her mom's voice. "Oh hello! It's nice to meet you!"

"It's nice to meet you too," said a familiar voice. She missed what followed, so she cracked open her bedroom door to listen.

She heard her mom say, "Traveling consultants! For what?"

A different, new voice answered her. "All kinds of things. We travel to all parts of the country to talk to people about the problems in their lives and teach them how to fix them. It's a very rewarding job. We have our own practice and a very generous salary." The owner of the voice sounded like he had a head cold and was reading from a bad script.

"Hattie? Hattie, come meet our new neighbors!"

Hattie went down the stairs into the dining room. Four strangers sat at the dining table, chatting with her parents. There was a man and a woman both with inflated, shiny, pink skin, butter-yellow hair, and forearms as round as hams. One of the people at the table was the boy from the woods. His eyebrows jumped when he saw her, but he quickly became interested in the half-eaten pizza on the table. The fourth person, a teenage girl, was skeletal with ghostly blonde hair like cobwebs and a dreamy, bored face. Her skin was so transparent that Hattie could see delicate blue veins through her arms and neck. She studied the floorboards and did not move to acknowledge Hattie in any way. One hand made secret movements, as if spelling words in air with her fingers.

"Everyone," said her mom with a gracious movement toward her. "This is my daughter, Hattie."

"Pleased to meet you," said the two other adults together, as if rehearsed.

"We are the Lipid family," said the man in a voice as high as a mosquito's.

"I'm Jack," said the boy, leaping up for a handshake. He gripped her hand until she squirmed. "It's nice to meet you," he said, holding her gaze. She caught the significance and, in confusion, could only nod. She guessed that he didn't want her to admit she'd been trespassing in front of his parents.

"This is Jane, my...cousin," Jack added.

"Hi," said Hattie politely. Jane ignored her.

Her mom didn't miss the rudeness, but also didn't call attention to it. Instead, she addressed Jack and Jane. "So what school are you two attending? Hattie's only twelve, so she'll be going to Applewood Middle School."

"We're not going to school," said Jack stiffly. "We'll be working with our uncle En Law in his practice and then we'll move to another town."

"Unfortunately," the fat man squeaked, "because there are so few specialized consultants in this world, we must travel to make sure as many people benefit from our services as possible. And En Law is the best. Everyone wants to have him."

"Maybe we can meet him sometime," said her mom. "Where is Mr. Law's practice?"

"En Law," said the woman, enunciating each word. "His first

name is two words. Common mistake. His practice isn't on the main road. Take Gunter Road through the forest straight there and you can't miss it."

Hattie's dad was standing a little off to the side, nodding occasionally and eyeing the half-eaten pizza. At last, he tore his eyes away from it. "What does he practice?"

"Sorry, what?" asked Jack after a moment. Jane had frozen. Her hand clenched.

"He's a consultant, right? Is he a law consultant? Tech? Finance?" He continued amiably as Jack and Jane caught each other's eyes. "I used to be a tech consultant before we moved. Well, I'm still a consultant, but an in-house one. How is he able to support a small practice all the way out here instead of in the city? I'd love to know."

Jack's face was neutral the way a schoolboy's face was neutral before telling a whopping lie. "Why don't you come visit? He'd love to tell you how."

"Will do," said her dad cheerfully.

Hattie thought the visit would never end, but finally the four guests said their goodbyes. Her mom sighed happily. "We're so lucky to have good neighbors this time. Remember the Hutchinsons?"

Her dad grabbed the remaining slices of pizza. "It would be nice if they were law consultants. If my employer wanted to expand, they could partner with them."

"They were kind of weird," Hattie pointed out.

"It's not polite to say so." Her mom pinched her lips as she cleared the table. After a moment, she admitted, "They are a little strange. That girl gives me the goosies."

"I don't think they were normal."

Her mom gave her a hard look. "What did I tell you about being nice?"

"I didn't say it to them! And you think so too!"

"It's a good thing they didn't find out how you really behave.

They probably would have suggested that I take you to a behavioral consultant!"

"Girls," said her dad soothingly before his attention drifted to his phone.

Hattie muttered something about going to bed and escaped up the stairs. Each stomp was a satisfying boom in sync with the three words running through her mind: I-hate-them-I-hate-them-I-hate-them...

Tomorrow will be better, she thought and tried to force herself to cheer up. There was nothing to worry about. She would simply avoid them.

"It *will* be better," she said to the ceiling.

* * *

Her mom announced at breakfast that she was going to host a block party Sunday night to get to know the neighbors. "We'll have it in the backyard, hang some lanterns on the fence, make some good food..." Her mom, buoyed by her own cheer, bobbed away. Hattie knew this meant more work. She scarfed her pancakes, grabbed her backpack, and snuck out.

It was a clear and sunny day, and the town of Applewood was not so far away that she couldn't walk there on her own. The rolling prairie surrounded the town like a reef, golden green with switchgrass, bluestem, and coneflower; it lapped at the apartments which lined the city center. Sleepy cafes clustered inside them, toward the center. Their patios were full of parents gossiping with one eye on a group of children who scribbled on the sidewalk in the nearby park. The park was scruffy with dried grass, and at its center, a fountain blossomed into a leaf-choked pool. Applewood looked nice in the way that meant everything interesting happened elsewhere.

After she browsed the dusty windows and read the menus taped to the cafe windows, she found herself looking into a narrow alley. On a wall, just above eye level, hung a small brass sign with an arrow pointing into the alley: *En Law's Consulting Firm*.

When she ventured farther into the alley, she saw a plain red door with another sign: *En Law's Consulting Firm. No Legal Advice.* *Then what does he do?* Hattie wondered. She circled the building. Shops below, office space above. No clues. Why did they have a consulting firm here? Wouldn't they be downtown? Nobody would find them here except by accident. But she didn't know a lot about consulting. Maybe there was a good reason. Eventually she gave up, opting to kick rocks around town and browse the windows of the few shops until she grew bored and started back home. Maybe she would find something in the neighborhood.

The road leading from Applewood to the neighborhood cut straight through the prairie. Though she was short, she could see for miles. The prairie was so empty to either side of the road that she noticed a black speck in the distance, like an inkblot on the sky. The speck looked like a person walking with a sway like a heat wave. It might be a statue, albeit an ugly, abstract one. But then how could it walk? And who would make a statue with a face as featureless as the surface of an egg and a body dripping black? It dragged its melting feet through the grass, and a long slick of oil marked its trail far beyond the hills. Beneath the oil, the coneflowers wilted, and the smell of petrol blew across the prairie.

Hattie watched it trudge through the grass. She was weirded out by it, but more than that, she wanted to know what it was.

"Hey!" she called. It moved on methodically. "Hey! Can you hear me?"

Nothing. Hattie found a decent rock and winged it at the thing. The rock clipped its shoulder with a splatter of oil and bounced into the grass, but otherwise the thing did not respond.

"Hey!" The boy from before, Jack, stood near the Applewood city sign holding grocery bags. His horrified gaze switched from her to the thing.

"What?" she called back.

"Is it yours?"

"No." Why would it be hers? "What is it?"

He gave her a baffled look. When he'd called out, the faceless head had turned, as if looking at him. It slogged in a broad arc and clumped toward him. Jack's face changed from confusion to alarm.

He snapped, "Hey, stop it!"

"I'm not doing anything!"

But he strode off at a clip, glancing back over his shoulder. Perplexed, Hattie watched him go. The thing sped up. It struggled forward, squelching as it passed her, and slimed onto the road after him.

With nothing better to do, Hattie followed it. How did it move? It seemed to be made entirely out of oil. How did it not lose all the oil? It didn't seem to be getting smaller or drier. What was it? She couldn't get too close to it. The smell was nauseating, so she held her T-shirt over her nose and mouth.

A young man in a button-up and slacks talking on his cell phone hurried into their path. He veered into the oil-thing. Hattie winced, but he kept walking and talking; his shirt was spotless. Maybe he'd missed it? A car honked behind her. She hopped to the curb to get out of the way. The thing didn't. The car smashed through it, oil showering its hood, and all that was left was a smeared puddle. Passing cars tracked the oil across the road, but the tracks shrank back into the puddle. When no cars passed for a minute, the puddle shivered. The surface bent as if someone poked a finger into the center. Stretching, stretching, stretching, high into the air until, with a *plip*, the point separated from the puddle and hung in the air like a suspended marble. More drops quickly joined the first drop as if magnetized, raining up to it until the surface of the liquid funneled. The oil sculpted itself and reformed the oil-thing again. Finally, it trudged onward to its destination. Not one of the mothers sitting at the cafe spared a glance. The children, who definitely would have done something had they seen the oil-thing, continued playing as if nothing beyond their game existed.

Excited, Hattie kept close to it. It slopped down the sidewalk, seemingly heading to the alley. Hattie heard someone hammering on a door. Jack's panicking voice rang out, "Hey! Guys! Let me in! Is anyone there?"

Worry crept in. The thing was crawling faster. She ran ahead of the thing and saw Jack peering through the windows of the practice. She shouted, a moment before the oil-thing sloshed into the alley, a moment before Jack's face distorted with terror, and a moment before the thing arced in a long jet of oil and pounced on him.

Hattie screamed as Jack grappled with it. Its limbs flowed around the thrashing boy. Each of his blows landed with a sucking noise, but did nothing. It enveloped Jack, who fought desperately and yelled. "Help! Jane! En Law! Help!"

Hattie trembled. She needed to stop it. She needed to run. She needed to get help. She needed to hit it with something...

The hands melted together and draped across Jack's mouth to smother his cries. Hattie slung her bag off her shoulder and whammed it into the thing's head with a shriek. The head exploded with a magnificent splatter and showered them both in reeking gunk. Jack staggered out of the loosening grip. Oil was smeared across his stark face and dripped from his ruined clothes. The oil body toppled and splashed into a puddle of itself.

All became still. His grocery bags had spilled apples, peaches, and cans into the oil. Two of the mothers from the cafe craned their heads into the alley, their cell phones lifted to their ears.

Jack looked from her to the puddle, then to the women watching them. His expression changed from shock to forced determination.

"We need to go," he said. He dug through his pockets and took out a fistful of oil-soaked receipts in a wad. He lobbed them at the patch of oil. "It'll re-form. Come on—go!"

They ran past the women, though they called out. Jack dashed down the prairie road toward the neighborhood, but after a few steps, he veered off and sprinted into the forest. Hattie followed with burning lungs, stumbling as the undergrowth whipped and stung her bare legs. Before long, they were engulfed by the wind-whispery sycamore and locust, as if they'd vanished from the world.

They stopped their breakneck pace when Hattie finally fell, scraping her knees and palms. Jack paced as she got up, muttering, "Come on, come on."

"Can't," Hattie wheezed. All her days of sitting inside and reading were catching up to her. She pulled herself up using branches to lean on like an old woman. Her thoughts were scrambled.

Jack's eyes darted to everything that moved. His cheeks worked as if he were biting them. He stopped pacing. "Are you really human?"

Hattie gaped at him.

"Say something!" He seemed poised to hit her.

"What?" she said dumbly.

"How can you see and touch the stroilman?"

"What?"

"Stop saying what!" His cheeks worked harder and he began pacing again. "You could see it, right?"

"I—yeah."

"What did it look like?"

"A person made of oil."

"And you have no idea what it was?"

"No."

"And when we first met, you had no idea there was a boundary between the orchard and the forest."

"No."

He threw up his hands. "What is happening?"

If he didn't know, who would?

She asked, "What was that thing? The stroilman?"

The wind strengthened, carrying a whiff of gasoline. Sniffing deeply, Jack's expression strained. "Listen. Go home and take a bath. Put on fresh clothes and don't keep anything that you wore today. Dump it all far from your house, so the stroilman won't find you. And stay inside for a few days. It might be roaming around looking for you or me. Since ordinary people can't see it, it can go anywhere, including your own house."

She imagined the stroilman oozing up the stairs one step at a time.

"And please, please don't tell anyone else what I've told you. Not Jane, your mother, *nobody*. Got it?"

"But what's going on?"

Jack looked at her with such fright she knew he'd been about to ask her the same thing. "I don't know. I'll find you later." He ran into the orchard and was swallowed by the trees.

The water gushed from the showerhead with a rolling, scalding cloud of steam. Hattie scrubbed herself all over until she felt boiled. As she stepped out and redressed, she was careful not to touch the clothes heaped on her floor.

Her mom was folding the laundry in her room, entranced by the food channel. Hattie, counting her blessings, picked up her clothes with a pair of salad tongs and dumped the whole lot into a plastic garbage bag, tossing the tongs in, too, just in case. She did not trust Jack, but she trusted her gut and it said to bury her clothes in the forest far away from her house.

She left by the back door like a thief. The sky blushed with evening light. Crickets chirped and the porch of the house across from hers was filled with murmuring neighbors sipping iced tea. Hattie tried to look as casual as possible as she walked down the road toward the birch forest with her bag of clothes. She waved to them and smiled but once out of sight, she sprinted into the woods. How far did she need to go? Could the stroilman follow her back home? What if there was more than one? What if it was watching already? Driven hysterical by her imagination, she flung the bag at the base of a tree and frantically scraped dirt over it until it was completely hidden.

The sun had sunk when she finished, and the deep turquoise sky was freckled with stars. The night wind ghosted through the treetops, whistling. She walked home quickly with the hairs on her neck rising like a million antennae. It wasn't safe here, she could feel it, so she took off in a blind panic. She slipped and scrambled to her feet without noticing her stinging knees; her breath sawed through her throat. When she reached the neighborhood, it was agony to walk normally again, let alone briskly, while smiling, waving, and trying to breathe naturally.

The windows of her neighbors' houses seemed like spotlights. On her driveway was a shining patch of oil. She squeaked and backpedaled, but there was no trail leading to or from it. It was only a genuine oil patch.

She didn't turn off the lights that night; her sleep was shallow and dreamless.

🎇 2 🎇

FREE GIFT

Hattie's night passed like a bad dream. Only when sunlight touched her corner of the Earth did she feel safe enough to crawl out of bed and peep outside. The wind ruffled the birch leaves, making them wink silver and green.

There was a note at the breakfast table next to a peanut butter sandwich:

Meet me in the backyard after breakfast to set up for tomorrow.
—Mom

In the backyard, her mom stood on a dining chair, straining to reach a branch where she could hang a streamer. Rolls of crepe paper streamers in tropical colors dotted the grass around her. Boxes of paper lanterns, coils of Christmas lights, and a disassembled picnic table leaned against the fence.

"Hattie, go find the outlets. They're supposed to be on the side of the house. I bought extension cords, but if they can't reach then I'll take them back."

"When did you get this?"

"This morning." Her mom threw the streamer roll over the

branch and it ribboned to the ground. "Phew! I should have done that first. I went while you were still asleep."

"Leaving me at home alone is child endangerment."

"Nobody's going to steal *you*, sweetheart."

The picnic table was moved a hundred times in exponentially smaller degrees. "To the left...my left. Not that far, go back. No, *too far.*" And there were a million things to do inside.

"Clean the grout in the bathroom with an old toothbrush so you can get between the tiles. The last owners didn't do it." Number forty-five. "Hang the summer wreath above the mantle." Number twenty-nine. "Scrub the refrigerator." Number thirty.

Unlike her old house, the new house had an upstairs and a downstairs, both of which she had to clean. *But who was going to be upstairs?* Weeding the garden, cutting the grass, doing the laundry, and cleaning the windows, floors, and doorknobs left her mind much too free to wonder what Jack was up to and what would happen next. Every few minutes she glanced at the orchard. The wind-tossed leaves frizzled her nerves when they scratched across the windows, and her skin prickled. If she'd turned around just a little faster, she knew she would see something there, watching. But nothing out of the ordinary happened.

"Oh, you're almost done?" Her mom poked her head in through the door. Hattie had just finished ironing the tablecloth. "Good job! Now, we have to go get new outfits for the party tomorrow, and there are a few boutiques in town that I want to visit. Go shower. You don't need to wash the curtains. I don't think anyone will notice. Since the party is going to be outside, I doubt many people, if any, will be in the house."

"Nobody's going to be in the house?" Hattie asked in a strangled voice. She was dirt-smudged and aching. "Then why—"

"*Because if they do,*" her mom said in her no-arguing voice.

Only when Hattie ducked into the car did she wonder if they would be driving through the area where she'd run into the stroilman. And yes, the car followed the same road Hattie had walked along, heading for the same apartments and park.

Excuses bubbled up her throat. *We should take a different way to town.* But there were no side roads. *I heard that there were shops elsewhere.* She imagined her mom saying, *Where? And who said that?* Her stomach began to hurt; her mom always knew when she was lying. She slouched below the window and peeked out as they passed the alley. Not even an oil patch marked the struggle.

The streets widened and became busier. Boutiques and restaurants lined the streets, and people flowed along the sidewalks. Maybe they would be safe here. Why would monsters go shopping?

The first dress shop was library-quiet. Dresses fluttered from the door's movement and settled. The air smelled of laundered linens. Western relics adorned the wall: lassoes, a pair of antlers, spurs, a horseshoe over the door, and a framed picture of a cowboy. A saguaro cactus in the middle of the room held spare hangers on its prickly arms like a butler, dignified and patient. Her mom began pulling out dresses and throwing them over her arm. "I think a coral pink would look good on you. With some sequins, of course—good ones. Or maybe a muted violet..."

"Ma'am." A woman materialized. She had white hair braided round her head and flinty green eyes. Hattie's mom froze. "Please do not pull out my dresses." It sounded like an order rather than a request.

Her mom looked flustered. "I'm sorry, but—"

"They are quite delicate," she went on. "My designer makes them out of a special blend of silk and cotton using cactus needles. She prefers that I recommend our one-of-a-kind clothing to customers based on their personal taste and needs. When you have chosen your design, we will tailor the dress—a complimentary service—and send you on your way to enjoy your new clothing. Please, call me Matilda."

Her mom relaxed. The woman had said all of her favorite

words: *service, one-of-a-kind, designer, clothing.* "I would like a party dress for my daughter."

Matilda gathered the dresses from her mom and replaced them, smoothing the wrinkled fabric. When done, she turned her unnerving eyes on Hattie to inspect her.

"I was thinking Hattie would look great in a pink dress." Her mom followed her like a puppy. "With something sparkly on it to catch the eye."

"I think," the woman said, removing a blue dress made out a heavy, satin-like material, "this would look better on your daughter. Besides, we don't have any dresses that are pink or have sequins."

"Ah." Her mom looked crestfallen. Hattie breathed.

To Hattie's surprise the dress fit well. Her mom smiled, but Matilda frowned.

"It's pretty."

"It's not quite right."

While her mom was stunned, Matilda went back to the racks to sift for another dress. "Try this." A long purple and silver dress. "Not your color combination. Try..." A full-skirted, red one. "Mmm, closer, but no. Try this one."

Hattie lost count of how many times she went back into the dressing room. The rack beside the dressing rooms sagged with each rejected dress until Hattie tried a simple mint green cotton dress with small white bows at the shoulders.

"It's a little plain for a party," said her mom, shifting her weight from foot to foot. She swirled her finger in the air. "Do a twirl, sweetie." Hattie turned and the dress flowered around her knees, swaying before it settled.

"It brings out her features beautifully," said Matilda serenely.

"I like it," said Hattie. "Can we get it?"

Rarely did Hattie admit liking any article of clothing. Her mom's eyes flashed. "How much is the dress?"

Matilda named her price. The cactus smiled, seemingly glad they had a sale.

The cactus smiled.

It had simple black dots for eyes, a curved line for a mouth, and fringes of thorns rimmed its eyes like eyelashes, fluttering as it blinked. Hattie stared at it, wondering what she was looking at. It blinked again. The smile faded. Its amiable expression changed to dismay. Hattie's jaw dropped.

"Matilda!" it whispered, keeping its eyes on Hattie. "She can see me! Emergency! Do the check!"

Matilda had been holding a dress up to Hattie's mom as she held out her arms. Her shoulders stiffened. A moment later, she wheeled around wearing a strained smile. "Do you like my cactus? Her name is Sonorra and she's about forty years old."

"If you can hear and see me, say, 'Wow, that's forty laps around the sun!'" whispered the cactus.

"Wow, I didn't know plants lived that long," said her mom absently, taking the dress from Matilda's limp hand. "I'm going to try this on."

"That's forty laps around the sun!" Hattie shouted.

The shop was as quiet as the moment after thunder. The cactus and Matilda stared at Hattie, looking as frightened as she felt.

"Yes, sweetheart, it is," her mom said in her special patient voice from behind the curtained dressing room. "I never thought of it like that. Can I have this one altered?"

Matilda hastened to help her. Her mom held out her arms and studied her turquoise wrap in the mirror while the woman pulled out more dresses.

"Can you really hear me?" said the cactus softly, bug-eyed. Hattie nodded as minutely as she could. "But how?" She raised her shoulders slightly. "Are you human?" That was the second time she had been asked. She nodded but wondered.

The dress woman returned with her mom, a second dress, and a small patterned bag.

"For all my customers," she said, lowering the bag by its drawstrings into Hattie's hand. "A gift."

"Thank you." She was about to open it, when her mom hooked their arms together.

"Thank you for the lovely dresses and the gift. Have a good day!"

The woman lifted her hand in farewell as they left. The cactus gawked until the door closed behind them.

* * *

In another store, while her mom tried on shoes, Hattie inspected the bag. It was a palm-sized pouch. The drawstrings looped long enough to wear as a necklace. Its fabric was actually leaves of scarlet, yellow, and green. When held to the light, the veins stood out like fine rivers beneath the colors, and the tiny stitches followed the edges so that they fit together like a puzzle. She could feel a lump nestled in the bottom and something else, like a card. Hattie teased the bag open.

Inside was a business card and a metal bead. She pulled out the business card and read out loud, "Matilda and Sonorra Redhorse, Owners and Seamstresses of Redhorse Dresses." Beneath the title was a store address, an email address, and a phone number. Her mom caught her with the pouch open. With a frown, she told her to look at the gift at home.

Once in the car, her knee jiggled all the way to the house. Her bedroom door had just clicked closed when Hattie dug through her pockets for the dress woman's gift and dumped the contents in her hand. Her palm sizzled, she yelped, and the bag dropped. The card fluttered to her toes, and the bead rolled to the wall. The fingers that had touched the small piece of metal throbbed and stung as if she'd touched a hot coal instead. She ran to the bathroom and trickled water over them. When she returned to her room and when she was sure the door was closed, she knelt as close as she dared to the bead to examine it. It was about the size of the end of her thumb, dull grey, and it wasn't a bead; it was a bullet.

The bag was probably made to hold it because she hadn't felt the burning sensation until she touched it directly. Her hand quivered, and she clenched it to make it stop. She set the bag on the floor, propped open its mouth with a pen, maneuvered the bullet inside with another pen, and drew the strings tight. Now what? First, she would have to visit the shop another time without her mom to get answers. But was it safe to return? Who would give a bullet as a free gift? Why would a bullet hurt?

Maybe it wasn't a gift. Maybe it was a warning.

"Hattie!" Her mom called up the stairs. "Help me set up!"

"Coming!"

She ran out, slipping the leaf-pouch around her neck as she went.

✵ 3 ✵

INCENSED

T he sky had just turned to twilight, cooled to Neptune-blue, seamless, and transparent as water. Paper lanterns illuminated the backyard. Perched on the tables and strung along the fence, they clacked in the wind and made shadows as wild as firelight. Hattie thought the lanterns were the best decorations and made sure to tell her mom.

"Thank you, sweetie," said her mom, shapely in a turquoise cocktail dress. "Now go say hello to our neighbors. Help the elderly ones into their seats." She slipped into the crowd and introduced herself to a pair of young women.

Hattie positioned herself by the garden gate and welcomed everyone who walked through. Most came in pairs and said hello quickly before going back to their own conversations. The ones who came alone were the most interesting. A little old man wearing a grin and a dapper orange suit strode to the fence and vaulted it, much to the astonishment of those who noticed, before handing a bottle of wine to Hattie with a wink. There was also a single young lady like a stork, near-sighted with a tight matronly braid, who stammered a greeting. Hattie gave her the wine and later saw her weaving through the crowd, pink and bright-eyed with her braid undone and beautifully disheveled. A tiny girl her age waved at her from between her mom and dad. A toddling boy with curly gold hair took his hand out of his mouth to wave at her.

Jack stalked through the gate, more pale and strained than usual. "I need to talk to you," he whispered, scanning the crowd and forest. His fingers plucked at his white button-up shirt tucked into black trousers, held up by odd suspenders. He looked like he'd come from a different time.

Hattie's mom stood on a chair and clapped to get everyone's attention.

"I'm so glad everyone could come tonight," she said in an adoring voice. "I have invited all of you to our home so we could become acquainted as new neighbors. Also, my husband returns from his business trip tonight, and..." Coyly, she put a finger to her lips, "...this is his surprise party. So, if you see him, yell surprise!"

The crowd cheered with scattered applause.

"Let's talk out front," Hattie said, leading Jack through the side gate. From there, the party's music was far away and tinny. Headlights swept the darkness as a car rushed like a yellow-eyed phantom down the road and out of sight.

"Listen," said Jack. His skin was chalky, and he glanced impulsively over his shoulder as he spoke. "Our little problem brought friends to your party."

"More stroilmen?"

"They're in the orchard. More than a handful. Maybe a whole barrel."

"Mom," breathed Hattie, outraged and terrified all at once. "Dad!" Would all these people be in danger?

Jack glanced toward the party. He trembled harder than when they had run from the first stroilman. He spoke as if trying to convince them both. "They won't attack you or the party, I think. Stroilmen are like machines that do one thing: find one orex, and capture, kill, or hold them. They aren't here for you. You'll be safe. I think." He checked round the edge of the house. "He's not here yet. Your mom invited En Law. When he shows up, the stroilmen will probably go ballistic trying to get him...probably."

"Probably?"

"I don't know who else they'd go for!"

"We have to get everyone out of here! If the stroilmen get them—"

"They'll be okay. They can't see the stroilmen, so they might not be targeted. Even if twenty of them came through and danced, nobody would see or hear them. If they touched anyone, people who got touched would just think they touched some greasy food." He twisted and clenched his hands together as if to break them off. "En Law is strong enough that we wouldn't be in any danger...except it might be more dangerous to attract *his* attention than the stroilmen's. He'll protect me and Jane, I think. My parents aren't real people. They're dolls," he added, as if clarifying. "If they get destroyed, it won't matter. And the stroilmen probably don't know about you. But you did hit one, so maybe they will be after you. Hide in your room until this blows over."

"What are orex? Why are they here?" After a pause she asked another question she'd been wondering. "Why are *you* here?"

"I work for En Law," he said in a strained voice. "I'm an orex, and so is he."

"What is he going to do?" she asked, watching Jack retreat, shrinking, shaking his head, stricken. "Jack..." There was something terrible about this night, and she was acting in all the wrong ways. Stroilmen loomed in her imagination, attacking the lady with the braid or the man with the wine, smothering them, oil filling their mouths. "You tell me! What is he going to do? Why are you here?"

"I can't—"

Yellow lights swept across the house, and his expression turned wary as tires crunched over the driveway gravel.

"Dad!" Hattie leaped away from Jack to the car. The porch light flicked on. Her dad ambled into the light. "Hey Hattie. What's going on?"

"Hello, Mr. Flores," Jack said in a stiff formal voice, holding out his hand.

Her dad shook it warmly. "Hello! It's great to meet you again..."

"Jack."

"That's right. What are you doing with my daughter all alone?"

"Nothing!" Jack and Hattie both yelled at once, and her dad laughed.

"Nothing? Too bad." He craned his head over the fence. "What's all the noise?"

"Uh...it's a surprise party! For you!" Hattie tugged him toward the backyard without any clue as to what to do next. Jack followed, looking ill. Maybe she should corral her dad the other way.

The backyard was full when they returned. The air was vibrant with conversation; if Hattie closed her eyes, she could hear the smiles. Everyone stood loosely, laughing with others in pockets of conversation under lanterns like strands of glowing pearls. Giggling children slalomed around them and crawled under the picnic tables. Patches of sweat were like handprints on the smalls of the backs and like rings around their throats.

"All this for me?" her dad asked, flabbergasted. "Cassandra!" He navigated through the crowd to the table where she held court. He hugged her tightly once he reached her. "You sure know how to keep a marriage alive. Where did you get all this?"

Her mom smiled. "Oh, it was nothing. How was work?"

"Dull and lonely without my girls," he said fondly, ruffling Hattie's hair. "But hey, I convinced them to let me work at home. Pajamas are the new suits."

"Tanner, let me introduce you to our new neighbors."

"Hello!"

"When will En Law get here?" Hattie whispered to Jack.

"Soon. You better go to your room now before anyone sees you."

"What is he going to do? Can I stop the party? What will stop them?"

He gazed into the orchard with real fear. "I can't. You've got to go, *now*."

"No! What about mom and dad?"

He grabbed her by the shoulders, spun her around, and shoved her toward the house. "Get out of here!" His voice had gone high with terror, and his eyes were ringed with white.

She ran behind a tittering couple and through the garden gate, into the side door that led to the garage. In her room, her fingers touched the light switch before she realized, *They'll see my lights on*, and left them off. But who were *they*? She wedged open her window, and the warm spring air curled through her room, ferrying the sounds of the party, fluttering the loose papers on her desk. There was a great weight crushing her chest. The world seemed to deform before her eyes, so the backyard beneath her window was a tiny embroidered patch, and the orchard beyond the fence was a vast black tide. From the dark orchard came an outline of deeper dark. When it reached the garden gate and the light washed over it, she saw it was only a man. But like a panther, he moved with deliberate, deadly quiet. He was only slightly taller than her, and wore loose, straight, black trousers and a long-sleeved shirt of the same material hemmed in crimson. His hair was Mars-red and scrubby, so his lead-white skin combined with the fierceness of his hair made him look like a candle, complete with flame. Smiling seemed alien to his nature, kindness against his creed. And like Jack, there was something about him that looked warped. He could only be En Law.

He slipped through the gate to the backyard and stalked

through the crowd. He carried a brass ball hanging from a chain, swinging it smoothly like a pendulum. Silky grey smoke leaked from holes in the ball and threaded through the crowd. The people closest to him edged away uneasily. They seemed unable to look at him.

Hattie's mom spotted him and called out something lost in the murmur. En Law's gaze cut to her, and he stopped and watched her approach. Hattie could not see her face from her vantage point, but she seemed to say something to him, as En Law's eyebrows arched. He stirred the brass ball, and its smoke looped around her head. He moved on; she stayed, standing as if still speaking to him. All around her, the voices in the crowd were extinguishing, and soon the backyard was full of people who stared at each other, smiling, without speaking or gesturing. Hattie slid down beneath her windowsill with her hands crammed over her mouth to keep in a building scream.

There was a noise like hot oil sizzling on the wind. Something incessant and growing. She peeked over the sill. The forest seemed to be crawling in the moonlight. The forest spread. No, a pool spread from the trees' roots and crept toward the party, a thick murk.

En Law had stopped at the backyard gate. His eyes were locked on the tide that oozed forward in the lantern light. The liquid splashed, and the splashes clotted to form stroilmen. An elderly couple were nearest to the tide. Hattie's scream whispered out of her, but the stroilmen seeped right through the couple. Oil soaked the guests' shoes, but the guests were otherwise untouched by the stroilmen. Melting figures sprouted, collapsed, reformed, and strengthened, swaying upwards, bodies stretching like taffy toward the house.

She whirled to run downstairs but stopped. Something knocked below. She cracked open her door and peered down the stairs and screamed: oil spilled *up* the stairs. She slammed the door and stuffed dirty clothes under the door. The door rattled. Licorice-like liquid squirted between the hinges and under the door, and she gasped, backing away. The puddle under her door grew. A hand reached out of the puddle; then a wrist, forearm, elbow, shoulder, and a melting head as if a person was climbing through a window.

The window! Hattie threw her legs over the sill. Her foot slipped on the shingles and she scrabbled but managed to jam her shoe into the gutter just in time. Her arms trembled as she hauled herself up. Hand over hand, she pulled her way along the roof by gripping the clapboards. The wind tangled her dress about her legs, blew her hair into her eyes, and numbed her hands, making her fumble. Inching along, her mind screamed with static as the squelching and slopping continued on her heels.

Beneath her, the party guests trickled into the forest. Nobody looked up or noticed the stroilmen sludging toward the house, though the monsters had stretched and towered higher than the roof.

Hattie screamed down at the partygoers. "Hey! Wake up! Heeeeeey!" Her voice rose until her throat tore. "Come on! *Wake up!*"

Not one person—not the funny old man who gave her the wine, the tipsy lady who had come alone, or the girl her own age —looked up.

A gurgling noise came from her right, followed by a splatter. A glob of arms, legs, naked shoulders, and heads squeezed out of the window and dribbled down to the shingles. From the ball of limbs, a head emerged like a worm from a rotten apple. Streams of oil spilled as the neck stretched, and the head turned. It had no eyes, but curves on the smooth head where eyes should be. Little whines escaped her. She clambered away from the hideous mass as the many arms pulled and the many feet pushed.

When her foot dipped into empty space, she knew she had run out of roof. The ball crawled faster, trailing oil that bubbled as it went. Hattie lay flat and dangled her legs off the roof, but there was still ten feet of air between her and the ground, and another stroilman, twice that height, was reaching for her.

But someone else ran toward her with arms outstretched. The person caught her as she dropped, and together they bounded over the fence and sprinted into the orchard. Jack looked down at her and smiled. His eyes were pitch-black and without pupils or whites. His body had stretched like a rubber band to twice his usual height. His torso was as thin as a light pole, and his legs sprang yards with every stride. The stroilmen in the yard turned to follow. Their comrades oozed out of the windows until Jack leaped the fence and ran into the orchard.

"What's going on?" she called.

"Don't worry. I'm taking you somewhere safe!"

"But what about my parents?"

He didn't reply, and she couldn't tell if he hadn't heard or hadn't wanted to answer. They flew by more and more of the partygoers, until the trees fell away to reveal a clearing. A billowing tent of brightly colored silks sprouted from the mud like an anemone. The guests shuffled into a slit in the tent wall. She grabbed the hem of his shirt and yanked. He staggered but stopped.

Jack ducked behind a tree and craned to see the clearing.

He whispered, "It's not safe for you to be here."

"Then why did you bring me here?"

"They'll never look for you here! They'll never suspect you're still..."

Alive?

The tent breathed and exhaled like a soft-bodied thing digesting its prey. A sweet odor stung her nose and fogged her head. "What is in there?"

"Processors." His face twisted as if to prevent himself from crying. "I'm sorry."

She slurred, "What does that mean?" Did her brain not work? Her fear dulled, which she knew should scare her, but even that thought didn't possess the edge it should have.

"We have to hide you. The incense—"

"Can't you walk in there and take them out?" Hattie asked hopefully. Jack's face collapsed further. The wind picked up, brushed away the incense, and her mind cleared. "Will En Law notice? Or I could do it. It won't take more than three minutes..."

"He'll know."

"Put me down. I'll get them."

"If you went in there, the smell would get stronger and it would drug you. You'd lose control. And then you'd lose your self. Your body would be stored in a tag and put in a record book. Your self would then be used for...I don't know. You can't do anything. I can't do anything. That's it!"

Hattie didn't understand. How could anyone do whatever horrible thing that was being done to her parents and her neighbors?

"Is this real?" Her voice broke. "Why is this happening?" A thought lifted above her horror and the fog. "This is your job?"

His face twisted further.

"You *knew*."

His face warped and broke. "I'm sorry...I'm so, so sorry..."

"What are you doing?" A skeleton emerged from the orchard like a harbinger, all polished ivory and hollow eye sockets. Yet, somehow it seemed familiar.

"Jane." Held closely to his chest, Hattie could hear his harsh breathing.

"One escaped?" she asked, peering at Hattie. "Does En Law know?"

He spoke quickly and disjointedly, backing away. "You can't tell him. Something weird's going on, and there's a lot happening. If you're my friend—*please*—you won't tell him about Hattie. She's just one self. She doesn't matter."

"What's going on?" Jane's voice sharpened.

"Tell En Law I'm directing more humans. Please."

"Jack!"

He bolted. The tent vanished in a flash and its crimson, sulfur, and toxic green colors slivered to nothing in the black trees.

"Put me down!" Hattie screamed and kicked. "Put me down, put me down, *put me down!*"

"Stop fighting!"

"My parents are going to die!"

"They won't die!"

She bit his shoulder through his shirt. He gasped, but he did not stop. Tasting tears, she twisted and dug her teeth further into his skin, and blood worked into the shirt. Jack lurched to a halt on the edge of the orchard. She wrestled out of his grip. When her foot touched grass, he lunged and pinned her down.

"Stop it!" With his wild hair, super-black eyes, and ghoulish, stretched features, he looked like a nightmare. Hattie shrank back into the grass. He saw her do it and his face twisted. "I'm trying to save you! Why don't you see that? Why won't you let me help you? I'm trying to save you!" His face crumpled. "I'm sorry."

She could not speak. Tears slid down her temples, spreading warmly into her hair.

A smooth new voice like the incense filled their minds. "Jack, do you have something you want to tell me?"

En Law, Jane, and a monster stood just beyond the fence watching them. The monster was double her dad's height and walked on crooked legs bent backward at the knee like a cricket. Its thick, hunched back swayed jerkily as it moved forward. It had a gruesome, flabby, pale head like a grub, set with huge oily black eyes that had no pupils, and a slit for a mouth. No hair grew on its head and its ears were shrunken and withered like dried mushrooms. The monster had Jane held tight in one giant hand; she looked as sorry as a skeleton could. En Law held the metal ball, which wreathed him in the fragrant, numbing smoke. He observed them without emotion.

Jack got up warily and put Hattie down. En Law's black eyes fell on her.

"She was at the party watching from the dwelling," En Law said. "Why isn't she with her parents?"

"She wasn't affected by your incense," Jack said in an unnaturally calm voice. "She was in her room on the second floor."

"Why do you know this?"

"I caught her as she fell from the roof."

"Why did you save her life?"

"She saved mine, sir," he replied. "I was attacked by a stroilman in town, and she made it liquify long enough for us to get away."

The monster then spoke in an oily, but articulate voice that startled her. It sounded too urbane for the way it looked. "Dear human, what do we look like to you?"

Hattie's throat had closed. Jack spoke. "She could see the stroilmen—"

"I asked *her* what *we* looked like. Do not speak again."

Her voice shook. "Y-you look like a monster. Jane looks like a human skeleton. Jack is stretched out and very tall."

"Interesting. Another one who can see us." Its voice seemed to coil in her chest, like a poisonous snake, heavy and deadly.

En Law held up his left hand. "How many fingers?"

"Six," she said nervously.

"Interesting," the monster repeated.

Hattie's thoughts scrambled. En Law's eyes lingered on the bullet pouch. "The stroilmen were probably after her bag. What were you doing with her, Jack?"

"I thought we'd be even if I saved her self from being taken," said Jack reluctantly.

"I see." He paused. "We've met and exceeded our quota many times over tonight. We'll let her go."

"What?"

But En Law was walking back to the tent. "She isn't worth the trouble." Flabbergasted, Jack looked from Hattie to En Law, hope faintly returning. "We have to place the selves in preservative tags before we leave. We don't want them returning to their bodies."

He's not going to take me, Hattie thought in relief. The selves could go back to their bodies? She had to make him stay. She blurted, "What will happen to my parents?"

"Their bodies will continue to live without them, automatically performing daily tasks necessary to keep them alive such as eating, sleeping, and working." He continued to walk. "As for their selves, they will be used for research."

"What about me?" It sounded like the whine of a left-out child.

En Law stopped and eyed her. "Do you *want* to be taken?"

"I want my parents back! Can't you research me...or, or, *something*? There has to be something I can do to get them back?" En Law's expression changed so slightly she wasn't sure if she'd imagined it.

The monster laughed creakily. "His descriptive is 'Merciless,' dear, but mine isn't." It leaned close. "A willing research subject is valuable. And I was unable to find the research subjects from the original experiment," it added to En Law. "If we take her, body and soul, it would help me reconstruct the experiment."

"In exchange for my parents," Hattie said. "I'll do what you want."

The red-haired orex did not move his gaze from Hattie's face. "There is no room on the ship for another body. Even if there was, your parents are too valuable to buy back—not that we would pay to study you. You are not worth both of your parents. What can you give me that is equivalent to their worth?" En Law moved his gaze to Jack. "Jack has connections which make him valuable. Jane has special powers which make her valuable. If each worked for five years, they could buy your parents. What do you have that is valuable? Merely being able to see orex isn't good enough. Being human isn't enough, either." He paused. "We cannot take you with us, but if you have something to offer us, my office is in Baba, the Red Hen Casino southwest of New Sprout, east of the Noh Forest. I want to leave as soon as possible. We have work to finish."

Jack stood as if unfolding. He looked relieved. But he couldn't be relieved for her, because he'd helped take her family away. And now he was walking with the orex and leaving her behind. Alone.

❧ 4 ❧

THE DRESSMAKER'S SHOP

The grass, grey and soft as if penciled, hissed in the night breeze. The stems cut blood-beaded lines into her bare legs, but she couldn't go home and couldn't slow down. She was afraid to look back in case she saw fluid movements in the shadows. At last, the road to town came into view and she picked up speed. She tumbled into the ditch, clambered out, and ran wheezing.

The confrontation with En Law sucked out all spare ingenuity, and she could only think on repeat, *the dressmaker's shop, the dressmaker's shop*. There were orex there who didn't seem to be evil and who might be able to help her. She had no good reason to believe they weren't evil—who gives free bullets?—but what else could she do? More importantly, she remembered that she needed to go to the Red Hen Casino southwest of New Sprout, east of the Noh Forest. Irrationally, she thought that if she could get to the dressmaker's shop, everything would be solved.

These thoughts looped through her head as she trudged into the light of a streetlamp and slumped on a park bench to rest. The roads echoed with emptiness. Outside the islands of light on the sidewalks was the night, which held shapes that could be anything or anyone.

Her imagination invented movement, whispers, eyes, an oily sheen. The wind had cooled and kicked up loose papers and trash bags along its path. Every movement made her flinch. As she passed the large reflective windows of shops and cafes, her reflection rippled darkly, as if swimming underwater, and her pale face frightened her into thinking she'd become a ghost.

Soon she was at the dressmaker's shop. The lights were on, and voices slipped out from under the door. When she knocked, the voices stopped. The door swung open to reveal the green-eyed, white-haired woman from before.

"Yes?" she said irritably. "The shop is closed." But her expression changed as she took in Hattie's haggard, muddy appearance and her panicked expression.

From inside the shop a voice rang out. "Stroilmen!"

Her eyes flashed. She yanked Hattie inside and slammed the door. Something on the other side collided with the glass and it cracked.

Hattie shrieked, "They'll come under the door!"

"They can't," the cactus said, "There's not enough to break down the barrier."

The woman gripped her shoulders and steered her onto a couch near the changing room. "How many are there?" she asked the cactus.

"Three whole barrels."

"For her?"

"I guess so." The cactus twisted in its pot to stare at Hattie. "Yeesh, what did you do?"

"I hit one." Her voice broke as she fought to speak through her rising tears. "And now they've been chasing me instead of the guy they were supposed to be after, and I should have let them have him because—" A sob escaped and her tears poured out after it. Whatever strength had carried her through the night washed away as she cried.

"Oh no, she's leaking!" The cactus looked gobsmacked. "What do we do?"

"We can't help you if we don't know what's wrong," Matilda said in a severe voice that failed to hide her quaver. "Spit it out."

"Let's start at the beginning," said the cactus soothingly. "What happened?"

"I—*hic*—saved someone's life and—*hic*—he helped En Law kidnap my parents' selves."

They exchanged dark looks.

"What an ingrate," the cactus said. "But what about the stroilmen? And who is En Law?"

"I don't—*hic*— know." She tried to breathe and speak clearly. "The stroilmen—*hic*—were after the one guy I saved."

Matilda knelt in front of her and pried her hands from her eyes. "Look at me." Her green eyes were penetrating. "I know you've just suffered something terrible, but this is very important. Do you know why they are here?"

"They were stealing human selves. They took my mom and dad and my whole neighborhood."

"An entire neighborhood," murmured the woman. "How awful. It sounds like Ran Corp."

"I don't know. En Law said they were leaving tomorrow at noon." The woman and the cactus relaxed.

"Well, if they are leaving tomorrow, the stroilmen may follow them. But will you be okay on your own?" asked the cactus.

"I have to go to the Red Hen Casino. I have to get my parents back." Hattie said miserably.

Matilda grasped Hattie's arm, pulled her off the couch, and headed for the door. On the other side of the cracked window in the door, black shapes squirmed. Hattie fought, screaming.

"Please don't! I'm sorry—I'm sorry!" She dug her heels into the rug as Matilda dragged her toward the door.

"Matilda!" Spines rocketed from the floor and criss-crossed over the door like a fence. Matilda snatched her hand back from the knob. The cactus glowered from her pot, her spines bristling. The pot had cracked on the bottom. Her roots had gone down through the floor and speared upward. "What are you doing?"

"I want nothing to do with Ran Corp again. What if they come back for her? What if she's an orex?"

In a severe voice, the cactus said, "She's not an orex. She's definitely human. Remember? We did the check."

"But Ran Corp—"

"We don't know if it's Ran Corp, and if it was, they probably took advantage of her. That's what they do. She's scared and trying to make the best of a bad situation. Is that why you came here?" Hattie nodded, sobbing. Matilda's hands were like shackles. "Now, just to be safe, I'm going to ask you some questions. Is that okay?" She nodded again. Her breath sawed against her throat. "When was the first time you encountered stroilmen?"

"F-f-friday."

"How did it happen?"

"Jack—I-I didn't know he was an orex. I was going home and saw the stroilman in the grass. I didn't know what it was. It went up to Jack and attacked him. He thought I'd been ordering it around 'cause I was standing near it."

"What happened when he was attacked?"

"I tried to help him. It was trying to swallow him with its body. I threw my backpack at the stroilman's head and it exploded. We got away, and he told me to bury my clothes in the woods." It sounded lame and unreal when she retold the story, like she was describing a dream.

"It exploded?" Matilda *tched,* and the cactus gave her a warning look.

"Y-Yeah."

"Then what?"

"Mom had a party and Jack and some other orex showed up. So did a lot of stroilmen. Jack tried to save me, got caught, and En Law and this... monster... I don't know," she said despairingly, "They looked like they were in charge. They found out that I could see orex."

"And they let you go?" asked the cactus.

Hattie couldn't believe it either, even though it had happened to her. "The bigger one wanted to study me, but the small one, En Law, said there wasn't room in the ship to take me."

"How do we know she isn't lying?" Matilda shook her by her shoulder lightly.

"The zenzen I've been sensing lately matches up with what she says. The stroilmen around the school and in the neighborhoods, the mass atmosphere generated tonight southwest of town. Her story matches up with what we know."

Matilda released her arm. Hattie rubbed it and moved away from her. "I'm sorry. Ran Corp is not a business we want to be involved with." She did look sorry, but Hattie turned away.

"Why did you give the bullet to me, anyway?"

The cactus answered. "Because we thought that if you were an orex, then giving you that bullet would have ripped away your disguise. The question we asked you and the bullet are part of our security system, so to speak. We don't want to be found by other orex for...reasons. But you didn't have a disguise and you walked out of the shop with the bullet, so we knew you were human." Her blood curdled; they hadn't meant to offer help at all.

"We've never met a human that could see orex or spirits," said Matilda. "Are you sure you're human?"

"Everyone keeps asking that. Stop!" she shrieked, making them jump.

"Okay, okay, calm down." The cactus glanced at the window. Oil coated the glass. "You've had a bad night. Why don't you stay here until you can leave?"

"But what about my parents?"

"Why do you *have* to go to Tsava?" asked Matilda. "Don't you have other family who could take you in?"

"What's *saw-vaw*? I have to go to the casino."

The cactus replied, "The casino is in Tsava. Tsava is where we're from. Another world."

Both cactus and woman were mute for a time. Matilda took a breath. "We both escaped Tsava. After the war," she added, as if clarifying. But it was terrifying. There were wars there. "And we left our families behind. If we'd stayed, we would have died. It's better to think of them as dead."

It was the most absurd, cruel thing anyone could have said to her. Hattie said, "They aren't dead."

"But it's better to—"

"Matilda," the cactus interrupted.

"There isn't a way for her to get them back. Ran Corp is enormous. It has probably grown larger since we've been away."

En Law's words still echoed. Hattie groped for ideas aloud. "En Law said that Jack and Jane, his workers, could buy my parents back if they worked for five years. He said they could work for him because they had something to offer, but I don't have anything. I'm not special."

The cactus wiggled, as if shaking her head or shrugging. "Do you really have nothing? You seem pretty smart to me. You didn't freak out when I talked to you for the first time. You came here immediately after your parents were taken, even though you were in shock. You escaped Ran Corp. Not everyone could do what you did tonight. That proves you have something."

Hattie's mind churned. "If...If I did something...If I proved to En Law that I have that *something*...What would I have to do?"

"That's the question, isn't it?"

"You aren't serious about this," said Matilda, astonished.

But Hattie was. "Ran Corp got to Tsava by ship. How did you guys get here?"

"A friend swam us across—" The cactus began, but Matilda interrupted.

"Don't tell her," she snapped. To Hattie, she said, "You can't go to Tsava."

"If she's sure, we should help. We were helped, remember?"

To Hattie, the cactus said, "We know someone who can take you. What do you need from home?"

"The stroilmen might still be in my house." She imagined the scattered lawn chairs and the paper lanterns rolling palely along the oil-brushed ground as grass. And the uneaten and congealing food picked at by birds, raccoons, and mice next to the discarded trampled jackets and purses ruined by mud. The floors of her new house were likely stained black. "I don't know if I can go back."

"And you can't waste time, either. Fine, don't go back," the cactus said grimly. "We'll call Kometa. She can take you to Tsava."

"We?" Matilda had stood a little ways away while the cactus talked, staring out the oil-smeared window. She dropped the curtain and turned with her hands on her hips. "They might come after us."

"Good! I have a few things to say to them!" The cactus bristled. Her spines lengthened, glinting. "Aren't you angry with them?"

"Of course I am, but I'm doing the best I can to move on!" Matilda's voice built to a scream.

"How can you, when this happens? They're a ball and chain, and we just found out how long the chain is. I can't ignore this."

The spines elongated and angled toward the wall. They caught the pair of antlers on the wall and lowered them into Hattie's hands. The wood-colored bone split at the base and branched. Holes drilled into the base allowed for a black ribbon to anchor the antlers to the head, and the base was cupped underneath for a small skull and padded with brown velvet.

"Wear those. You'll look like a cervid, a type of orex." The cactus's expression changed. "Oh, Mota, types of orex. There's hundreds!" Matilda turned her back on them and glared out the window with her mouth set.

"You'll have to learn as you go," said the cactus. "All right. Let's call Kometa."

✣ 5 ✣

GOLDFISH IN THE DARK

T he cactus, who had introduced herself as Sonorra, sat in her pot on a trolley pushed by Matilda when they left the shop bound for the fountain in the park. The click and bump of Sonorra's trolley over the buckled sidewalk made Hattie flinch. Could stroilmen hear? The roads smelled of petrol. Was it from the stroilmen or the cars? The park was as motionless and lunar as the bottom of the ocean, and the fountain water was murky and had a sheen of cold grey moonlight.

Matilda parked Sonorra in front of the fountain and rummaged through her pockets. Like Hattie, she glanced over her shoulder, her eyes jumping from shadow to shadow. Sonorra seemed wary, but more self-contained.

Sonorra whispered to Hattie, "Do you know what a wanderer is?"

"No. I don't know anything about Tsava."

"A wanderer is a special orex. They're usually immortal, usually large, always powerful, and extremely territorial. Kometa is a wanderer."

"Wanderer, monster," said Hattie anxiously.

"Not all. Kometa's nice. Nicer than most orex or humans.

Their territory is Mota's Space, or the motaspace. And the motaspace is the space between Earth and Tsava. You can't cross it on your own. You need Kometa."

Matilda wedged a cellphone under her chin to shine light on her hands as she scribbled something on blank business cards and dropped them in the water.

"Ah, *tags*," said Sonorra in despair. "You should learn about them, too."

"Tell me more about Ran Corp." Questions boiled in Hattie's head and she couldn't ask them fast enough. "What do I need to know? What should I do when I get there? Why did I—"

"Ran Corp can trick you if you don't know the law. They're scum, but they abide by their contracts. Read carefully, take your time. Ask for help when you're there, but don't let them know you got help."

"Help? From who?" Hattie nearly choked.

"We're helping, aren't we?" The cactus' simple, honest face soothed her. "Matilda? You got anything to add?"

Through Hattie's tears, Matilda's face swam like a severe moon. She enclosed Hattie's cold hands in her own. "I think," she said after a time, "that you shouldn't be going after your parents. You're too young to commit yourself to a life of hardship, too young to bleed and sweat for them!" She stopped. When she resumed, her voice was tight. "But now things are the way they are. I wish we could go back to Tsava and live a normal life with our family and friends. But we can only have peace on Earth." Her own words seemed to sink in. Her expression softened. "You don't have to go. You can stay. You have family here. Won't they take you in?"

Hattie hesitated.

Matilda persisted, "Why don't you want to stay? Ran Corp fulfilled their quota, didn't they? They won't come back for you." Hattie hesitated again. Matilda's voice rose. "You're a child! You think you can win your family back from the most powerful company in Tsava? They caused the war. They're the reason hundreds of orex are dead! They're the reason we're hiding!"

"Matilda!"

"No! I want to know why!"

The water shivered. Something under the surface winked in the moonlight. Hattie thought it was a penny until it swam under a leaf: a goldfish.

Sonorra said in a hard voice, "She has to go."

"She shouldn't have to do anything." Matilda's grip numbed her arm.

A spine lanced between Hattie and Matilda and separated them. "We can't make her decisions for her!"

"*She is a child!*" Matilda clawed for Hattie around the spine. "This isn't right! She'll die!"

Newly terrified, Hattie jerked out of Matilda's grasp and toppled backward into the fountain. Sonorra and Matilda's shrieks were cut off by the crash of bubbles. Icy water engulfed her, and her entire soul electrified. Hattie had fallen into an abyss. The motaspace was depthless and vast. Moonlight spotlit down into the void as pearly columns, and the light diluted without hinting at a floor or walls. The leaves above her drew back over the hole she had made. The dark became darker.

Panicking, Hattie swam up toward the leaves. As her head broke through, she gasped for air. But the fountain was gone. She was still in the motaspace. Cautiously she inhaled and exhaled. No bubbles. She could breathe whatever cold, stagnant medium the motaspace was made of. Sipping breaths so as not to choke should the water return, she looked around.

"Kometa?"

The goldfish wiggled out of the leaves, orbited her head as if drawing her attention, and swam down past her feet. Though there was no apparent light source, Hattie could see herself and the fish as if they were outside during a sunny day. She retied her antlers, as their strings had come loose when she fell, and swam down after the fish. She didn't want to be alone in the dark, though descending was nearly as bad. She began counting heart-beats to keep time. After 321, she had settled into a paddling rhythm. It was like swimming in frigid water. Her hair clouded around her ears. She had no idea how far she'd swum.

It was 757 heartbeats before something glinted in the deep. Then many things, like sequins, stirred. They moved together in a flock—no, a school. Thousands of goldfish swam toward her and surrounded her, kissing her face curiously, exploring the folds of her dress and the strands of her hair. Each touch was dry and hot, not like earthly fish at all. Chimes sounded inside her head like a series of shaken copper bells. Were they speaking? The fish darted away from her. The school condensed, the fishes' bodies melted together, and an enormous goldfish twisted into being. Its veil-like fins floated around its red-gold body, as large as a whale, as it circled her.

"Are you Kometa?"

Another chime, a larger bell. Something like a yes.

"Will you please take me to Tsava?"

Another. Kometa glided next to her and rippled its upper fin. *Take it.* The fin was thin and slippery. Kometa beat their tail and powered forward. Hattie's hands slipped, and she clamped her legs and arms over the giant fish's back; it was like riding a muscular rocket that flexed. The invisible medium of the mota-space made no noise as Kometa swam.

The fish chimed a complicated series of notes that went up at the end like a question.

"I'm sorry, I don't understand."

The bells changed tones; it sounded melancholic. The fish didn't speak again.

She continued to count heartbeats and focus on holding on. Counting prevented her from thinking about Matilda and Sonorra, or falling off Kometa and being forgotten. Avoiding thought had been easier on Earth, with the stroilmen and En Law and the monster and everything happening all at once. Her arms and legs cramped as she gripped with all her might, but with Kometa undulating underneath her and their smooth scales, her grip was loosening.

Her hands lost contact and she yelled, "Kometa!" As she floated off the fish's back, she froze with horror. Kometa tore beneath her and rocketed into the darkness. "Kometa!"

Soon the fish was a glint, then gone. Hattie screamed and screamed into the blackness. She was sure she was screaming at the spot where Kometa disappeared, but everything was the same. What if she wasn't screaming at the right place? Or loud enough?

Soon she was screaming through sobs, her throat aching with the force of her voice. She curled into a ball and cried. Eventually she stopped crying and a cold dullness came over her. She couldn't think her way out of this. She had no idea where to go and could only hope Kometa noticed and returned for her. She couldn't tell if her eyes were open or closed. She could hear her shuddering breath and nothing else. Maybe, soon, she would hear both stop. Her thoughts accumulated, orbiting around one big thought: *I'm going to die.*

She'd never thought about death before. Death was what happened to cats who ran out into traffic and classmates who went away for a week unexpectedly and came back quieter and greyer; it was something that happened elsewhere to other people. Death meant going away and never coming back. But going away where? Here.

Hattie thought, *I'm already dead.*

She uncurled and looked into the motaspace. It seemed to be full of faint, colorful, pulsing shapes. She knew her brain was creating the shapes in response to stimulus. She could hear her breath going in and out like a tide. It was almost as if she was in her bed with the lights out, her eyes closed, waiting to fall asleep.

If I die here, that's it, she thought. *But if I don't...could I go back to Earth? Kometa would probably take me back if I asked.* She imagined surfacing in the fountain and arriving for the second time that night at the dressmakers' door. Matilda would probably be relieved, Sonorra regretful. She could talk with them about what she would say to her grandparents to explain her parents' change. She couldn't imagine that they wouldn't change after having their selves removed. She imagined that being without a self was to be bland, agreeable, and inwardly dead. At best. Could she keep what happened in her memories for the rest of her life?

No. I don't want that. She couldn't imagine what would happen if she went to Tsava. To her, Earth was her old neighborhood and old house with her mom and dad; it was the halls of her old school and her friends. She couldn't imagine what Tsava might look like—maybe a fantasy world with dragons and wizards and talking animals—but her parents' voices shone clearly in her memory: her mom, brisk, clear, and commanding, and her dad, friendly, patient, and generous. In the silence of the motaspace, she imagined she could hear them distantly, though she couldn't make out what they were saying. It was as if the millions of cells in her body turned into compass needles and strained toward the sound. And despite the situation and despite her fear, one of those compass needles pointed toward Tsava.

If I'm saved, I'll go to Tsava, she thought. *If Kometa finds me again, I'll know I have to go. And if I die here, that's it. Heads I win, tails...something loses.*

"Hey! Heeeeeeeeeeeey! Kometa! I fell off!" She shouted until she was tired. She continued for a few minutes, then stopped to rest before starting again. The weight pressed deeper on her chest. Dying was boring and taking too long.

Finally, she screamed, "Dammit, you stupid fish!"

And something winked in the dark. Kometa torpedoed through the dark and crashed into her, falling into sparkling little fish that swam around her, kissed her face, her hands, her neck, her legs, and chimed over and over like copper bells. Stricken with mortification, Hattie protested, "I'm fine! I'm fine! I'm sorry I yelled." The weight eased, letting her lungs fill with laughter. "Oh my God, I'm so glad you came back!" Kometa condensed into one big fish and smooched her. "It's okay. I'm okay." She laughed until she was limp. "Let's keep going. But make sure I stay on this time."

Kometa let her climb on again and swam, more carefully, onward. Hattie clutched their fin with tears rolling off her cheeks.

Many heartbeats later, the darkness lightened from absolute black to charcoal grey, then ash to oyster. Above, a pool of light wavered, distinctly separate from the dark. Kometa swam for it and broke through. They had arrived in a forest pool with a glassy-black surface. On dry land, trees the size of spaceships rocketed into a sky feathered with cirrus clouds. Cold air burned into her lungs as Hattie took her first breaths in Tsava.

While Hattie knew it had been night on Earth, shafts and spears of an evening light played across pond water. How long had they been in the motaspace? She swam to the ledge, dragged herself onto the warm rocks, and lay across them, exhausted. Kometa rested their head on a submerged rock beneath her.

"Do you know where we are? New Sprout was a town, so this is the Noh Forest, right?"

A firm chime.

"So, I go east." When she got up, her dress dripped with pond water and the pale-green fabric was stained with algae. She wrung out the liquid from the fabric as best she could. "Do you know how long it will take?"

Several firm chimes. Kometa broke into the thousand small goldfish, swarmed, and remerged. It could have meant anything. Hattie chose it to mean that she should get going.

"Thank you again for everything." It seemed so inadequate to say. "Will you tell Matilda and Sonorra that I'll be all right?"

The Kometas blew bubbles and merged to one Kometa. The fish thrust its tail, lifting their head out of the water, and kissed her forehead. Their lips burned, and when they slid back, the warmth spread from the spot and traveled throughout Hattie's body. Somehow, she knew that Kometa was trying to tell her something important. The great fish dissolved and, as a school, wriggled back into the dark.

"Thank you!" She waved until she could no longer see them. The wind's touch made her jump. "Okay," she muttered to herself. "Let's go." Carrying the burning inside her like a torch, she retied the antlers firmly onto her head and walked away from the pool.

Since the sun was setting, she followed her shadow east through the forest. It could be that the sun did not rise in the east or set in the west, but she had nothing else to go on. There was little undergrowth to block her way, but the tree roots were like the veins of giants, and she had to climb over the bigger ones. The air creaked with unknown insect and bird calls. Her wet dress clung to her legs and chilled her. Her fortitude wore away like chalk in a stream. She tried to think about what she needed to do, but she was too exhausted. How could she get into the casino? They probably wouldn't let in a dirty little girl who asked nicely. She would have to clean up, or sneak in, or both. Or...

The light faded. The stars blinked awake, and the sky cooled to velvet blue. She emerged from the forest onto a hilly meadow silvered with grass and studded with large stones like the backs of grazing animals. Around the stones were long ribbons every color of the rainbow which were tied to the top of an enormous and bizarre building planted in the center of the clearing.

The building resembled a colossal pinecone, both beautiful and strange. The shingles were scales painted in bright, childish colors, and between the scales of the pinecone nestled ten tiered floors set with windows. Alien figures passed behind the golden-lit glass. The building was supported by two legs round as grain silos, both scaly, knobble-kneed, and four-toed like chicken feet.

As she watched, one of the feet lifted, cracked a toe with the sound of timbers breaking, and settled on the ground again. Orex flowed into an entrance on the other side of the building she couldn't see; the line trickled from a road with bright white round lanterns bobbing on it. Was this the casino?

Between her and the chicken-legged pinecone building was a long, low building. Hattie bent low and crept through the grass; the tips tickled her nose. The building looked like one of the longhouses she'd seen in history books: mud-sided and thatch-roofed, with smoke cottoning out of the top and no windows. She pressed her back against the wall once she reached one side of the structure. She could hear orex talking at the front. Unlike Jack and Jane, they were clearly not human or even human-shaped. They spoke in mutated growls, squeaks, and mechanical voices, yet she could understand them. She passingly wondered why but ignored the thought.

"...Soth, you're working on the third-floor balconies. Xnth, you're working on the main floor with Ahk. Mushio, you're with me and Nim on the second floor..." She peeked around the corner. One appeared to be reading from a list. "...and that's it. En Law returns tomorrow. Remember to use our summer greeting. Remember to use the stairs instead of the elevator. Blah, blah, blah." The orex, who resembled a furry, upright alligator crumpled the list. "All right guys, we get through the night and then it's the weekend!"

The orex chuckled and drifted off with their lanterns. He mentioned En Law. This *had* to be the casino. Could she pretend to be one of them and sneak in? Though it was hard to see, she could tell they all wore something like uniforms. Maybe she could steal one? She checked the other side of the longhouse. There were laundry lines and a water pump with a drain, all empty. Maybe inside...

She tiptoed to the front and knocked. "Excuse me, is anyone in there?"

She felt electrocuted as someone called, "Yes, one *second!*" The door opened and an orex loomed out. The creature was a many-jointed, glassy humanoid with a floating head and a face hewn from crystal. "I'm coming! Oh." The crystal's planes shifted as they frowned. "Are you lost?"

"Yes," she said at once. Rolling with their assumptions seemed like a good plan. "Nice to meet you. I hope you don't mind, but do you have a spare uniform or something I can wear instead of this?" She spread her dress to show off the stains. "My mom will kill me if I go inside looking like this."

"Uh...yes, ma'am." They bowed. Hattie breathed. "I can't offer you a spare uniform, but may I offer you laundering tags?"

"Yes, please."

They reached into the pocket of their uniform, pulled out receipt-like slips of paper and presented them to her with all four hands. She froze. How did she use them? What could she do?

Several moments passed. The orex asked the floor, "Ma'am?"

A memory blazed: her mom holding out her arms as she was fitted for a dress. Hattie held her arms out and said firmly, "Please."

The orex lifted their head and their eyes popped. "Oh! I'm sorry, I didn't realize—" He pressed the tags to her skirt, back, and chest, flustered.

"No, I'm sorry. I should have explained: I don't know how to use tags. I was always told to let someone else do it," she added, to make him feel better and so that she could possibly learn. "I've always wanted to learn how to use them..." This only made them more flustered.

"No, no, no, everything's fine. We just press them on and..." The tags absorbed the dirt and water and dropped off after they filled, leaving cleaned fabric. "Ta-dah."

"Thank you," she said sincerely.

"Of course. Would you like succor?"

"Sorry?"

They pointed with a slender feeler. Mud was pasted to her ankles. Cuts oozed through the mud, and one of her toenails was cracked and purple. Scratches criss-crossed her arms from pushing through the forest. Seeing them, pain throbbed all at once. She pressed her mouth and tightened her eyes to prevent herself from crying and giving it away.

"Are you all right, ma'am?" asked the orex timidly.

"Yes." She rubbed her eyes. "I'm just worried about my mom. I'll take succor."

"Succor" was first aid. The orex used different tags to sponge off and dress her wounds. One smoked and stung, but she bore it rather than complain, afraid it would give her away. When the dress was clean and pressed and she'd wiped her eyes, Hattie asked the orex, "Would you escort me to the casino? When I get inside, I can find my mom from there and I'll let you go to work."

"Uh, yes ma'am. Do you not have your tickets?"

"Mom has them."

"I see." The orex steered her down a dirt road. Ahead, wide stairs led to crimson-colored front doors two stories tall, which were guarded on either side by hulking automatons who collected tickets from the orex lining up at the door. The orex walked to a guard and whispered to them. The guard waved them through the doors into blasting light and sound.

Everything was bright, moving. Playing cards slapped against long tables of green or red felt. Hulking gold slot machines rolled symbols and spat coins. The ceiling, ringed with balconies draped with ribbons, yawned, and the roof was painted with a night sky more beautiful and transparent than the one outside. Like moons, luminous balloons floated above their heads, shedding light on the crowd.

She wished she could see in two different directions like a chameleon. There was an orex with a mess of squid tentacles for feet and eyes on the sides of their heads. Some had scissor halves for claws, there were mannequins of porcelain who wore outlandish costumes, and insects with mournful human-like faces. A beautiful Hattie-sized hummingbird laughed once, and she ached to hear it laugh again. There were half-human, half-animal or plant or machine floating objects with painted black eyes that blinked and mouths that talked, along with some so indescribable she thought they weren't orex at all. They created a din like a mixture of all the sounds in the world.

"Thank you," she said to the orex. "I think I'll be fine now. What's your name?"

After a pause, they replied, "Lirk."

"I'll be sure to mention how helpful you were. Have a good night!" She waved goodbye to them and moved into the crowd. *Okay,* she thought. *Almost there. Act like you belong. Now, his office.* Her stomach growled. She remembered she had not eaten anything for hours, and thought, *Now, food. Find out where the office is while you eat.*

There was a bar at the far end of the casino-ballroom. An orex like a human with a bat head mixed glasses full of colorful liquids. Her ears, as large and full as satellite dishes, twitched in all directions, and her gelled mousy brown fur had comb tracks.

"Yes, miss?" she said in a clicking voice.

"A menu please." Hattie remembered she had no money. She wouldn't get to eat after all. But maybe she could find something out by sitting and listening. She wasn't so worried about being discovered now that she knew she could pass as an orex.

"Aren't you a bit young to be drinking?" said the bat-orex wryly. "Where are your parents?"

"I don't know. I'm supposed to go to En Law's office to meet him when he gets back, but I don't know where they are, and I don't know where the office is." She found that telling a vague truth was easier than lying. "I don't want to go, but if I don't, I'll be in trouble."

"Would you like us to send out a call over the speaker? For your parents?"

"No!" Hattie said too loudly. The orex frowned. Hattie lied quickly. "They're crazy. I need a break."

The bat chuckled, clearing dishes. "I understand that more than you know. Your parents are meeting with En Law?"

"Yep. They're making a deal with him."

"That's pretty rare, to meet with him in person."

"I didn't know," she replied after a pause. Admitting when she didn't know something seemed to be working out, and the bat didn't pursue it.

"Who are your parents?"

"Cassandra and Tanner Flores."

"What are their descriptives?"

"Descriptives?"

The bat's watchful attitude chilled her. There were other customers at the bar, and she ignored them, though some were trying to get her attention.

"Yes, descriptives." She leaned in. "What are they?"

"They don't have any. We don't use them."

"Where are you from that you don't use descriptives?" Two tiny white fangs glinted in her teasing smile.

Nervous, Hattie tried to joke. "Ever hear of a place called Earth?"

The bat laughed. "Good one. But where?"

"Earth. Seriously."

"Uh-huh." She put a glass of water in front of her and a bowl of pink jelly cubes wrapped in leaves. "Complimentary. I can tell your parents haven't fed you." Hattie tried not to wolf anything down, but the cubes were gone too quickly. They tasted like cold, gelled chicken broth wrapped in a mint leaf. "Do your parents have a tab? I can't give you much that's complimentary."

"No." The bat seemed to expect more. "Cheapskates."

"Ah. Not as surprising as you would think here." She gestured at the crowd. "Why are they meeting with En Law?"

"To make a business deal with him." Hattie focused on the water glass rather than meet the bat's gaze. "I don't know what it is, though."

"Mm. Have more." She put another bowl in front of her. "It's strange how they know when En Law will return," she said in a low, silky voice. "Not many orex know he's out. And," her voice became lower, "the orex who aren't supposed to know aren't allowed in Baba."

Hattie's mind blanked. "Who?"

The bat blinked. Some of the customers cleared their throats, rattling their glasses of ice, but she ignored them. "Well...you know about the Alate."

Hattie had meant, who was Baba. "The who?"

The ears twitched again. "You've never heard of the Alate?" A robot whirred to the bar, dressed in a bright green tux and bowtie. Two metal arms snaked from the robot's sides and wound around her. "You are a suspicious little orex."

She felt like she'd been shoved down a flight of stairs. This was why she was getting caught? "I'm being arrested for not knowing who the Alate are?"

"No, because your heartbeat says you're telling the truth."

"I'm going to be detained for telling the truth? That's not fair!"

The orex at the bar were watching her now, curiously. But the closest orex gazed at the bat with something like outrage and alarm.

Struck by inspiration, Hattie said to the closest orex, a ghostly women with fangs jutting over her upper lip, "Did you hear that? She just accused me of being from the Alate!" Some orex frowned, but the ghost woman and two others stiffened. One orex gasped, "I heard!"

"Ma'am," the bat began in exasperation.

"Do you know what they do in the Alate?" Hattie whispered this question to the orex who'd spoken, a humanoid with the head of a white horse, hoping they'd would tell her.

"No," she whispered back, scandalized.

Hattie knew horses could be spooked by even a frog, and she hoped it was the case here. She breathed, "They poison people. And she accused me of being from the Alate. But *she's* the bartender." Both of them looked at the bartender, who looked incredulous. One orex held his drink to his eye. "Did she serve you last?" The robot was pulling her away. Hattie raised her voice. "I'm poisoned! This bartender just poisoned me! And they're taking me away to die!" A quiet bubble had formed around them. All the orex at the bar examined their drinks. "She probably poisoned everyone! *She poisoned me!*" The horse-headed orex leaped away with her dress tearing on the barstool.

"Ma'am!" said the bat in alarm.

To Hattie's triumph, the orex screamed, "The bartender's from the Alate and she's poisoned everybody!"

The crowd screamed and recoiled. Food and drink splattered on the carpet as the crowd stampeded for the doors. The robot moved into the crowd with Hattie and blared soothing words: "Please remain calm. There is no threat." Orex knocked into him as they ran blindly. Hattie couldn't protect herself and was hit hard several times by swinging limbs, purses, trunks, and wings. A giant orex slammed into the robot and its arms released her. She fell to the carpet. A hoof dug into her stomach, and she curled up in pain. Another foot smashed into her legs.

With a jolt she realized she could be trampled to death. She scrambled on all fours through the crowd until she could clamber to her feet and run with those around her. She glimpsed side doors and ran through them into a hallway full of towering hookahs, their smoke made the air heavy and spiced. She dodged huge orex lazing on cushions who craned their larvae heads at the havoc through the doors. Another door led to a kitchen which smelled so good she wanted to hide in it. Beyond that was a smaller, less-furnished hallway. At one end was a lobby with another exit open to the night and a desk with a bee-orex receptionist.

Hattie ran to the desk.

"Where's En Law's office?" she gasped. "Emergency!"

"What is going on?" the receptionist asked in concern, rising from her seat.

"Please!"

"Third floor, end of the hallway. You can take the elevator—"

"Great! And call security!"

"What! What's going on?"

Hattie was already running. When she reached the end of the hallway, she stopped. There was no elevator. In the center of the ceiling dangled a dainty silver bell on a blue satin ribbon. A sign on nearby wall said: *one ring to summon the elevator*. She swatted it.

Chiming, it swung once—*Bang!*

Hattie squeaked as a huge box materialized with an explosion of steam. It was painted deep red with interlocking lines of indigo next to silver trim. The doors parted like sideways eyelids into a pale yellow and green room—the elevator. A lantern orex standing inside said cheerfully, "What floor?"

"Third, please—hurry! There's a riot downstairs! Someone got poisoned!"

"Holy Mota! Yeah, let's go!" The doors snapped shut and the elevator leaped, knocking her onto her rear. The orex was a large paper lantern. Light diffused from the translucent paper, ribbed and tapered to rings at both sides of the cylinder of its body. Someone had drawn a straight line for a mouth, and simple black dots for eyes. He was just like Sonorra.

"What happened?" he asked.

"The bartender's poisoning everyone!"

"Chiros? No way, I thought she was nice!"

"You can't trust anyone around here," she said grimly.

The doors dinged open. Hattie prepared to run out, and the orex shouted, "Wait! Unhook me!" He struggled to get free of a metal hook attaching him to the elevator. "I don't want them to get me!" Hattie unlatched him, and the lantern zoomed out ahead of her.

A lengthy corridor stretched straight ahead to a black door. The floor were bare, dark wood, and the walls were covered in pale, spring-green fabric spotted with blood-bright poppies. There were no windows; light came from lantern pairs—not orex lanterns, regular lanterns—burning along the corridor. A fragrance like charcoal undulated in grey smoke threads from brass burners on either side of the door. The riot sounded muffled, like a TV turned low.

Hattie walked toward the door. The orex zoomed in front of her and blocked the way.

"You can't go in there," he said. "I'll get fired."

She grabbed him. He squeaked as she tucked him under her arm. "Sorry." Her voice cracked.

Beyond the doors was a magnificent room. Paneled walls rose high and arched over their heads to a domed ceiling. Cabinets lined the walls, holding a thousand treasures: small engines, glass bottles, calipers and pencils and lightbulbs and botanical drawings. Hundreds of shelves illuminated by thousands of candles, their lambent faces wavering. Here, the riot was only a murmur. Something ticked on a shelf.

A broad blackwood desk sat in the middle of the room. Behind it, one chair; in front of it, two. Hattie sagged into one in front and released the orex. He bobbed into the air and brightened, looking around.

"You know, I've never actually been here. I guess that's a good thing." He hovered over the desk, inspecting it.

She didn't respond. Sleep caught up to her like a fog, and with it, all the delayed aches and pains. Her feet throbbed. She felt drained yet heavy at the same time.

The orex drifted back to her, looking concerned. "Are you okay?"

"No," she said thickly. She drew her knees to her chest and laid her head on them, letting out one ragged breath.

"Oh. Don't worry. There's a nurse downstairs. When everything is over, I can take you to her." His cheer was like the sun shining in her eyes. "What's your name? I'm Limn the Bright."

"Hattie."

"No descriptive? Where are you from?"

"Earth."

"Earth? Ha, that's funny." He paused. "Unless you aren't

joking. You're not laughing. Oh my stars, you're serious." A nearby *bang* made her start. Another *bang* and then voices.

"She said she was looking for his office—"

Hattie leaped up and staggered. Her vision tilted and her legs buckled, but she caught the desk before she could fall completely. She slid down to the carpet and leaned against the desk, dazed and panicking.

"Oh, it's Chiros!" Limn soared to the door. "Chiros! In here! We're all fine!"

The doors burst open. The bat plus several other orex streamed into the office. The bat looked battered, with tears in her eyes and mussed fur.

"Where's the little orex?" she barked at Limn.

"She's over there. Whoa, hey, what are you—" The bat bared her fangs and aimed the crossbow at Hattie. Limn dropped in front of it. "The safety isn't on!"

"She's with the Alate!" the bat snarled, pushing him out of the way.

"No! We're running from them! Right?" he asked Hattie. She nodded. "See? Listen, see if she's lying."

An orex she hadn't seen before said in a deep voice, "She's responsible for the riot downstairs. She's with them."

"She did that? But..."

"She shouted in front of a hundred customers that I'd poisoned her, and that I was with the Alate. Nearly everyone left the ballroom. Thousands of petals in damage. More in lost revenue. Someone will pay for everything and it won't be me."

A horn popped out from the desk and all jumped. It blared, "Move off the pad. En Law's coming."

"He's back," one of the guards muttered.

"Early," said another. "Mota and Atom, he's going to kill us."

After an ugly pause, she and the others backed off a design in the carpet Hattie hadn't noticed. The orex muttered and Limn dimmed until he was barely as bright as a tea light. Finally, the design flashed, and En Law, Jack, Jane, the crooked-legged monster, the receptionist, and a few other orex Hattie hadn't seen before, materialized.

En Law snarled, pale as lightning, "Why is my office populated when I gave strict orders—"

Hattie stood up. En Law's eyes turned ultra-black, colder than deep space. A strained moment passed before he said, "you."

"Beat you," she said hoarsely.

The monster laughed his creaky laugh. "Splendid!"

"Creon," Chiros stepped forward. "This young orex is responsible for the riot that occurred on the first floor. I strongly suspect she's with the Alate."

He answered, "She's not from the Alate, and she's not an orex. How do you know she caused it?"

"She sat at my bar and we started a conversation. Her heart rate was abnormal to start, and she had strange reactions to questions. I called a guard to restrain her. She made a scene and accused me of being from the Alate, which a customer believed. Then, the customer panicked and inadvertently helped her start the riot."

"Which ruined an entire night," En Law finished, eyes on Hattie.

"Yes, sir."

"Interesting," Creon said. Jack stood behind them. He was trying to catch her eye, but she ignored him. "When did you discover the existence of Tsava? Orex?"

Hattie whispered, "A few days ago."

"Clever. And you escaped the stroilmen horde and the numbing incense. Clever, clever." He spoke of her like a dog that had done a neat trick. "Shall we take her gambit as her interview, En Law? Tack on the night's losses to her parents' price, and make that her debt?" Chiros and the guards' expressions changed slightly. "Five years?"

"Yes." En Law's expression had cooled. He went around his desk and picked up paper, pen, ink, and a stamp. "Your parents' selves plus tonight's debt is five years of work. Normally that would be the sum of the contract, but I believe there are a few conditions I must add due to the nature of your origin." He wrote swift black strokes with the pen. "While you work for me, you will give no information about your origin or nature. You are an orex for the next five years. I will give you a few things to aid you with this, and you will work closely with Jack and Jane while you learn about Tsava."

He addressed everyone in the room. "If it becomes known where she is from, I will blame you and take appropriate action. Understand?" They nodded. "I expect you to help her maintain the illusion that she is an orex." He thrust the paper at her. "Hattie, sign."

"How do I know you will give them back?" she asked.

"The contract is binding for you and me. I would not stay in business if I did not keep my word." His nostrils flared. "Sign." She pushed herself up to the desk, took the pen, and signed: *Hattie Anne Flores.* When she finished, the paper folded itself smaller and smaller until it disappeared. "Jack and Jane, take her to the longhouse. The rest of you, go help clean and repair Baba. I must speak with her tonight."

Jack and Jane stepped out from behind him and lifted Hattie up by the arms. Being set back on her feet was like stepping on nails. If either of them let go of her, she would jellify and collapse. Instead, she floated out of the rooms hanging on their arms like a worn-out shirt. Half the guards watched her with pity and fear. The other half watched En Law with fury and hatred.

Jack and Jane carried her to the elevator and it shuddered as they entered.

"You did it," Jack said as the doors closed. She hated his voice. She wished she could lunge over and bite him. "I can't believe you made it. How did you get here?"

Hattie didn't speak. The elevator juddered to a halt and the doors opened to a gloomy, cramped hallway. One wall was punctuated with thin needles of light. The hallway echoed with their footsteps. Orex passing in front of the slits made the light tremble.

They carried her to a door at the other end and passed out of the casino into the night. Hattie remembered the yellowing light of the longhouse, unfamiliar eyes, and being set down. Nothing else.

❧ 6 ❧

HATTIE THE FLORES

Something small, wriggling, and heavy dropped on top of her. Hattie woke with a suck of air and flailed on her pallet. A little girl rolled off her stomach.

"New girl! New girl!" the little girl yelled. "There's a new girl. Wake up!"

The girl ran through the slumbering workers, pounding on their backs until they groaned awake and swatted at her. They were in a long low room with woven walls. The floor was rush mats covering dirt, tamped down and hard from traffic. Along the walls were pallets, folded blankets, and pillows. Some orex still slept against the wall, mounds of blankets gently rising and falling. The orex-girl was about the size of a five-year-old and was dressed in a scarlet silk poncho marked with black dots. Her skin seemed armored in pure black scales and two wiry antennae sprung from her tightly curled black hair. At first Hattie thought she wore faceted sunglasses but quickly realized those were her eyes.

"Everyone up! There's a new girl!"

"Shut up!" A pillow collided with the little girl and she fell face-first into Hattie's lap. "Can't you be quiet for ten minutes?"

She popped up and attacked the speaker with a shriek. Orex

shifted and murmured sleepily. *This is Tsava*, she thought, waking completely. *I'm really here. Sleeping with aliens.* Her legs ached when she moved and dirt crumbled from her feet when she rubbed them together. Hattie hid under her blanket to fix her antlers because they had slid sideways during the night. When she emerged, she mimicked the orex clumsily, her nervousness ebbing, and her curiosity growing. The orex pulled on clothing with extra arm and neck holes. Robes with belts seemed to be in fashion, or were they a uniform? Some dipped their tentacles in oil and rubbed themselves down. Others washed their faces with water and soap. No two were alike. Nobody but the little one paid any attention to her aside from a curious look and a friendly *hello, did you get here last night? Oh, welcome.*

There was a knock, and Jane came through the door of the longhouse.

"Hey, guys." She sighed, stepping over the other sleepers. "Hey, Hattie." She handed her a loose dress of rust-orange. The fabric had been worn and washed many times to a soft thinness. It had a pattern of four white diamonds arranged into a larger diamond. "This is your work uniform. And I have to take you on a tour of Baba."

Hattie asked, "Who is Baba?"

"Baba is the building. Red Rooster is the name of the casino."

"Bye!" called the little girl-ladybug.

Hattie waved to her and tied her hair in braids as she hurried out the door with Jane. Baba loomed over the clearing.

"How was your first night?" Jane asked. Her bones clicked like bouncing dice.

It was a nightmare, and I can't believe I'm alive, she thought. A memory hit her. Jane was standing on the roots in the forest. Her stomach knotted until it threatened to break. For lack of anything better to say, she replied, "It was okay."

Jane chuckled. How? And it was a deep sound, a *hm-hm-hm* that would have been made with closed lips and in the throat.

But Jane was all bones. Was there any point to asking how things worked in Tsava? "First day's the worst day."

They reached Baba's side. Colored tiles patterned her square base in turquoise, poppy-red, spring-yellow, milk-white, algae-green, and oil-black.

"Blue, green, yellow," Jane muttered, pressing the appropriate tiles. "And backward..." The door swept open. Behind it was the corridor hidden on the first floor.

"This is the servant's entrance. Never go through the front doors unless it's an emergency. Try to whisper when you're back here, but you don't have to during the day."

At the end of the corridor was another bell on frayed twine. Jane swatted it, and the elevator exploded into existence. As they rode it, Jane explained Baba's schedule. Night workers employed during the regular casino hours every evening to early morning worked as waiters, maids, cooks, bartenders, and dealers. Day workers fixed and cleaned up from the previous night before preparing for the next round of parties from late morning to the afternoon. Most orex workers within Baba were one shift or the other, but there were other jobs, such as the receptionist, the doctor, the financial planner, and the assistants. Jack and Jane were En Law's assistants.

"You'll be working on the main floor for now," she explained as the doors opened to the fourth floor. "You'll have to stay in the longhouse until it gets less busy and he can put you somewhere."

The fourth floor was for workers only, with splintery floors, squinting windows, and crooked doors. Servants washed their clothes and bathed in a steamy, tiled room filled with shallow pools. Next door was a break room with a wall of jumbled lockers, mismatched chairs, a leaning table, and a couch leaking pale blue stuffing. Next to the break room was a communal office with an ancient printer who politely greeted Hattie and introduced herself as Krrrsch the Reliable, a phone that was not an orex, and a tray of paper, envelopes, and pens. Hattie would need to provide her own tags.

"That's pretty much it," Jane said. "Jack and I live on the fourth floor. En Law likes us close so he can call us in the middle of the night and tell us to bring him tea or something. Questions?"

Hattie's stomach growled.

"Excuse me?" Deep in Jane's eye sockets, a green light flashed.

"No, it's my stomach growling." Jane cocked her head. "I'm hungry," Hattie added.

"Why not just say so?" Jane led her back into the elevator.

"It just happens. I don't control it."

"Huh. Well, the kitchen is on the first floor. They'll feed you. By the way, what do humans eat?"

"Fruits and vegetables, meat, eggs..."

Jane inhaled. Again, Hattie wondered how. "*You eat dead things?*"

"Uh..." Jane wasn't wrong, at least on Earth. "Yes. But I could also eat the stuff the bartender, Chiros, gave me. I could eat that. The complimentary stuff." How much would she have to hide, if crying and stomach growling is so strange here? What if she couldn't eat anything?

Jane let out another *hmmm,* and led her to the kitchen she had run though last night. A small group of orex milled around the entrance, chattering. They too had the four-white-diamond pattern on their outfit. If Hattie pretended she was on a set for a fantasy movie, she could believe she was among humans. When a watery being engulfed a squirming plate of yellow slugs and their writhing shapes were absorbed into its body, the illusion vanished.

"Give us a little bit of everything," Jane told a blue-skinned, many-armed chef. "And mil-fle."

The chef ladled and scooped different soups, reddish bark,

jelly, and paint onto a platter. They thanked him and retreated to a counter to try everything.

"This is mil-fle." It was the jelly. This kind wasn't as pink and the leaves were different, but it tasted almost as good as it did last night. "It's made from mza." Hattie tried to pronounce the word but couldn't. "Just ask for the day mil-fle, and they'll know what you're talking about. This is saim." It was the bark, which tasted like cured meat. "These are puj, nareem, and kol." The first soup was bitter and nasty, the second edible and sweet, and the third so vile Hattie choked. "And this is loop." The paint-like sauces were actually paint. Hattie wiped her tongue on a napkin. "So, you can only eat essences and life-derived foods, huh."

"I guess?"

"For now, just eat mil-fle, saim, and nareem." Hattie repeated the unfamiliar names until she could remember them.

"You'll need to learn the names of all the food we serve. En Law wants you to stay off the night shift until you know more about Tsava. You'll be cleaning with the longhouse crew until you get the hang of it." Jane had led her around the fourth floor, and now they were back at the elevator hall. "Hey." Her voice lowered. "How did you do it?"

An ugly, burning feeling spread through her.

"Why don't you want to tell me?" She sounded genuinely puzzled. "I can keep a secret."

"You helped En Law kidnap my parents," Hattie said in a low voice. Her hatred nearly choked her when Jane had the gall to look surprised, then guilty. "Are you stupid? Don't be friendly to me. I hate you."

Jane backed away with her hands raised.

"All right, fine. I understand why you would be mad, but don't ever speak to me that way again." Her tone changed, defensive. "I'm your supervisor and you don't want to be fired. En Law's doing you a favor. I don't know why he's bothering to give you a shot at all. So, don't forget that." She lifted her chin. "Any questions?"

Hattie glowered. After a moment, Jane said, "Go talk to Chiros and Limn about helping you find your way around. I have work to do. And besides, I don't want to work with someone who hates me."

"Where are they?"

"You figure it out." Jane walked away without another word. Hattie burned with injustice and imagined her gaze boring a hole in Jane's spine as she disappeared through a door. The burning feeling ebbed, replaced by misery.

She swatted the elevator bell and the elevator banged into existence an inch away from her. She jumped away. What would happen if it ran into her?

The lantern orex from the night before bobbed in the corner as before.

"Welcome to the elevator. Where can I take you?" he said in well-worn cheeriness. He relaxed when he saw it was her. "Thank Mota. I thought it might be Creon or En Law."

"Hello. You're...Limn, right?"

"Limn the Bright," he said, smiling. "That's me."

"Uh, Jane said I was supposed to talk to you or Chiros about knowing where to go?"

"Yep, I was told not to let anyone know about you." He bobbed again as if nodding. "Hattie the Flores?"

"Hattie Anne Flores. Not *the* Flores."

"That's a long name. What's your descriptive?"

"What's a descriptive?"

He sucked in air and his inner flame flickered. "Ooo, we have a lot to cover. Okay. A descriptive is something your parents give you when you're five, and it helps other orex know who you are. How old are you?"

"Twelve."

His dot eyes expanded. "Don't tell anyone that, or you can't work here anymore. New Sprout law says that you have to be at least fifteen to work."

She covered her mouth to keep it from trembling. Another thing to worry about.

Limn continued, "Pretend your descriptive is Hattie the Flores for now. We'll have to think of a backstory for you. Why don't we say you're from beyond the mountains? Nobody knows what's past there, and you'll be okay as long as they don't ask too many questions." He paused. "Are you really from Earth?"

"Yes," she said miserably.

"Wow! Earth is real?" Limn flashed with excitement, beaming.

She covered her eyes with her hands and pressed on them to push back tears. The burning returned, hollowing her out.

"Oh, no, I'm sorry. Please don't leak." Limn's light peeked through the cracks in her fingers.

"Earth isn't...real?" Hattie choked.

"I mean, it has to be real, because you're from there. To orex, Earth is something our parents tell stories about. Like, 'The Human and the Monmouth Take a Walk.'"

"What's..." *Everything.* Which questions were the most important from the mountain of them? "Do you think I'll be able to get my parents back?"

Limn's light wavered. "I don't know," he said finally. "But I'll help however I can."

The elevator pinged. "I have to take this. Wait here. Actually, go clean yourself off. You still have dirt on you." He let her out of the elevator, and it vanished with a puff of wind. Hattie ran to the washroom, filled a basin with water, put her whole face in it, and screamed underwater.

Her heart felt bruised and every reminder of home pressed on it. She wanted to believe it was all a nightmare she would wake from, or that a miracle would occur and the orex who knew what was happening would storm En Law's office and demand the release of her parents. Then she would go home hand in hand with Mom and Dad and everyone. Or maybe she could morph into someone who was unafraid and fierce who could work tirelessly for five years. She would be seventeen when she finished. Would her parents recognize her? What if she was fired or found out? What if they died trapped wherever they were? What if she died?

There was a shower in the washroom. *At least they have showers in Tsava*, she thought. She wondered why Tsava looked like a mixed-up version of Earth. What does Tsava have that Earth doesn't?

This train of thought distracted her. She stripped off her new dress and showered in the lukewarm, slightly salty water. Dirt sluiced down the drain, and with it, some of her fear. When she was done, a tiny light blinked on over a pile of towels.

Of course Tsava would have towels, she thought, wrapping herself in one. *It's hard to improve towels.* She made a game out of spotting familiar things, like cabinets, doorknobs, and carpets as she dried her hair. By the time she was fully dry, she was ready to go out again.

The elevator was waiting for her when she exited.

"Do humans wear shoes?" Limn asked.

Shoes, she thought. "Yes."

"Let's go to Chiros then." The elevator doors closed. "Any questions?"

"What are you?" Limn's mouth vanished. She didn't know how to read this new expression. "I'm sorry if I said something mean," she said hastily. "Tsava and Earth have a lot of the same things, but Earth doesn't have orex."

He shook his body and his mouth returned. "No, no. Earth must be very different from Tsava. There are *no* orex on Earth? At all?" Hattie shook her head. "Wow." The elevator doors pinged open. "Hold on. Ammu! Ammu!" Ammu was like the ladybug-esque orex, except he was an iridescent green beetle about as tall as Hattie. He paused his sweeping. "Would you mind the elevator while I show the new girl around?" The beetle orex shook his head and held the door open for them as they filed out. "Thanks. See Hattie, orex are pretty friendly here. It's just that En Law isn't."

They were in a corridor that ran behind the main hall. Orex ran back and forth with supplies and equipment from different rooms. One room seemed to be full of pulsating, moist organs the size of beanbags that orex poured stinking liquids over. Hattie stared as much as she could before the door closed.

Limn caught her staring and laughed. "Those are Baba's organs. We have to take care of them or she dies."

"Are all buildings alive here?"

"Not at all. Living buildings aren't typical in Tsava. Baba's a molluska, one of the last of her kind. Actually, I think she *is* the last one. We're lucky."

"And a molluska isn't an orex?"

"Uh, yes. All orex in Tsava...are orex." Limn grimaced. "Ugh! It feels really weird to be explaining this. Hang on." He closed his eyes for a moment, before opening them with a decisive expression. "I'm an orex, but also a spirit. En Law is an orex, but he's also a monmouth. Baba's a wanderer, but also an orex...I think. Orex don't tend to think of wanderers as orex. But sometimes wanderers can also be spirits...maybe."

"Okay." If he didn't know, she didn't have to worry about it. "What is Ammu?"

"Ammu is a cryptidion."

"And Jane? Jack? What's a cervid?"

"Jane is an ossifel. I'm not sure about Jack. He might be a hybrid. A cervid is...well, it's what you look like now. Cervids are supposed to be extinct, so that's convenient for you. Cervids are from the Violet Hills and are supposed to eat grass. Can you eat grass?"

"Nope."

He led her to a storeroom where Chiros, the bat-orex from before, sharpened knives against a whetstone. *Knives are Earth things*, Hattie noted nervously.

"Hi Chiros. Hattie needs shoes," Limn said. Chiros put down her knife and looked at them with her oily eyes.

"I'm, um, sorry about yesterday," Hattie said timidly. "I didn't mean to start a riot."

"Who does?" Chiros smiled with her tiny white fangs. "So, it's true? You're from Earth?"

"Yeah."

"She's never met spirits before!" Limn said excitedly.

"Ooo, then you better represent." Chiros reached into a cabinet and pulled out boxes. As Hattie tried on shoes, Chiros leaned over, her eyes gleaming. "Can you tell me the whole story of why you're here?"

Hattie started at the beginning—the move—and by the middle, Chiros's fur bristled and Limn's light had a red tint.

"That is awful," Limn whispered. Heat poured off him. "That is evil. Why?"

"I don't know," Hattie said gloomily.

After a pause, Limn said, "You'll definitely get your parents back. You found a way to a world you didn't know existed the day before, beating your parents' kidnapper to his own office. Give yourself some credit."

"But if I hadn't...it was terrifying! I didn't want to do it!"

"I don't know if Earth has epics," Chiros said. "But in our stories, a hero takes a world-changing journey across land and time to do something incredible. The hero seems larger than life because you hear the story in a single sitting without all the extra stuff like being terrified or failures. The hero's achievement wouldn't be so awesome if you had to slog through the chain of coincidences, luck, fear, and little things. But epics aren't epic because the hero has no fear, they're epic because the hero is brave and bravery is being afraid and doing it anyway."

"That should be your descriptive," Limn said. "Hattie the Brave."

❦ 7 ❦

SICK BREAD

Hattie clung to her new descriptive like a talisman. She knew she'd been brave or they wouldn't have given her the descriptive. Having it helped her look orex in their many eyes, to not flinch when the elevator appeared, and when frighteningly odd monsters, such as a crawling worm with a rasping leech mouth, came around. The descriptive gradually fit her like an old shirt, and she stopped thinking about it so much. It wasn't that she became brave, but that she wasn't afraid of orex.

For a week, Hattie rose with the other longhouse girls, washed in the small shared washroom, and walked with them across the dewy grounds to the back rooms behind Baba where their schedules were pinned to the bulletin board. *Bulletin boards*, *schedules*, Hattie thought.

Hattie's tasks were to clean the casino floor along with the newest employees, the lady-bug orex, Doro, and the crystalline orex who'd cleaned her dress for her, Lirk. They picked up the biggest pieces of trash and swept with a vacuum spirit—a vacuum!—who sucked up the debris too small to see. Chiros showed her how to brush the velvet card tables, rub oil into the bar, shine the brass accents, and polish the floor. Each task reminded her of the preparations she'd made for the block party, and she bitterly suspected she would be reminded every day for the next five years.

Living in Tsava wore away its fantasy. There were always surprises, like the time Hattie got turned around while folding screens and hanging curtains in Baba's twisting sixth floor and became frantic until she turned a corner and saw a small pink tree blooming in the square-shaped light from an open window. Daily life was done differently, but familiarly. Some orex bathed in oil, some in dust, but all bathed. There were familiar chores like cleaning and gardening, but also chores like shoveling muck out of one long hallway whose walls glistened, fleshy and pink, and which kinked and doubled back. Night was spent lying on pillows in the longhouse, chattering about other places, other orex. She asked far, far more questions than she could answer. Luckily the girls assumed it was because of her foreignness and youth and were more than happy to explain things to her. *If I have five years of this*, she thought. *I think it'll be okay*. And she could sleep.

After another week, Hattie saw on the schedule that she was to meet Creon and En Law in En Law's office. Her mouth dried.

"What did you do?" the ladybug-orex asked, standing on tiptoe to read.

"I promised some things to them as part of my contract," Hattie said. "They're probably thinking of that. I don't think I've done anything wrong."

"You haven't." Lirk leaned over her to read the schedule. "Chiros reports to him on what you do. She said you're fine."

Still, Hattie's stomach was in knots as she rode the elevator up to the third floor. She hadn't been to it since arriving in Tsava. Despite the sunny day, the corridor was as musty as a funeral home. She knocked and stepped back.

Jack opened the door. "Come in," he said neutrally. They avoided eye contact as she stepped in. En Law stopped writing at his desk, shuffled his papers into a specific order, and stood. In his simple blue shirt and black trousers, he looked human. But there was something chilling in his gaze and, like Jack, something off about the way he moved, too fluid and quick.

"Good morning," he said after a pause.

"Morning," Hattie replied with restraint.

He examined her for a long moment. She bristled and bit the inside of her cheeks to not react.

"You look like monmouth. Do your bunkmates already view you as a cervid?"

"Yes."

"They don't suspect you?"

"No. I don't think so."

"Good." En Law folded his arms. "Dr. Creon has asked me to administer a series of questions about being human and the differences between Earth and Tsava. He kept a journal of all the crossover objects he identified both on Earth and on Tsava, making a game of how many he counted. When you have quiet moments, do the same. Write down things that are on both Earth and Tsava." It irked Hattie that she had been doing the same thing. "Question one. How did you follow us?"

"I didn't. I went ahead of you."

"Your method of travel. And do not give me smart answers, because I will fire you, or at the least add more time to your contract."

Hattie ground her jaw. Would the two orex in back Applewood be in danger if she answered? Would he know if she lied?

"I asked an orex how you traveled to Tsava and did what they said," she replied. "I swam through the motaspace."

A partial truth without naming names; she thought she'd nailed it. En Law raised an eyebrow.

"You *swam* through a metaphysical plane?"

"A meta-what?"

"An imaginary ocean."

"How can it be imaginary if I went through it? How did you get here?"

"A ship to protect and ferry us across the motaspace...which is supposed to be deadly to the touch." En Law examined her reaction as he spoke. Something about her bewildered expression convinced him and he went on, "Can you perform any zenzen?"

"I don't know."

En Law pulled a receipt and a pen from his desk and handed it to her. "Draw the most perfect square you can." Hattie used another piece of paper to draw straight lines and erased the overlap. "Now activate it. Imagine the square changing into a cardboard box."

Hattie focused. Seconds trickled past. She began to feel stupid.

"I suppose not." He made a note.

The questions afterward were unchallenging. What do humans usually eat? What is a day like in your regular life? Where else do humans live? What news was happening on Earth? And more that she could more or less answer.

En Law wrote her answers down, placed them in an envelope, and slid it into a drawer. "Dr. Creon has returned to headquarters to conduct research. When he returns in a few weeks, he'll be ready to study you. Do you think you know enough about Tsava to work the night shift?"

"I—no."

"No?"

"No, I don't know enough about Tsava," she said through gritted teeth.

"You will have to learn as you work. Tonight, you start."

With that, he dismissed her. She fumed on her way back to do chores with the longhouse girls. On the way down, Limn said, "What's wrong?"

"En Law," she spat. "Put me on night shift."

"That's not bad. Most orex love night shift. You're allowed to keep what you earn."

"It's not that..." She lowered her voice. "I hate him."

"Me too."

"Why do you work for him?"

"Well..." He sank into thought until the doors opened. "It's a bit private. Sorry."

"No worries. Bye."

It would have been nice to know what it was, Hattie thought sadly. If only to have someone else who was in a similar situation. Was he a special kind of spirit? She hadn't seen other lantern spirits around. Or maybe En Law had stolen something from him?

Hattie was allowed to leave early to sleep ahead of the night shift. In the evening, the girls shed their makeup, clothes, and exoskeletons, redressed in their formal wear, and headed out. Workers lit the lamps lining Baba's driveway and swept the road. Hattie ducked into the entryway and scanned the bulletin. She was with Chiros at the bar.

The casino floor hummed with last-minute activity as orex straightened tablecloths, stacked chips, and arranged flowers and crystals. At the bar, Chiros showed Hattie how to cut fruit and ice for drinks. *Limes*, Hattie thought. *But no lemons.*

"Just take orders and cut fruit," Chiros said, demonstrating how to pulp something like a dragon fruit. "The easiest way to make small talk is to ask questions. Orex love talking about themselves."

As the doors unlocked and orex flowed in, Hattie's stomach twisted, remembering her last journey through this same crowd. A walrus-like orex heaved himself into a seat and ordered. "Can I get a...uh...*a jus* old fashioned?"

"Coming right up," Chiros said smoothly. She juggled a pair of blue cherries as she poured a glug of straw-yellow seltzer, added a drop of some other smoking liquid, and passed it to the orex on a small red napkin.

The orex's proboscis snaked into the glass and the liquid level dropped. "Excellent," he grunted. "Put it on my tab."

Tabs, napkins, Hattie thought.

The night became so busy she forgot to be anxious. No orex talked to her unless it was to order. She found a steady rhythm between chopping, serving, and watching. Listening was too hard when she didn't know half of what the orex were talking about. Asking vague questions like, "What happened next?" and, "Why not?" helped the customers stay happy.

Her lack of knowledge almost got her into trouble. On one of her first night shifts, she couldn't stop staring at a magnificent orex, a living, crystalline giraffe, twelve feet tall, wheeling four stilt legs round an axis, casting rainbows on the crowd and walls.

Its twelve eyes made eye contact with her and it wheeled round like a haughty chandelier. Hattie froze and thought, *Gotta be suave, gotta be polite.*

"I'm sorry for staring," she said. "I've never seen anything like you."

The orex paused.

"I'm one thousand percent real, sweet cheeks," it said in a smoky, smug voice before sauntering away.

"Wow." Chiros smiled with her tiny fangs.

Other times did not go so well.

"Why don't all the doors have doorknobs?" Hattie asked Limn.

"Because most orex don't have hands," Limn explained as they pushed through the doors.

"Are there no door orex?"

"What?"

"What makes some objects alive and some not?"

Limn stopped and gave her an appalled, disgusted look. "Objects?" he repeated.

Hattie realized she had said something gross. She wanted to respond, yet she could feel the air literally heating between them.

"I'm sorry," she said meekly.

"Good." He floated on.

It still didn't answer her question. Why were so many things familiar? She stopped playing her identification game because more was familiar than not. She had an uncanny feeling that underneath everything, there was an order to why some things were alive.

* * *

One day, four weeks later, Jane caught her at the end of her day shift to tell her that En Law wanted to see her. He waited for them in the corridor with his hands clenched. Jack stood next to him, his hands clasped behind his back like a soldier.

"Can't you move faster?" he snapped. "Come! I have a job for you!" He stalked down the length of the corridor. Jack and Hattie followed as closely as they dared. The once wax-white skin around En Law's eyes had purpled, and his mouth was a taut slit.

Once in the room, En Law said testily, "Close the door behind you." Jack did so. "Hattie, you will go with Jack and Limn into the Noh Swamp and seek out the Sage of Fireflies. He has been preparing medicine for me. By the time you arrive, it should be finished. Limn will go with you as a light to talk to the lampyridae to guide you further."

"Yes, sir."

"When you have the medicine, flip this—" En Law gave Jack a gold coin the size of a quarter "—and catch it to return to Baba. Now go." Jack collared Hattie and led her out of the office quickly. They met Limn in the elevator. He was explaining how to operate the elevator to Ammu.

Ammu asked Limn, "When are you going to be back?"

"No clue," he said cheerfully. "As long as you don't let the elevator shake, you'll be fine, even if you get off at the wrong floor."

"Bye," said the orex gloomily as they got off.

"Is operating the elevator hard?" Hattie asked.

"Yeah," said Limn nonchalantly. "You need five different

dimensional operators and a binding design to make it move. It's a boring job, but not everyone can do it."

Hattie was about to ask what dimensional operators were but thought she'd better ask him later. Jack looked like he might snap if they kept talking. Once outside, they waded through the grass and entered the forest. As they hiked, the evening deepened. Light slanted through spaces between the branches with fine gold particles and simmered pleasantly on their skin before cool, purple shade glided over them. Limn's light fell around the trunks. Occasionally a stream trickled through the roots and stones. Hattie stepped from root to rock to cross the small streams. Jack often simply crossed them in a single stride. He'd been in his stretched form since coming to Tsava, though sometimes he shrank for convenience. She wished many times she could grow taller, too. Why did he work for En Law? And how could someone change their height?

Jack cleared his throat. "Limn, you know that Hattie's..."

"Hmm?"

"...human."

He paused. "Yeah."

"You know where Hattie's from?"

"Earth."

"Okay." The ground became steeper, and they picked their way down the rocky slope. When they arrived at the bottom, Jack asked, "Did you two talk about spirits?"

"A little."

"Okay. There's a bit more that Creon learned about spirits while he was on Earth. Don't tell anyone else what I'm about to tell you. Limn, I'm letting you in on this, because you already know about Hattie. Hattie, did you ever ask Limn about objects and spirits?"

"Yeah. How did you know?"

"Spirits are almost always inanimate objects." Limn scowled. Jack held up his hand. "To Hattie, inanimate means like lanterns, clouds, pencils, books, and things like that. That's what their bodies would be to humans, since spirits don't exist on Earth. And if spirits have living things for bodies, they're usually given the same status as wanderers, because if they can inhabit an organism, they're powerful. That's a gross way of putting it," Jack added. "Don't talk about spirits like they are objects. Their bodies are vessels with *telos*."

"What's *telos*?"

Jack and Limn exchanged significant looks.

"That is a deep philosophical question," said Jack. "Spirits think it boils down to purpose, other orex say destiny. We really don't know."

"Okay." Hattie cast her mind around for other questions. "How are spirits born? Do they just pop up, or do they..." A grin curled across Jack's face. Limn's light reddened. She said hastily, "Never mind!"

"Oh, come on, it's not like human reproduction." Hattie blushed, but Jack continued. "Spirits are objects to you, remember? They don't have any body parts to reproduce with, so most of them have to get...creative."

"Jack!" Limn and Hattie said in tandem.

"Fine. Spirits are born in a few ways. Objects that have strong emotional attachments to them can become catalysts for spirit-birth. Plants or animals that are abnormal are also candidates. Nobody knows why this happens. Usually, two spirits will get married, pick an object like them, and nurture it like an egg until the object attracts enough zenzen to become a baby."

Hattie imagined Limn as small as an egg and giggled. Limn was crimson with embarrassment and had begun to smoke.

"Spirits dying is another side. If their vessel breaks, wears out, or their plant or animal dies, they die. Most spirits without living bodies can't switch bodies, but plant or animal spirits usually can, and they can live for hundreds or thousands of years just switching from body to body."

From there Hattie became absorbed in listening to Jack talk about spirits and Tsava. He went over manners, like "don't use bodies without permission," their native home which was rumored to be Cosmos Country, important spirit countries like the Grass Union and the Federation of Tools, and how what they eat and how they sleep depends on the spirit's body.

Soon the ground squelched with each step. Water puddled in their footprints. The fetid smell of decay clung to every plant and rock. Frogs, insects, and other creatures creaked unseen. Branches thin, bony, and black like the fingers of witches, snared the fog. Marshes feathered with reeds held grey-green water where bubbles belched softly on the surface. As the light faded, Limn brightened. His light reassured Hattie. The shadows slipped too often and too quickly for normal shadows, and Jack wavered in and out of sight.

Out of the swamp rose a tree lush with white leaves. At least Hattie thought they were leaves, until one of them peeked at them.

"Hattie, come here *now.*" The fright in Jack's voice was inarguable. Jack scooped her up and tensed to bolt forward when he froze.

The peeking leaf had dropped from its bough and faced them. A white face, holes for eyes and mouth, floated at the level of Jack's eyes. It floated forward unattached to anybody, to any *body*. Then it smiled, frightening as her own face in a mirror at night.

"Hello," it whispered in a high sweet voice.

As it floated closer, Hattie's hair rose. Though it was the size of her head, its presence had a powerful pressure like the feeling before a storm. It smiled and more faces slipped from the branches like sheets of dropping paper; like masks. They hung in the air, smiling at her.

The first whispered to Hattie, "Do you like fengul?"

"I don't know. I've never met one before." The masks giggled.

In her ear, Jack whispered, "Be polite."

"But I think I like you," she continued.

"So formal!" said one.

"Kometa said most are ill-bred."

"Sick bread?"

"No, like pests."

The voices chattered over each other, gabbing and laughing; they finished each other's sentences and started others with different endings. When the wind blew in, they rose and swayed as if buoyed. Their mineral, musty smell flowed toward Hattie, Jack and Limn; an old smell.

One interrupted the rest. "Do you know who you are here?"

They all turned to Hattie expectantly.

Hattie answered after a pause. "What do you mean?"

"You are one thing on Earth and you are another thing in Tsava," said one. "A certain thing to Mom and Dad and a certain thing to En Law. Have you ever thought what you were to Earth? Or Tsava?"

"No. Sorry." Her voice shook. They sensed this and their buoyancy became more controlled, a swaying.

"Peace, peace," another said soothingly, high in the branches. "We only wondered about you."

Hattie asked, "What is it?"

"We don't know. That's why we asked." A giggle rippled through them. "But we know you are not an orex."

"How?"

"Don't worry about it," said one to Hattie. "See you soon!"

The wind gusted, and the things were whisked with a *wheeeee* into the swamp.

Jack watched the place where they had gone for a time. Finally, he set Hattie on the ground and with a jerk of his head, he continued on their path. Hattie followed, trembling. After staying with the girls in the longhouse, she thought she had a handle on orex. But these were *alien*.

After a few minutes, she ventured, "What were they?"

"Those were wanderers," Jack said in a clipped voice. "And *those* were fengul. Do you have something you want to tell me?"

"What? No!"

He rounded on her. "How do they know you're not an orex?"

"I don't know!"

"You keep saying, 'I don't know. I don't know.'" He towered over her with a knot at his temple. "I can't believe you. How were you able to make a deal with En Law, beat him to Tsava, disable a stroilmen without help, and all without knowing anything?"

"But I don't," Hattie said miserably. "I got a lot of help. Not with the stroilmen but getting here."

"Guys." Limn squinted at the dark places where the fengul had slipped away. "Let's talk about this later."

"Do you know what wanderers are?"

"Yes!"

"How?"

"The orex who helped me get here told me. And Limn told me. I didn't ask those things to talk to me!"

"Wanderers *kill* orex! Fengul eat orex's *faces!*"

"I didn't know!"

"What *do* you know? Who helped you?"

"I can't tell you," she growled.

"Guys," Limn said fearfully. "Please stop yelling."

Jack had an ugly expression. "How did you get here?"

"Leave me alone!" Hattie snapped. They had stopped and stood apart, each tense. Limn flared. The light stabbed her eyes and she winced. "Stop fighting. We're still in fengul territory. Jack, if the fengul like her, they won't be happy that you're yelling at her."

Jack twisted his mouth and said nothing else. Hattie fumed. He had no right to ask her questions or accuse her of anything.

They continued walking for several minutes until Limn said, "Look!" Phosphorescent lights the size of coins blinked among the roots. They rose and fell as if on an invisible sea. Limn pulsed in rhythm for a minute. Presently the fireflies replied with a pulsing of their own and bobbed into the swamp. Wearily they followed them. A clearing opened, and earth breached the swamp like the broad back of a whale. A little round red-brick house perched in the center of the swamp island, windows glowing and smoke piping from the chimney. A fence of gnarled wood circled it. Paper squares and rectangles were pasted onto the fenceposts, which extended to include neatly-tilled rows of vegetables waving in the breeze. The fireflies nestled among the purple cabbage and yellow peppers, clustered along the fence and around the steps, and twinkled in the dusk. There were so many that she felt she'd wandered into space and walked among the stars.

They stood for a minute, catching their breath.

Jack was the first to speak. "C'mon."

They trudged up the grassy slope. Jack reached out to knock, but the door flew open. A powerfully-built orex stood before them. His brown eyes jumped from face to face suspiciously.

"En Law sent you?" he asked harshly.

"Yes," said Jack. "We—"

"Come in and wipe your feet," said the orex irritably, holding the door open for them. He had the body of a catfish or salamander, brawnier and taller than a man. His dusky blue skin was slick with mucus which spotted his rough-spun robe, and gills fluttered on his neck as he snatched things off the shelves.

The three went in mutely and the door snapped shut behind them. The house was well lit and sparse. A rug of braided rags pooled beneath a rough-hewn table and a trio of chairs. Strings of herbs and plant bulbs dangled near the window. A lamp burned on the table with a soft, amber light. Books with titles like, *Fungis and Gurls You Need to Know*, and *Bio-chemicals in the Kitchen!* lined the shelves. A mortar and pestle lay on the table beside a plate of multi-colored powders and dried herbs, and a beaker over the lamp boiled with a clear yellow liquid. The air was musty and rich with a medicinal smell.

"So, do you know what kinds of medicines En Law ordered?" Limn asked her.

"Nope."

"Why would he need medicine? Do you think he'll die?"

"Nope." Hattie wasn't hopeful enough to think her contract would end so soon.

The Sage gave Jack a package wrapped in old newspaper and string. "Take it, give me my money, and get out. And don't lead stroilmen here again."

Silence fell like a sword.

"What?" Jack said.

The Sage pointed out the window. Three stroilmen stood amongst the reeds. They did not go past them as if there was an invisible fence. Their presence made Hattie cold. How close had they come to catching them?

Jack's eyes had blackened with shock. "We didn't do it! Why would we bring them here?"

"I would never summon impurities into my swamp! Get out!" The Sage threw a handful of herbs at them. They ran out and the door slammed behind them. Fireflies scattered in a burst of green sparks. Jack fumbled in his pocket and pulled out the gold coin. The stroilmen stretched and craned their bodies but did not seem able to come closer.

"Hurry! We're going back with the coin. Hattie, grab my shirt. Limn, sit on her shoulder." Hattie grasped his shirt, and Limn perched near her ear, paper crackling. "Everyone ready? Heads."

He flipped it. It rang a pure high note as it spun in a golden gleam high over their heads. When it fell into Jack's hand, the world warped. The stench of the swamp vanished, a breeze swept away the humidity, and Baba's steepled roof tickled the milk-white moon.

The trip to the office was noiseless. Jack and Hattie trembled, and Limn's light was dim. Meanwhile, En Law inspected the package.

"Good. It doesn't matter that he won't work for me anymore. If this fails, I was going to cut him off anyway. Your first mission is complete, Hattie. Now you understand what you'll be doing. My advice to you: do your missions well if you want to be released earlier. I don't have anything else for the three of you today, so you are free to go."

"And the stroilmen?" Jack asked tersely.

"They aren't from Ran Corp. I will give you oleophobic tags to use if they come closer. And I'll investigate on my own."

He dismissed them. Limn greeted the orex operating the elevator and chatted with him about schedules before saying goodnight. He floated over the grounds to one of the other long-houses. Hattie and Jack watched him disappear inside where his light shone briefly through the windows before dimming.

She expected Jack to go away, but instead he coughed and shuffled his feet. "I'll walk you back. It's not safe at night."

"Thanks, but I'm fine. Goodnight." She began walking, but Jack stayed by her side.

"No, night is when wanderers come out. I'll walk you back."

"Leave me alone!"

He threw up his hands in exasperation. "I'm trying to help you."

"Ooh, big help. Helping En Law kidnap my entire neighbor-hood," she said acidly. She was going to cry soon and didn't want him to see it. A liquid movement in the dark on the edge of her vision made her flinch, but it was only the grass. Anger flooded her and pushed tears closer. Jack noticed and started to speak, but she said bitterly, "When the stroilmen finally get you, you better hope that somebody else saves you. I wish I hadn't. I hate you."

He stopped walking. The wind-whipped grasses hissed as she trudged to the longhouse by herself.

8

THE ALATE

The days settled into a friendly routine. Hattie learned the nicknames of the longhouse girls. All were kind, some saucy and some dutiful, with nicknames like "Golden Fur," and "Fire Eyes." Since Hattie was new, shy, and didn't know enough about Tsava to join in conversation, she was "Quiet Girl". They swept and mopped wooden floors, scrubbed stone tiles, beat carpets, and dusted corners. Aching back, knees, and palms, no matter how many each had were soothed in steaming soaks in the shower room. Like the others, Hattie stewed in the hot baths, gobbled her food, and wormed into her sleeping pad at the end of every day.

She no longer worried about being caught as a human. There were few things that orex did in their daily lives that humans didn't also do, such as cleaning and setting schedules. As long as she remembered to retie her antlers occasionally, they thought she was one of them. Except for tags. The girls slicked the receipt-like papers over the windows and doors every day, torn from something that looked like a coupon book. The receipts had geometric designs on them like Celtic knots or mandalas and usually burned away the moment they activated. Hattie was given a "coupon book" of her own. Its cover was cardboard printed with cute pink flowers and said *Household Tags*. It contained four different kinds of tags: Pure Water, General Fabric Cleaner, Dirty Storage, and Clean Storage. Luckily there were diagrams for how to use them.

She tried each one in the bathroom when she was alone. When she ripped the Pure Water tag it shuddered, and water poured from the ripped edges like sugar from a packet. The water swilled down the drain and the pouring stopped after a few seconds. The tag dripped, but the paper was not damp. Hattie examined the paper by turning it over and trying to peel it apart to see how the water was stored inside, but it appeared to be only a coupon ripped in half.

General Fabric Cleaner was sponged over dirty curtains, clothes, carpet, or other things after she remembered Lirk had used it on her dirty dress. When ripped, Dirty Storage expanded into an opening the size of a plastic grocery bag that led to a trash can. This seemed to be a fixed position, as the same trash can would fill and be replaced every day by an orex she could sometimes see. She waved to them, and they waved back with a hand like a sea anemone. Clean Storage opened a window to a closet Hattie could reach into and take cleaning spray, laundered rags, towels, and other things. She always tried to take things as fast as possible in case the window closed and snipped her arm off.

As far as she could tell, zenzen was magic with a different name. She blanked when someone asked her to "scribble," "doodle," or "activate," but she managed to make excuses each time—that her hands were full, she had to run an errand, or clean somewhere else. Reluctantly, she asked Jack about it when he did his rounds to supervise the workers on the casino floor.

"Zenzen, huh," Jack said coolly. "All right. We'll see if we can have a lesson."

"Thanks." The other longhouse girls casually swept closer and closer with their ears pricked. "Anything else?"

"En Law wants us to run errands for him in New Sprout. He wants you to come."

"Sure."

"Jane and I will be waiting downstairs," he continued doggedly. "Let your shift leader know about it."

"I will."

The shift leader had overheard and approved. "Not much I can say if En Law wants you to do it." Hattie wanted to wash the dirt and cleaning fluid off before heading to town, so she hurried to the bathroom. It looked like a gym's bathroom, with several shower stalls and a drain in the center. Jane was there, scrubbing her bones with a toothbrush in front of the mirrors.

"Hi," Hattie told her coldly. She wet a washcloth and rubbed over her arms, legs, chest, the small of her back, and the back of her neck.

"Hi." After a minute of scrubbing, Jane asked casually, "Are you getting used to Tsava? Jack seems like he's been helping you a lot."

"Yeah. En Law makes him. He thinks I like him because I saved his life on Earth."

"Oh, that's right, you did." Jane responded as if Hattie had said she'd gone to the supermarket and bought him a bag of chips. Hattie felt like she was turning inside out with awkwardness and annoyance. Then Jane changed the subject. "You're washing before going into town? Why?"

"Because I've been cleaning all day and I'm gross." *Isn't it obvious?* she almost added. Her legs and arms were grey to her knees and elbows with dust and dirt, and her dress had bleach and blood spots from when she received a large splinter while cleaning the bathroom.

Jane shrugged. "I thought it might just be something humans did. Orex don't typically wash up before going out."

"Then why are you?"

"No reason." Her tone suggested there was a reason and it was none of Hattie's business.

She dumped a bucket of water over her skull. The sudsy water crashed to the tiles and spread to Hattie's toes. Dripping, Jane wrapped herself in a towel and slouched out. Hattie wondered what she was missing as she changed, re-braided her hair, and went downstairs to meet Jack.

Jane had beaten her to the lobby. A powerful smoky perfume coiled around her when she moved, like a lash to the nose.

"Notice anything different?" she asked coyly.

"Your perfume? It's kind of strong," Jack said. "Let's go. I brought a list of what En Law wants, and once we get that done, we're free to do whatever."

They took the main road, trimmed by trees which rained leaves like gold coins. Jack and Jane were both taller than her, and Hattie frequently needed to jog to catch up. Carriages, sleds, wheeled boats with sails, and palanquins moved past. Each vehicle was pebbled in gems, painted richly, or pulled or carried by uniformed servants. Once, a car rolled past, a large key in its back rotating. Farther up the road, the brick ended, turned to granite, and branched. More orex joined them. A quartet of ordinary-looking young men marched together in lockstep with a briefcase carried in their center. As they passed, Hattie saw their chests were joined by interlocking ribs which protruded between the buttons of their shirts. Another orex like a large fleshy root was being pulled in a cart by a cantering, many-legged machine. A flock of balloons drifted from the direction of town, arguing and making faces at each other using similar drawn-on faces like Limn's.

"Don't stare," Jack hissed, and Hattie dropped her eyes.

The town jumped out of the forest like a pop-up illustration. Buildings of every arrangement, size, shape, and color lined a grid of teeming streets. There was an enormous green glass bottle with a door cut into of it. A many-tiered birdhouse was stacked to the clouds, with forms flitting in and out of the holes. An entire street of lofts lined the forefront of the town; the largest could have eclipsed Baba and the smallest was a single matchbox in an empty dirt lot. Houses were shaped like shoes, giant cardboard boxes, geese, and there were even some shockingly ordinary ones whose inhabitants were the most unordinary orex. Fishbowls were alive with aquatic orex. There were plastic castles and apartments of shifting floors. Bicycle frames lifted into the air on humming dragonfly wings. A purple school bus on frog legs trundled through the crowd and other orex rode animals too strange to have an Earth equivalent. Among them were almost-people, hybrids, tribrids, and some orex Hattie could simply not describe. The sound of the milling orex was familiar, the same melody sung with different voices and instruments.

Jane stuck by Jack's side and tried to talk to him. Hattie tailed them, feeling relieved they weren't paying attention to her, but also bizarrely left out. They first stopped by a stall with a wall of pigeon holes. The orex took the slip of paper Jack handed him, bowed, and placed it in one of the holes. The paper caught fire and its smoke moved into the wind over the buildings.

"Was that a post office?" Hattie asked as they left.

"No, just a smoke signaler," Jack said curtly. "Messages within the city only."

"Does Tsava have post offices?"

"Yes. We're going to one."

The post office looked similar to the ones on Earth except more colorful. The aluminum post office boxes were bubblegum-pink and azure, but the building held the same long lines and rows of boxes and envelopes and it brought a homesick lump to her throat. They shuffled into line and swayed forward as the line shortened. Most orex busied themselves with their own packages, yet one orex wrapped in a sky-blue scarf stared. His scarf wrapped around his entire face except for his violet eyes, which gave him a crazed expression. When it was his turn, the orex at the counter had to call twice before he slowly, one step at a time and without taking his eyes off them, moved forward.

"Do you know that orex?" Jack said to Jane under his breath.

She glanced back casually and shook her head. "Let's go. He's weird." He led them to a dress shop, a machine store, then a pharmacy where the orex at the counter said, "Just a minute," and vanished to the back.

The pharmacy was a wooden building with drawers from matchbox-sized to stable-sized built into the walls. Assistants opened them, took handfuls of grasses, white powder, or knobbly roots, and hurried off to grind or boil them. Another orex at the counter, a tiny creature like a crow with muscular arms, extracted a pocket calculator, pen, and notepad from his cardigan pocket. "The order is being completed at this moment. Here is what Mr. En Law owes..." He pecked at the calculator with his beak. *Why not use his fingers?* Hattie thought. "And your total."

"En Law is paying by check," Jack said, passing a signed slip. *They have checks here?*

"Very good."

A second many-eyed, many-armed smokey wraith orex with hair whisping like steam offered Hattie and Jane handleless mugs with blue tea. The tea tasted fruity and dirty, but not unpleasantly so. Jack eased into one of the chairs by the door and fished a list from his other pocket. "Once we pick this up, we're done. Is there any place you wanted to go?"

"The music store. I want to look at new mallets." Jane flopped next to him with her limbs all akimbo so Hattie couldn't sit. Hattie didn't want to sit next to her anyway. Instead, she leaned against the wall and watched the pharmacy orex busy themselves.

After a few minutes of Jane trying to pull conversation from Jack, the crow announced, "Sir and madams, your order is ready." As they exited, a single, still orex stood in the swirling crowd. Hattie thought she could make out something blue, but it vanished.

Hattie jogged between them. "I think that guy from the post office is following us."

"He might just have the same errands, right?" Jane said uncertainly. Hattie's gut said he was following them.

"Let's take a detour and find out." They moved away from the close streets and shops of the downtown district and headed down a boulevard. Bricks of pale green paved the road in a herringbone pattern, and straight-trunked trees with yellow leaves like stars lined the sidewalk. The mansions grew more opulent. A golden castle gleamed on the corner, protected by a moat of cream in which chocolate geese paddled. For the first time, Hattie felt the urge to learn how to hunt. A soaring tower of braided morning glory vines and rainbow embroidery threads swayed to the clouds. Splayed next to it was a wooden pyramid of interlocking parts that shifted hypnotically.

Hattie craned her head to see the next building, but was disappointed. The next estate was only a giant hole in the ground large enough to swallow an apartment building. It was as if a giant hand had reached down, scooped out a plot of earth, and forgot to put it back.

Jack hissed, making her flinch. He snatched her up just as there was a shout and he and Jane bolted. Figures flew above them and landed just ahead of them on the road. They cloaked themselves with their wings.

Jack's grip on her tightened. He whispered in her ear, "Remember, you are an orex indentured to Ran Corp. Say nothing else."

The orex closed in on them. All of the figures wore pine-green ponchos with wide sleeves for their wings and had bird heads, some of which were real and others, clearly masks. The blue-scarfed orex was the only one without a bird head and had scarlet wings. A prominent nose peaked under his scarf, or maybe it was a beak. From beneath their ponchos they drew rope coils and lassoed Hattie, Jane, and Jack. The ropes cinched Hattie and Jack together. Her antlers scraped his chin though her feet dangled over his knees. Jane's eye lights flared and flickered like fire in wind.

"Who are they?" she whispered.

Jack replied, "The Alate."

The orex reeled them in and dragged them to the hole. Wind whistled cold from the hole. It looked bottomless. Were they jumping into the motaspace?

Jack flinched as an orex shoved him and yelled, "Move!"

Jack stepped over the edge. Hattie's heart leaped into her throat as they fell into darkness. They landed a moment later. Their landing jarred her and made her antlers cut into Jack's chin once again. The hole's mouth was a faraway blue circle, like a hazy eye, too faraway for the shortness of the jump.

The rustling and thuds of the orex landing beside them were the only sounds until another, "Move."

Jack walked forward gingerly. Hattie had a sense of déjà vu. He had carried her before like this not knowing where they were going or where they would end up. Being unable to see the floor or walls made her feel like she was floating in Jack's arms.

The air was cool, motionless, dry, and smelled earthen. Their breathing echoed off...what? Walls? There was a yellow light at the end of the cave. Closer to the light, they saw that the cave's dirt and stone walls were close and rounded, but so lavishly and haphazardly decorated that it didn't matter. A rich tapestry rug pooled on the ground with tins of hard candy littered about, their spillage crushed to sugar dust. Blades glittered on the walls and were propped above jars of bullets and shell casings. Bookshelves were sunk into the wall and crammed with cheap souvenirs. The books themselves lay like dead birds on the carpet with their pages torn and spines broken. Gold, coins and jewels in little piles shone here and there. Beyond the illumination, there was darkness again as if the gold was the only thing worth lighting.

An orex approached as gently as smoke. Long ears tilted to catch sounds in their pink, veined insides. The head was almond shaped and the body was built with balanced wires of muscles as he stood on long hind feet. All of him was covered in ash-colored fur. Hattie was fascinated by his eyes: marigold-colored with jet-black centers. He was a grey rabbit, only slightly taller than she was.

He flicked a sword as if it were nothing more than a silver needle to Jack's neck. Blood slid down in beads along the forged metal. Jack's breathing was shallow and quick. Jane was as frozen as death.

The rabbit raised his paw and gestured. More orex, at least ten, coagulated from the dark and stalked forward, clinking through the piles of coins. Jane gasped as three appeared behind her as well.

"Okay, we grabbed those guys you wanted, Ven. Now what?" asked one of the bird-headed orex, a heron.

"Hold them ransom," said the one with the scarf. "All three are valuable. The tall one is Jack the Bastard. The ossifel is inherently valuable. If the third is who I think it is...Well, we'll find out. Tie them up. You, put the little one down," he told Jack gruffly. Jack awkwardly set her down and she slipped out of the ropes when he stood up. The orex tied her wrists together and then to a dresser.

"Well, well." The rabbit admired the three of them. "Three of En Law's workers imprisoned, and I didn't even need to leave the house. Though we might need to leave this location soon."

The orex with the scarf stepped closer to Hattie. He was staring at her, his violet eyes unblinking.

"This one," he said suddenly. "She's human." Terrible new questions shot across her mind. How did he know about her? How did he know about humans? What would happen now?

"Really, Ven?" Another orex, a raven-headed one, stepped forward to examine her. Jack's face was rigidly controlled. "How do you know?"

The orex, Ven, grabbed her antlers.

"Humans don't have antlers!" he said triumphantly. The strings hidden in her hair cut into her neck. The orex yanked until Hattie wheezed, tears springing to her eyes.

"Ven!" said the rabbit in alarm. "You're going to pull her head off!"

"Don't worry, the antlers will come off!"

"Let go!"

"This will only take a moment..."

Her neck popped audibly, and she let out a high rasp. All the orex shouted and the cave echoed with their voices. Ven let go and leaped back with popping eyes.

The orex gathered around her, making noises of distress as she slumped against the dresser. Her neck didn't hurt. She'd shrieked because it startled her, but the orex acted as if Ven had broken something.

"No, no, no, no..."

"Rostom's going to kill you!"

"I didn't—I didn't mean—" the orex with the scarf sputtered. Hattie seized the opportunity and pretended to cry and shrink against the drawers. The strings were tougher than they looked; the antlers had not budged.

"She's *leaking!*"

"Oh, Atom, no, this wasn't supposed to be—" he moaned. "Those aren't real antlers. They were supposed to come off..."

"She isn't a human, you idiot!" Jack yelled over the crowd. "She's a cervid!"

"Aren't cervid extinct?" one orex asked to nobody in particular.

"That's probably why she's valuable to Creon. Sounds like something he would do. Hire an endangered race for appearances."

"It's okay. You're not hurt." One of them patted her arm gingerly. "Shhhh."

"Rostom's going to kill you," another repeated.

"They aren't real antlers," he moaned.

"En Law's going to notice they're missing," said an orex with the head of a goldfinch. "Are we going to kill them or do something with them?"

Everyone tensed.

"Ah. Well then, we have our list of demands. We can let one of them return and let the rest go when the conditions are fulfilled." Ven straightened. "So...which one? Not the human of course."

"She's not human," said all the orex in the room.

"We don't know that for certain. Since we aren't sure why she's valuable to Creon, we should keep her and find out. Jack isn't worth so much anymore. We can let him go."

More than a few Alate orex hummed in skepticism.

The rabbit flattened his ears. "I don't like this argument. The ossifel is the most valuable, clearly, but the cervid could be worth something."

"Fine. Call Rostom, let him know what we are doing. You, Jack, tell En Law and Creon that we will release your friends if he releases all debtors in New Sprout from servitude." One orex cut the rope holding him. "And tell him we know about the human."

Jack unfurled to his full height. His head brushed the top of the cavern, dirt trickling to his shoulders. The orex shifted, their hands on swords as their breaths caught. Thin-lipped, Jack evaporated bit by bit. He did not turn his back on Ven. Their eyes remained locked and their bodies tightened for a fight. Gradually, he disappeared into the darkness. His narrow face glowed like a mask before fading away.

"Go find Samara and tell her what happened," the orex called Ven said to the goldfinch, who flitted deeper into the cave. Hattie watched all this from between her fingers. Who were they? Why did they become flustered when they thought they'd hurt her? It sounded like they weren't evil, but it didn't explain why they threatened Jack and Jane.

The rabbit approached and squatted to study her. His nose twitched. After a moment, he said, "You aren't a cervid, yet you have antlers. A new species of orex? Where are you from?"

She did not respond and shrank further into the dresser. The wooden knobs bit into her spine. *Be quiet. Don't move.*

"You have nothing to fear from me. I have a daughter a tad older than you, in fact. We won't hurt you, whichever way you say."

You don't know that, she told herself. She kept her eyes pressed into her knees. *Don't look. Don't speak.* He was so close to her she could smell him, a smell like musk and dry grass. He touched her antlers and traced his claw to their base. "Ven? I think you're right. If you examined her, she can't possibly be a cervid. Oh!" His claw caught the string hidden in her braids. "The antlers are tied on!"

"You see! She *is* human!" Rapid footsteps. "How could you mistake her for anything else? This proves Ran Corp has been to Earth in the past month! Creon made an error by bringing a human back to Tsava!"

"*If* she is human, *if* she was brought from Earth, *if* Earth exists," said the rabbit warningly. "Which you still can't prove. Why would Ran Corp go to Earth? Resources? The humans themselves?"

"Humans are supposedly intelligent, tough creatures. Imagine having one to do your bidding. Legend has it they can split atoms."

Hattie faked a sob. Inside, her head spun. How was splitting atoms a legend? The atom bomb was made at least seventy years ago. That wasn't long enough to be legend. And how did they know?

"She doesn't look very tough or intelligent." Another voice. "She looks like a scared little orex wearing antlers. Do you know what humans look like?"

"Wait," The rabbit lowered his voice. "En Law or Creon may have ordered her to be quiet. Maybe the presence of the ossifel..."

Ven's eyes flashed. "Take her inside. Hern and Jan, watch the ossifel."

They untied Hattie from the dresser, hoisted her to her feet, and led her deeper into the cave. The light slid over the piles of coins, swords, whips, daggers, and chains. Wooden crates lined the walls. Some had been arranged into a makeshift set of table and chairs, and what looked like a map lay open on the table. The group stopped there, and one of the orex folded the map and tucked it into his cloak.

"Well, little girl," said the scarfed orex, in a kinder voice. "Please, speak the truth and we will let you go free."

"No," said Hattie at once. "I'm going to get in trouble."

"Are you human?"

"I can't say."

"Because of En Law?"

"I can't say."

"Can you say what he is keeping from you?"

She wavered. Could she? "I don't know. I don't want to risk it."

"He does not keep his word," he said gently. "You have not been in Tsava long enough to know this. He is a liar."

"I signed a contract! Aren't there laws?"

"Who witnessed it?" He interrupted.

Could she tell him this too? The orex around her pressed close. "Jack did."

"And you trust Jack?"

"Mostly, yes."

"Mostly," repeated the goldfinch. To Ven, he said, "If she cannot answer without breaking her contract, then we cannot continue questioning her safely. It's telling that En Law placed a gag order on her."

"Is she important enough that En Law will retrieve her himself?" asked the rabbit. "If so, we need to leave."

"Why are you trying to help me?" Hattie interrupted.

"Because we are the Alate," said the scarfed orex. "And we help all orex."

Her first instinct was to take their offer of help and never go back to the casino. But she remembered what happened when she helped Jack. Her parents and the neighbors that she still hoped to rescue were trapped inside Baba. She didn't know enough about orex or Tsava to trust them.

"No thank you."

"This is a waste of time," said the raven-headed orex. "We can't get any information out of her, and she's one out of hundreds of indentured servants. We need to get the details of these contracts out into the open, and then we can help."

"And then what? Harness mob mentality? Yes, we do need to get those contracts out in the open, but we must first obtain them in such a way that En Law cannot deny their authenticity. Otherwise, we risk losing our rightness, and nothing will be done. Who here is in the raiders unit?" Many of the orex held up wings, arms, paws, and tentacles. "And those two— Hern! Jan!" He called the two orex who were guarding Jane. They were standing together as if discussing something. Neither acknowledged him. They continued to face each other as if they could not bear to tear their eyes from each others' faces. "Hern? Jan?"

No response.

The rabbit lashed out with his needle-like sword. Hattie squeaked as Jack spun away from him and retreated further into the cave. He had snuck up on them from behind. His long legs picked over the piles of coins as quietly and precisely as a spider. He wore a paper mask over his mouth.

"Too late," he said in a muffled voice.

The orex stiffened. The scarfed orex plunged his hand into his pocket and retrieved a fistful of paper, which he stuffed under the fabric at his neck. The rabbit froze mid-swing with a stifled growl.

"All right Hattie, let's go," Jack said briskly, striding into the midst of orex. None tried to stop him. They jerked and quivered but could not take a step nor raise their wings. Except Ven, who took a step to the side and wrapped his arm protectively around Hattie, drawing a sword.

"How can you bring yourself to work for him?" asked Ven. The contempt in his voice made Jack's lip curl.

Hattie headbutted Ven with her antlers. The tips cut into his cheek and he jerked away. Jack lunged, grabbed Hattie, and planted his foot in Ven's chest. Ven sprawled onto his back. Jack hoisted her onto his hip and bounded to Jane. Ven screamed and hurled a small silver flitting thing at Jack. Jack grunted and stumbled but regained his balance before he grabbed Jane and threw her over his shoulder. "Hold onto me!" His breath burst in Hattie's ear as he spidered up through the shaft.

Hattie held onto Jane's collarbone, hoping the skeleton wouldn't come apart in her hands. The circle of sky widened just before Jack crawled out, clawed to his feet, and ran straight through New Sprout along the road, ducking into the trees. He jogged to a halt just out of sight of the path and leaned against a tree, wheezing. His body was slimy with sweat. He dropped Jane and Hattie onto the grass.

"You...guys...all right?" He gasped. Jane muttered something. "Sorry." Jack put a receipt on her skull. The paper smoldered and curled to ash, and Jane moved and stretched.

"Thanks," she said in a dry voice that failed to cover a tremor. "Nice to know En Law cares, huh?"

"I didn't...go back. I bought the tags...at a shop. What did the red-haired one say to you guys?"

"He took me aside and tried to get me to admit that I'm human," Hattie said. "I didn't say anything."

"The Alate knows you're human," Jack muttered. "En Law's not going to be happy."

"Who are they?"

"They hate Ran Corp and do everything they can to stop them."

As he hoisted Hattie back over his shoulder, she thought of the scarfed orex's offer and wondered if she'd done the right thing.

❧ 9 ❧

A BLADE OF GRASS IN A JAR

En Law took their report with a face like thunder. "Hattie, return to the longhouse," he ordered. "Speak to no one you do not recognize and only listen to Jack or Jane if they summon you to me. Jane, stay. I want to talk with you alone."

Hattie and Jack left the office and took the elevator without a word. Limn wasn't there. The humming of the elevator was unbearable. Jack's back had a stripe of blood where Ven's thrown thing had hit him.

She was the first to break the silence. "Are you okay? You're bleeding."

"I'm fine," he said flatly.

She probed again. "What did they mean when they said you were valuable? Are you famous here?"

"A little. My mom is." His tone brooked no further questioning.

"Isn't your descriptive Long-legged?"

He twisted his mouth. "Not legally."

"Oh...okay." She knew she couldn't ask more about it but couldn't stand the quiet. She searched her memory of the near kidnapping. "What's an ossifel?"

"It's what Jane is. On Earth, they're skeletons, but here, they're just another type of orex. Maybe not *just* another type. They're special, I guess. They can do things with zenzen that ordinary orex can't, and Creon was really happy when she showed up. I'm nothing special."

Once outside, Hattie realized she didn't want to return to the longhouse and have to deal with more orex. "Why do you work for En Law?"

Jack eyed her. "Because of money. That's it. No good reason like you. I'll see you later."

He left so abruptly she wondered if she had asked something rude. She thought about why on the walk back to the longhouse. It was blessedly empty. Light painted bright windows on the floor. It was only about four o'clock. Now what? It didn't feel natural to have free time. Maybe a nap. She pulled her pallet to the floor and sank into it. Like a moth, a slip of paper shushed to the floor from her pillowcase, and something spiny poked inside the linen. Frowning, she pulled it out. It was a pinecone.

Doro, she thought fondly. The little ladybug-orex loved to give the longhouse girls presents she found while working. Hattie had already received a glass button. She unfolded the paper, expecting a badly misspelled note about the pinecone. It was startling to see the neat block print:

Dear Hattie. I am the orex who knows you are human. I know you doubt my words, but I can help you retrieve your parents and your neighbors alike. I will leave proof for you under Baba's northern foot tonight. If you accept my help, leave me a sign there. Otherwise, I will leave you alone for good. Ven.

Questions sprouted in multitudes. How did he know she lived in the longhouse? How did he spot her for a human in the first place? Why was he trying so hard to convince her? Maybe she could trust him. But he was part of a group that openly hated Ran Corp. He could be trying to lure her out to get to En Law. Maybe she couldn't trust him. *Maybe*. And proof would be under Baba's foot tonight.

She pressed her palms over her eyeballs and colored dots swam in the darkness. *If you accept my help, leave a sign there. Otherwise, I will leave you alone for good.*

If he was telling the truth.

It all came down to whether En Law would return her to Earth. But there was the part about the neighbors. Few knew about that. It proved he had been on Earth.

She had to know. She would risk losing her contract and her parents, but she had to try.

Hattie pretended to sleep as the girls bedded down around her for the night. When it was dark and there were no sounds other than soft deep breathing, she rolled down her bedsheet, pausing to see if anyone heard, and crawled between the blanketed bodies. The door whined when it opened, and she held her breath until it clicked shut. The new night was clear and violet as Hattie snuck through the grass and stole beneath Baba. Beneath the foundations, a white stone glowed in the dark. Beneath it was a folder with documents and a single pen. Cautiously, she stayed within the fold of shadows and slid the documents into the moonlight.

Proposal for Earth Expedition, put forth the First Month of the Hundredth Year of Existence.

We, the senior officials of Ran Corp, put forth this document proposing an expedition to Earth for the purposes of surveying and accumulating rare resources for research and sale, i.e., human selves, and analyzing the condition of the original base for resuming activity.

The document was typed in tiny letters, and the wind flapped it in her hands so she had to put her face close to the page to read it.

Human selves are important for numerous reasons: (1) their zenzen content exceeds the telos property first defined by Ulrik the Perspicacious, which is the...

A long list of reasons followed, none of which Hattie understood. But there were a lot of reasons human selves were important, which was proof enough. She skimmed to a part she understood.

...must capture in a way that other humans will not discover our presence. If they did, the consequences would be dire. They may even invade Tsava. Thus, I propose we capture humans individually, similar to the plan used by the first base and survey the conditions in Prior for potential re-establishment. For this reason, I plead for more funding in order to explore the possibilities.

She turned to the next page, and found that it was only a handwritten page from Ven.

Dear Hattie. My companions in Tsava found this document a year before Ran Corp's expedition. We tried to stop the tragedy but were unsuccessful.

Her throat closed. Seizing the red pen, she scrawled in large letters across his note, *You had a year to stop them!* She underlined *year* twice, tears dripping onto the paper and smearing the red ink. *You suck!* She stabbed the pen through the paper and the grass so he would find it, creeped back into the longhouse, walked over the beds, and cried into her pillow knowing nobody could save her but herself.

It seemed like she had just closed her eyes when sunlight blazed across her face. Jane had thrown open the door to the longhouse. The orex around Hattie curled inward, groaning.

"Hattie, get up. We have stuff to do." She slammed the door.

"Who spit in her breakfast today?" Hattie whispered, and a few girls snickered.

Jane waited for her outside, tapping her foot.

"So, what are we doing today?" Hattie asked.

"Cleaning the closet."

"You got me up early to clean the—"

"En Law will get you up whenever he wants," said Jane silkily. Hattie had a feeling it wasn't En Law who woke her up early but didn't press the point.

Jane led Hattie to En Law's office. She braced herself to see him, but mercifully, he wasn't there. Jack was there, reading a slip of paper.

"Morning," he said as he looked up. "Ready to clean?"

"Hattie's going to clean for me. I have to finish some security checks for En Law."

Jack's eyebrows drew together. "But some of the stuff in here is dangerous, and Hattie barely knows zenzen." Jane tossed her hand dismissively. Jack shot back, "What is your problem? You've been acting weird since we went to New Sprout!"

"Figure it out!"

Hattie shrank away from them as their argument escalated and tiptoed toward the door of the closet. She slipped inside. The door snipped off the end of Jane's words. After yesterday, she didn't want any more trouble.

High shelves on either side of her stretched into the darkness. They were full of interlocking white boxes, some as tall and deep as an elephant and some as thin as a lamppost. Some more fragile containers were no bigger than her little finger. Tags fluttered from them, withered soft with age. The ceiling was patterned with curling ferns and flowers. Dust neutralized the sound of her steps, as if she had cat feet. Time felt suspended and ageless here in the dusty air. The closet depths invited exploration.

Great pearls of opalescent light bobbed on the walls like weather balloons; their halos pushed back a musty blackness that smelled of formaldehyde and old paper and hung over the shelves beyond her row. One of the pearls detached from the wall and floated down to Hattie. A string trailed the ground like a tail. Hattie grasped it.

"Are you a spirit?" Hattie asked the balloon. No answer. "Guess not."

Hattie reached out to read one of the tags, but snapped her hand back as the door crashed open and Jack and Jane strode in. Jack was flushed from their argument.

"Don't wander off," Jane snapped. "Take these." She shoved a box of tags into Hattie's arms. "Jack will show you how to label. I've got better things to do than cleaning out En Law's closet. It stinks in here."

"Are you sure it's not you?" Jack yelled as Jane slammed the door. He deflated, simmering. "What's her problem?"

"I don't know."

"Here." Jack showed Hattie how to label and tie the tags to the boxes. "I don't know why En Law decided that the storehouse needed cleaning today. All I know is that we have to do it. Some of the stuff here is really dangerous, so let me check it before you label. I don't think your reflexes are up to dodging the tongue of a clover-headed nibbler. En Law mentioned there is one in a box somewhere...I need to talk to you about what the stuff in the boxes are and you'll learn more about Tsava, so listen hard. Got any questions now?"

Hattie thought for a moment as Jack pulled down boxes from the shelves. "Why does Ran Corp want selves?"

"I told you. I don't know."

"Then what is a self? I always thought personalities and things like that aren't things that you can take away and use, but here it's different."

"First..." Jack peeked in a box and set it back on the shelf. "...selves and personalities aren't the same thing. A self is what ties the soul to the body, like string," he added, wiggling a string at her for emphasis. "Take it away and the soul just kind of sits in the body, and if the self is gone long enough, the soul floats away, too. Souls are great for making special tags because they are so hard to get. Bodies are all right. But selves...." He shrugged. "Not enough research. Orex used to think they were vestigial metaphysical elements of the soul."

"Huh." Hattie wished she had kept the document that Ven had left under Baba's foot. *Figures*, she thought bitterly.

For the next hour he opened boxes, described what was inside, and, while Hattie wrote the description on the tags, fit the boxes together to make a new shelf. There were some ordinary things that she expected to be in a closet, like old shoes too scuffed to be worn without embarrassment and clothes of past fashions, but there were also things like...

"Number 3468: one preserved specimen of spirit grass."

Hattie paused in her scribbling. "It's a blade of grass in a jar."

"A blade of *spirit* grass," Jack corrected. "It used to be inhabited by a grass spirit but got left behind when the spirit changed blades. Good for manipulating zenzen without tags, lots of properties. Medicine, exorcism, distilling...supposed to make you live longer if you drink tea made from it. Next."

"What exactly is zenzen? I think it's magic."

Jack snorted. "Don't ever tell another orex you think it's magic. They'll make fun of you. Zenzen is particles of telos...or so quanta think. Quanta are orex who study zenzen, which is...zenzen is to the motaspace what atoms are to the physical space. The physical space being this world, Earth, and other things like it. And tags, not like these labeling tags but the other ones like you use for chores, they finagle zenzen into doing stuff. It's hard to explain. And nobody really knows what the motaspace is, either. Orex don't think it exists."

As Jack put away the tagged boxes, he tried to relate the contents to Tsava or point out things he thought Hattie ought to know. She was starting to make sense of this world, and of Jack. He acted as if she hadn't told him she hated him. She no longer hated him and was ashamed for saying that to him, yet she hadn't forgiven him, either. He spoke politely and but seemed too timid to ask her about herself or how she was doing.

Finally, he stopped to sigh and wiped his forehead.

"That's enough for now. Let's get something to eat. Hey!" His face lit up. "Maybe I can get En Law to take you to the convenience store!"

"Tsava has those?" *Another thing for the list.*

He looked crestfallen. "Earth has convenience stores?"

"I've never seen one in Tsava, though," Hattie pointed out. "They would be different."

"True. Let's find Jane. She was supposed to bring us fans an hour ago, but I bet she skipped out on work."

Beating dust from her dress, Hattie rose and followed him out of the closet. Jane and En Law stood in deep discussion by his desk.

"Creon's experiment won't work without empty vessels. And there's no such thing as an empty vessel that isn't also dead." Jane shifted her weight to the other foot.

En Law motioned Hattie and Jack over. "I sent workers to bring your belongings to your new room. I was foolish to think you could blend in with orex so soon." Hattie blinked. New room? "Also..." He leaned in close enough that Hattie could smell his peppery breath. "...You are not to go anywhere outside Baba without another orex beside you." He raised his eyes to Jack. "I expect her to be well-versed in local culture and history by the end of the week and have a general understanding of the world by the end of the month." He switched his gaze to her. "You humans are supposed to be smart. The faster you learn, the sooner I'll give you your parents back."

Cold with hate, Hattie replied quietly, "Yes sir." She and Jack bowed as En Law and Jane swept away without saying goodbye.

When they left, Jack lifted his head. After a pause, he said, "We'll do the convenience store some other time and pick up where we left off in the afternoon."

Her belly thundered quietly in the gloom of the closet. Questions rose but died when she glimpsed Jack's strained expression. Why was he angry? He stepped out to grab food from the kitchen while she kept working. When he returned, he slammed the closet door, and she flinched.

"Sorry," he muttered.

The afternoon passed, in the dark, in silence.

* * *

After they had sorted the afternoon specimens, Jack led her back to the elevator to the fourth floor and down another corridor, also made of wood. Instead of being closed off and lantern-lit, large round windows let air and light stream freely through the passage. Doors in bright yellow, blue, green, and red lined the way. Jack pushed open the red door, revealing the best bedroom Hattie had ever seen. There was a lush carpet that looked so much like grass, she had to reach down and touch it. A bed made up with a voluminous quilt patterned with red and white checks stood under a window with a view of the longhouse. Opposite the door, there was a bookcase on the wall to the left, a dresser with a mirror on the right, and a nightstand with a bubble-shaped lamp next to the bed. The mirror's silver surface seemed deeper than any mirror should be and the furniture legs ended in hands so intricately carved and veined they might have belonged to real people.

Jack leaned on the door. "Do you like the room?"

"Yes. Definitely." Hattie touched the bedspread. It sank beneath her hand, warm and deep.

"En Law usually gives it to visiting lunaries." He seemed overly relieved that she liked it.

Wondering what it could mean, she joked nervously, "I'm surprised he didn't put me in a closet instead."

He gave her a strange fearful grin with all his teeth. Then he blurted, "About Earth." Hattie froze. "I'm sorry. I'm sorry I helped En Law take your parents! I hate that I did it. I wish I could go back and stop him somehow, but I can't! That's why I've been trying to help you!"

"I know," said Hattie hastily, sensing the situation was starting to spiral out of control.

"I've tried everything!" Jack's voice rose on the last sentence and he towered with a distorted expression.

For an electrifying moment, they stared each other down. He shrank abruptly. His face flushed and he dropped his eyes.

She fumbled, "Five years."

"I know."

"Do you?" Tears were rising. She spoke faster and her words jumbled. "I'm supposed to be in school. In five years, I'm supposed to be finished with school. So when I'm out of here, I'll be five years behind everyone. How can I tell my parents, 'Sorry, I went to another world to save you and that's why I don't know anything.' And what about my grandparents? They're probably wondering why we haven't called them back." Jack looked sick, ashamed, grey. "In five years, I'll look different. How am I supposed to pick up my life when I've been away from it for five years? Will my parents recognize me? Sometimes I don't think I'll ever get my parents back. I don't know anything. *Stuff* keeps making everything harder." Trying not to cry, she snapped. "So what if you're sorry? They're still gone and I'm still here!"

His face twisted as if he might scream. Instead, he shrank to human size and hunched into himself as if she'd stabbed him, and left without another word. Her righteous anger drained away. She didn't feel better. She was tired of being angry, but what else could she be, even if he was sorry?

PARTY TIME

T he days whisked by like leaves before a broom. Jobs came and went; cleaning Baba, sorting things in the closet, running errands for En Law, directing customers to different games in the casino room. Since colliding into the Alate, she did everything she could to pretend she was an orex. She held her breath when customers peered and blinked with many curious eyes. Chiros, Jack, and Jane made excuses for her. She wore the mask of Hattie the Brave over Hattie the Human.

Since the day she moved into Baba, Jack treated her with a distant manner that was a step away from fear. Jane treated her with a new gleeful vindictiveness. The longhouse girls realized something had changed between them when Hattie moved out. When they worked together, they rarely spoke and resentment simmered below the surface the few times they did.

True to his descriptive, En Law awarded her with difficult tasks she was forced get help with, fearing he would add to her debt. But there was one bright star that helped her get through the days: Limn, whose chatter sometimes surprised a smile out of her.

"Done for the day?" he asked one evening as Hattie tramped

into the elevator covered in grey-green mud. "What did he make you do?"

"Landscaping for the stupid anniversary gala," Hattie said, disgruntled as she pulled off her muddy shoes and dropped them onto the floor. Ran Corp had been planning a gala for their fiftieth anniversary two weeks from now. *Fifty years of crap*, Hattie thought. And she was expected to help set it up. "And when I say landscape, I mean, digging holes for flowers in the front yard. Who plants new flowers for a gala?"

"Don't drop your shoes in here! I have to clean this thing! So have you had a free day yet?"

"A what?"

"En Law gives everyone one free day per month!" Limn flashed like an arcade game to emphasize. "You've been here close to a month, right? You should have one coming up pretty soon."

"En Law gives breaks?" Hattie said incredulously. "Nobody told me!"

"Yeah, he likes it when we forget. What are you going to do?"

This stumped her. It had been so long since she'd had free time to do whatever she wanted that she didn't know what to do. And how did you have fun in Tsava? Maybe she should keep working and get her parents back sooner. But they wouldn't want her to suffer, would they?

"The convenience store is always fun to go to," Limn offered. "All my friends hang out there. The appliances will heckle you if you don't buy anything, but the calculator who runs the place will give you discounts if she likes you."

"Where is it?"

"About a thirty-minute hover, or walk for you, to the east, near New Sprout."

"That's a good idea."

"If only everyone thought I had good ideas." Limn sighed as the elevator doors opened with their familiar *ding*. "Then the world would be a better place. See ya."

She learned a great deal about Tsava from Jack's lessons, chatting with Limn, and what she gleaned from overheard conversations. Creon, Jack, and Jane were lunaries, as were the majority of customers who frequented Baba. Both lunaries and sublunaries were orex, but lunaries were orex who were "so rich they could vacation on the moon," as Chiros put it. Hattie also learned that the moon and the continent of Tsava had been easy to travel between until Cosmos Country closed for unknown reasons, and the lunaries couldn't take their rocket ships there anymore. But the name stuck.

"There goes Chopin-daal," Jane whispered to Hattie as she taught her how to deal with customers. Hattie had moved from working behind the bar to working the floor. She knew enough about orex by now that she could more easily pass as one. The crowd milled, their chatter cresting and falling. The identified orex had large needles for arms and legs, a wooden body, and a china-doll head. She stumbled across the carpet due to her leg-points getting stuck.

"Her husband got rich off the poppy stock a few years ago, but I bet she'll gamble it all away tonight, she's absolutely fizzed. There's Cadmium Len. But what's he doing?"

A dull yellow robot clunked repeatedly into a wall. Jack sprinted out of nowhere and whacked the head so that it spun completely around on its socket.

Jane giggled. "Probably has a screw loose. He had a really expensive upgrade recently, too. Absolutely useless. He's still a dump." She sighed contentedly. "I love orex-watching. It's so much fun just to stand around and judge them. There goes Cadmium..." The newly-dented robot wobbled away to the bar.

Jane perked up. "I think somebody's not supposed to be here. Follow me."

She threaded through the crowd. Near the doors, a frog-type orex pleaded with three guards.

"I am allowed in, you know. It's not illegal for me to be here!" he said in a high voice.

The guards were car-sized hulks of welded-together machine parts, armor, and plants. They were one of the more difficult orex to approach. They smelled of damp and rust and spoke in beeps and tones. Hattie didn't know them well.

"What's happening?" Jane's tone was friendly, but Hattie knew this was a bad sign.

The frog bowed. "I am a reporter for the *New Times*, and the paper is doing a segment devoted to the influence of the Alate on lunary social lives. I came to your illustrious establishment to interview folks."

"That sounds really interesting," Jane pulled the saddest face a skeleton could pull. "But you aren't a lunary yourself, so you can't be here. Kick him out." The guards grabbed the frog around his arms and legs.

"Hey! You can't do this!" The frog kicked out with shockingly long legs at the guards and Jane, yelling as he was carried away. "You can't operate a business that is discriminating against—" A guard punched him in the stomach and the frog doubled over, wheezing. Hattie started with a yell in her throat.

Jane leaned forward and said in a low voice, "Remember your debt."

The frog stopped kicking, appalled, and looked between Jane and Hattie. Hattie dropped her eyes to the floor, her cheeks coloring. She felt the frog continue to stare until he was taken out of sight.

"Good job, Hattie." Suddenly Jane hissed. "Fix your antlers!"

Automatically her hand shot up to her head, but Jane spoke again, "Not here. The washroom!" Jane pushed her along, discreetly shielding her with her own body until they reached a door in an adjacent corridor. "In here!" She pushed her into a mirrored, marbled, and gilded bathroom. Jane forced the antlers back into position and cinched the string under her chin until it pinched. "Did that journalist see? I bet he did, he was staring at the end." Antlers in place, Jane pushed her out into the crowd again.

Loud voices boiled out of the general noise. "This is exactly what we are fighting to end! Unjust social order and slavery!"

"It's him again!" Jane stalked through the crowd, but before she could take more than ten steps—

BOOM!

Orex screamed. Paper balls shot in all directions.

"The Alate will rise against injustice!" shouted the frog as he brandished what appeared to be a tube for launching fireworks. "Read and be aware!" The frog swung at the nearest guard.

"Catch him!" Jane shrieked. But the guard collapsed and in the chaos, the frog vanished.

"Hattie, clean up those balls. Don't let anybody read them and don't read any yourself. Montmorency, calm everyone."

Hattie scooped up the balls. Her hands were crushed by the crowd several times, and she was knocked from side to side. During the confusion, she slipped one into her pocket.

It took several minutes to calm the orex. Jane desperately explained to the remaining few, "Look, he's gone now! There wasn't any danger. En Law would've smashed him out of existence if he'd pulled anything."

"Why didn't he?" rumbled a humanoid orex who looked like he was made out of melting blue candle wax. Bits of wax flew out of his mouth when he spoke. Hattie could see Jane wincing as they landed on her. "I want a refund!"

"Those damn Alate! Ever since Golden-Back joined them, their activities have gotten more brash!" A horse-headed orex set his fizzing juice down so hard it slopped onto the bartop. Hattie hurried to her station to swipe at the spill with a rag.

"You'll have to excuse him," said the wife apologetically as her husband whinnied and tossed his head. She was a glossy chestnut; he was grey and dappled, and both had manes done up with ringlets. "Golden-Back raided our pastures a few weeks back. My husband is still furious, as you can see."

"Furious? She stole our ancestral arrows and bows! She even took our kitchen knives! An outrage! The House of Equinine will not rest until Golden-Back is chased away! When Allnon sent me a message yesterday saying she'd stolen his priceless dreamcatchers that very morning from his bower, I said, 'I will come to your aid...'"

The wife slipped Hattie some red disks after the meal and said, "for listening to him so I don't have to." Hattie took them to Jane, who informed her that they were marks and that En Law allowed workers to keep whatever tips they earned. Excited to have her own money, she stuffed them safely into her leaf pouch with the bullet. Luckily, Hattie wasn't blamed for the incident.

Later in her room, she uncrumpled and smoothed the paper. On it were crude, hastily-printed words.

We are the Alate!
We will not allow you to enjoy your stolen wealth in peace. Your good time depends on the suffering of kidnapped humans. Renounce your support of Ran Corp, or else.

A chill radiated through Hattie when she read the note. She braced herself to be called into En Law's office, but it never happened. The casino continued its business with extra guards. When they were prepping at the bar before the next night, Chiros told her, "I doubt the lunaries care where their money comes from, so long as it comes."

"Humans," chortled one orex. It was the same horse-headed orex who'd come the previous night. "They aren't *real*. And if they were, what would Ran Corp do with them? Make them split atoms?"

His wife replied, "It's a funny thing to accuse someone of doing. The Alate might be terrorists, but I didn't think they would believe in fairytales."

Chiros had one ear swiveled toward Hattie. Despite the glass being spotless, Hattie rubbed at invisible watermarks.

The husband sniffed. "So let's think for a moment. If Ran

Corp kidnapped humans, what would be the most profitable thing to do with them?"

"Ziti, that's a nasty question!" He flinched. The wife's ears were flat against her head. Hattie picked up another clean glass and inched closer.

"Well, I just think...say, hypothetically—"

"You and your hypotheticals."

"—that if Ran Corp did kidnap humans, where would they find them? Why not tell anybody? Wouldn't they get more money in the long term for discovering a legendary species? Think of the marketing! Unless humans have something about them that makes them profitable, the discovery could be a chance to advertise a commitment to scientific discovery, which would reflect well on their company, especially after the war. I know Creon has been working on Ran Corp's image."

The wife was quiet for a minute. She replied deliberately, "The war was fifty years ago. I would think, given the nature of what they did, that working on their image would mean being kinder to other species, working to repair the damage to the land where the battles took place, and giving reparations to the parties involved."

"Parties involved?"

"You know what I mean."

They bickered good-naturedly for the rest of the night and didn't return to the topic. After the night was over, a paper airplane glided from the ceiling and beelined to Chiros.

"En Law and Creon want to know what we heard about humans," she said, showing Hattie.

"Customers don't believe the Alate," she replied. "Tell them that."

Chiros wrote it down on the airplane and launched it back toward the ceiling. It disappeared like a prayer beyond the wooden beams. That night, Jack left a coupon book of defensive tags under her door, though she had no idea what they did or how to use them. The next night was quiet, and so was the night after that. What happened wouldn't be the last time the Alate would do something, she thought, and dared hope that they would do something else.

* * *

The day before Hattie's day off, En Law called her into his office. Jack and Jane were there. Jack looked uneasy and Jane sulked.

En Law's gaze pinned Hattie to the floor. "There is a special customer visiting today. She is the mother of all fengul. And she requested you. Why?"

Jack's head turned ever so slightly to her. Did he not tell En Law what happened in the woods? But even then, Hattie couldn't understand why the fengul cared about her in the first place, or why their mother would want to see her.

"I don't know," she replied. "Who is she?"

"She is one of the most elusive wanderers in Tsava. Do you know what a wanderer is?"

"Yes."

"Then you'll understand that they don't usually pay visits to ordinary orex."

Hattie stood rigidly so as not to squirm. Her voice sounded unnatural to her own ears. "I don't know why she wants to see me, or how she knows about me."

"Do you think the Alate told her?"

"I...don't know."

"Have you had any communications with the Alate at all?"

"No! How would I?"

"How are you able to see orex? How do the fengul know about you? How did the Alate discover Ran Corp had been to Earth? So many questions surround you."

His gaze skewered her, and she felt like she was bleeding, growing faint.

Jack spoke. "If she came through the motaspace, the fengul would know about her. And if they like her, then they wouldn't be happy if we treated her badly." He was repeating what Limn had said. She held her breath. "And, as someone who has been working with her and who has to hear everybody else's' complaints, if Hattie has been faking ignorance about Tsava and orex, she's a natural liar."

The prick of annoyance wiped her mind clear for a moment. But maybe now, instead of being fired for the fengul's and Alate's attention, she would be fired for being a bad employee.

Jack continued, "Is it really so hard to believe that the Alate would find out about our mission to Earth? They've raided offices, attacked upper management, and stolen and damaged property long before Hattie came along."

En Law's silence stretched on. At last, he said, "No matter. Creon plans to begin more serious experiments after the gala. If there is anything you are hiding from him," he turned his gaze to Hattie, "he will find out." More calmly, he continued. "For the gala, you, Jack, and Jane will end your normal shift at eight o'clock at night, bathe, and change into fresh, proper clothing. The queen will appear promptly before the gala begins. We will decide what to do as we go."

Dismissed, they filed out. If the fengul liked her, didn't they understand the trouble this was causing her? She could lose her job! But then again, if you lived in a big colony in the forest and kill orex who came in, you probably didn't know or care about regular jobs. She decided that when she saw the Fengul Queen, she would tell her to please leave her alone and let her do her job.

When they reached the hall, the bell for the elevator was missing.

"Where is that elevator?"

A note was attached to the far wall. Hattie read aloud: "'Elevator broken—use roof ladders.' Are there no staircases here?"

"Not very many," said Jane as she opened the window. "The spine is a staircase, but Baba doesn't allow anyone on it. Baba is a living creature. Remodeling any part of her would be like doing surgery. We have to be careful about what we put in her. Furniture made out of certain woods gives her allergies. Elevators are all right." She landed cat-like on the roof and began creeping toward a ladder.

"Wait, are we...?"

"Until the elevator is fixed, yes. By the way, don't bother to report workplace violations. Ran Corp owns the whistleblower association."

Jane spidered across the shingles and took hold of the rungs. Hattie gauged the yards of air between herself and the ground. *Just take it slow,* she told herself and threw her leg over the sill. *You did this before.* She felt around with her foot for better purchase on the slippery tiles. Her shoe slipped, and her hip hit hard against the roof. Jack paused and looked back but did not extend his hand. She cautiously let go of the sill and moved slowly across the roof to the ladder.

"It's not like we *couldn't* add an extra staircase," Jane mused to Jack. "But you never know with Baba. Being the only hen-house known to be alive, we can't allow her to get constipated from all the stuff we put in her."

* * *

At eight o'clock that evening, Hattie excused herself from cleaning duties and returned to her room. Jane slouched against her door.

"En Law sent me here to teach you how to wash up," she said in a bored tone. "Doubtless you already know what to do in the shower, but in Tsava we have to be a little more thorough. Now get in the shower."

"Not if you're coming in with me," Hattie said warily.

Jane snorted. "As if. I'm going to tell you what to do from outside."

Feeling as if she was heading into a torture chamber, Hattie gathered her clean clothes.

"Not those. En Law got you a new dress." Jane pushed a shift nearly identical to the one Hattie wore every day into her arms. "This one isn't as worn out, and it comes..." Jane flourished a pair of tulip-yellow trousers, "...with pants. Now shower. Hurry up!"

Hattie scrubbed all the places Jane yelled at her to scrub with soap that smelled pleasantly of lemon tea, and combed her hair hurriedly, wincing at the tangles. The moment she set foot out of the bathroom, Jane pounced.

"Put the towel under your hair so you don't get the back of your dress wet!" she snapped as she forced Hattie into a chair in front of the mirror. Small tubes, jars, and a tiny glass pyramid of wine-dark liquid littered the dresser. A large jar filled with brushes balanced precariously near the edge. Jane plucked up one of the brushes and a thumb-sized box.

"You've probably never worn makeup before, have you?" Jane daubed paint on the edge of her nose. "Close your eyes." Her face became strange to her. Her lips were black. Three thin black lines striped across her nose and a wide green stripe covered her eyelids. The makeup didn't make her beautiful but added force and weirdness. "Shoes." Hattie tied on the cute red silk slippers she would have admired more if she weren't busy hating Jane. "Take a look at yourself and meet Jack and I in the hall in about ten minutes. We have stuff to tell you before you meet the Fengul Queen."

Hattie re-braided her hair. Her throat cinched tight, and she took several deep breaths. Again, she was going against her instincts to run and hide.

Jack and Jane were already there and dressed more carefully than usual. Jane had changed into her skeleton form and was painting her clavicle with tiny, intricate blue flowers and yellow lace. Jack wore makeup of his own, black dots and lines along his brow and nose, and had changed into stovepipe pants with suspenders and a frilly white shirt. He plucked at his shirt irritably as Jane groused. "We have thirty minutes. Hattie, did you smear your makeup on your hand? Don't touch it, you'll make it worse!" Jane cracked her knuckles and paced the floor. "Jack, did En Law tell you about the seating arrangements?"

"Yes," he said, still messing with his shirt.

"We'll be the ones serving the queen. And we're serving her while we have other customers who'll be watching us, too. They're all En Law's best customers. Does my mascara looked smudged?" she demanded.

But Jack was still absorbed in setting the ruffles on his wrists just right and merely glanced at Jane. "Oh, yeah, yeah...it's fine."

"Okay? Like, not smudged?"

"It's not smudged," he muttered, straightening his collar. Seeing them nervous made Hattie's stomach churn.

"We have to go." Jane opened the window. The night wind clutched at them as they crawled down the roof.

"I can't believe they didn't fix the elevator, especially on this super important night!" Hattie complained, but both Jack and Jane looked at her askance. "We're climbing the roof in event clothing! And why are you looking at me like that?"

Jack said, "You never complain about anything."

"Yeah? Maybe I should start." Maybe it was the makeup, but Hattie remembered how picky her mom was about events and hosting. She amused herself thinking of how her mom would react to Hattie climbing the roof in special clothes.

Jane led Jack and Hattie to the lobby and through the halls to another set of doors to the kitchen. A few orex ran around the room smelling, testing, ladling, and garnishing. Their movement stirred the hot, delicious air, so thick Hattie breathed a new feast with each inhale. There were dishes as varied as the orex who ate them: glass containers of colorful, swirling gases, liquids dancing on their own, stews of shoes, meals made entirely out of plastic like children's toys, a bowl of luminous green jelly speckled with cream that Hattie longed to try. Little bowls the size of her cupped hands squirmed with tentacles. A ceramic oil lantern puffed steam, whistling and emitting a mouthwatering beef smell. Another bowl held iron filings. Hattie knew *nothing* that was before her on the cart. She'd never seen this served to the normal customers on any ordinary day.

Jane noticed and said like a slap, "Just do what we do."

Hattie's stomach lurched as the doors swung shut behind them. Where sumptuous carpets once lay now gleamed with lacquered wood, reflecting the light of drifting luminous balloons like the ones En Law had in the closet. The slot machines and card tables had been replaced with many square hovering slabs of glass tabletops at which lunaries laughed, gossiped, and chatted. Energy buzzed continuously through the air. At a long floating table near the end of the hall, En Law and Creon sat with ten fengul, the two of them on one side, the fengul on the other. In the center of the fengul was the queen. Hattie knew it was the queen because unlike other fengul, the queen's mask-body was not pure white and smooth, but wrinkled brown and pliable as leather. Frost-white hair coursed down each side of her mask. The holes of her mask did not echo of emptiness, but were clear, dark, and aware of everything. She levitated above the seat of her chair.

The queen smiled at her when their eyes met. "Hattie...I'm sorry my children frightened you."

Hattie said, "Oh, they didn't do anything." En Law's expression darkened like a lightbulb blowing and she knew she would pay for her mistake.

The queen's laugh was a sound like pebbles crackling. "That is good. I asked her not to tell you my children inspected her," she added to En Law. His expression lost its stark rage, retaining embers of annoyance. "I would like to talk to her in private. Can that be arranged? Then I will make my announcement."

En Law looked to Creon, who watched them with great interest.

"Yes," said Creon after the briefest pause. "The dinner is starting in a moment, but there will be a lull when everyone is eating that you can talk. What, may I ask, is it about?"

"I must discuss it with Hattie first."

Creon tilted his head. "For what reason?"

"You will know, after I speak with her." The Fengul Queen did not drop her serenity.

"As her employers—"

The queen's serenity dropped and a blank, terrifying expression took its place. Softly, she corrected, "As children of Mota and Atom."

Creon regarded her for a long moment. "Forgive us. Do as you will."

The queen's serenity returned. "I will. Run along, Hattie."

Hattie looked to En Law, who jerked his head toward Jack and Jane. Jack motioned her over to where he and Jane leaned against the wall.

Hattie bowed and trotted to Jack and Jane, bewildered. The pair loomed over her.

"What were you doing?" Jack's eyes flashed. "That was the queen!"

"She talked to *me*!"

"Creon's about to make his speech! Shh!" Jane flapped her hand at her. Hattie ground her teeth.

Luminous balloons dimmed until the hall was amber-colored and mysterious. Creon took the stage.

"Good evening honored guests. It is my pleasure to welcome you to the 50th Anniversary Gala. My name is Dr. Creon the Unfeeling and I am the current Chief Executive Officer of Ran Corp. I have had the privilege of leading this historic company from its humble beginnings in the Ferric Dunes, built by one in-debt orex with a shack for a factory, to a business that spans Tsava with a revenue exceeding one billion petals."

Jack hid a yawn behind his hand. Hattie, bored, scanned the crowd to see if anyone else was paying attention. Most listened raptly, gasping in all the right places. A few did not. An elephant-headed, pot-bellied behemoth jangling with gold bangles and long beaded necklaces had taken out a scroll and surveyed it with his massive head resting on his fist. A pair of televisions with long, spindly legs whispered to each other with lowered volumes, ladies with gluey skin and raisin-dot eyes picked flies from their arms, and a group of five orex wearing the same sky-blue scarves and tomato-red suits played a game with napkins and sugar packets. The last group caught Hattie's attention.

Their faces are covered, she realized. The scarves wrapped around their heads, not neatly like a regular piece of clothing, but like they had done it hastily to hide. One had wrapped theirs over their nose, mouth, and forehead, but not their eyes, like a bad mummy. Another had wrapped theirs around their neck and hunched into it, so it looked like their head was sinking into a whirlpool. Only their glittering eyes showed.

A smack on her head brought tears to her eyes. Jane glared at her and jerked her head toward Creon. Hattie pointed to the five orex. Jane glanced at them then skewered Hattie with a vicious look.

"Is it okay for orex to hide their faces?" Hattie whispered. Jane stared at her, nonplussed and angry. To clarify, she whispered. "They have their faces covered."

Jack overhead and casually looked at the group, as if checking to see who was winning the game with the sugar packets. his voice was almost drowned out by Creon's droning. "I'll tell the guards to keep an eye on them." He slipped into the kitchen, making no more noise than the massive floating lights drifting above.

Jane crossed her arms and returned her gaze to Creon. Defeated, Hattie leaned against the wall and tried to pick up on the speech.

"...a great honor for an industrialized nation to bend down and offer Ran Corp a chance to transform the Noh from rural country to developed state...the Monarchy has graciously allowed us some small protection from the roving thugs and anarchists clogging our rivers, highways, and passes..."

One of the scarfed orex turned away from his table to stare at Creon. Another, eyes focused on the sugar packets, dealt out a few to the other three, who kept their eyes rigidly fixed on the table. The first one's mouth moved angrily under their scarf.

"I'm happy to announce a partnership with the Monarchy to eliminate them. Their ideals are childish, their objectives ridiculous, and their actions laughable. With our targeted approach to eliminating unrest, backed by data, we estimate that the Alate will be destroyed in less than a year."

Scattered clapping like fitful spits of rain spread throughout the crowd. The first scarfed orex stood. Another orex in a tuxedo stood, probably thinking he was giving a standing ovation. The first's orex's hand closed on something underneath his cloak, and his fist stood out hard.

The luminous balloons exploded in a blaze and thunder.

❧ 11 ❧

DESCRIPTION

Concussions rocked the hall. The ground leaped, and Hattie fell on her hands. Specters, monsters, half-animal, half-machine, all orex, flew around the hall shrieking and crying like wild things in the night, blurring with frenzy and buffeting her. She was already lost in a maelstrom. Fearful faces strobed in and out of her vision. Arms, legs, and tails smashed into her. In the thick of it, she couldn't tell who was what or where. Her sensations were so muddled that she didn't know if she'd felt them or had a concussion dream. She struggled through the confusion. An elbow caught her in the throat. Oxygen was crushed from her lungs in the next second. She fell, a foot pulverizing her fist and then more feet on her back. Panting, she clawed up the wall to regain her footing.

"Jack?" Hattie called hoarsely, scanning the crowd. "Jack!"

Another explosion blocked out her words and her head struck something hard. Her vision dulled. After a moment, her head ached and rang like a funeral bell. There was a metallic tang in her mouth.

Moaning and weeping filled the smoky room. Embers smoldered in the carpet with soft sizzling sounds. The paintings had been blasted away. The blazing balloons trailed smoke as they sighed to the floor. Three of the scarfed orex scanned the hall and two ran toward the guests. Windows fractured as hard things hit them, but they didn't break, and frantic forms darted behind them.

With eyes sparking, En Law sprinted toward the three orex with one hand on the hilt of a sword and the other clenching large paper tags. One roared a warning but it was too late; En Law lunged, struck, and retreated. As one collapsed, the fight was on. When En Law avoided a blow, he reared then rushed back blade-first, but the two remaining Alate were determined. They danced and lashed at him with barbed-wire whips that sang with the high, thin whine of a hornet. Blood blotted his sleeves and back. Only seen as a silver wink in the air, En Law flicked his sword and a head rolled.

The last of the three screamed and chopped wildly. En Law leaped back and pulled a tag from his pocket. The other two remaining Alate, who were still bullying customers and whipping them out the doors, balked at the tag.

An explosion smashed through the ceiling like a fiery fist. Splinters flew and beams wheeled through the air. En Law glanced up, and the orex before him plunged his hand into his pocket.

En Law threw his own tag at the orex like a knife, but with a whirl of scarlet a cardinal shot over the crowd and vanished into the night sky. The paper tag slapped uselessly to the floor, glowed green, caught fire, and smoldered to ash.

Speakers popped out of the walls, and a soothing voice said, "Please stay in your seats. I am preventing the Alate from coming in. If you open the doors to run, they will come in. Please stay in your seats."

Some lunaries were huddled together in the back of the hall. They gazed at everything with hollow eyes. Their finery was ruined, and they looked pathetic and lost. Hattie pressed against the wall. Debris still rained from the ceiling.

En Law hissed in annoyance. "Jack!"

"He went to get the guards," Hattie called. "He never came back." En Law gave her a strange look, as if he hadn't expected to see her.

"There are probably more Alate upstairs." He swept into the hallway. A second later she heard him roar, "*Why isn't the elevator working?*"

Hattie went to the lobby, where En Law slapped a tag on the wall. It melted into the wallpaper like a water stain. A speaker popped out of the wall.

"Baba," he said. "Tell me where the Alate are."

The voice from the speaker was female and dignified. "There are several Alate on the third floor, going through your office. One is in the closet." En Law stilled, as if stabbed. "There are several more Alate on the seventh floor, holding Jack and Jane captive. They are discussing trading them as hostages. I've called the Monarchy's hotline for backup. They will be here in thirty minutes."

Out of the rubble, fengul lifted off like windblown paper. They sailed to Hattie and swirled around her.

"Hurt?" they repeated. "Hurt? Hurt?"

"I'm okay," she said, hyper-aware of En Law and his incredulous gaze.

"What is this?" he demanded. "How do the fengul know you?"

"We know her. She does not know us," one replied.

"We are her servants," another said.

"I didn't ask them to. I don't know why," Hattie said hastily, confused.

En Law eyed them for a moment. "Order the fengul to help you clear out the Alate on the seventh floor." The fengul hissed, but he replied brutally, "Unless you're happy to let the Alate kill them. And remember, you work for me. Do you want to be fired?"

"No!"

He swept away without another word. The fengul glowered at his retreating back.

"Guys," she whispered. They turned to her. "How are we going to do this?"

"We'll eat their faces! That always works," said one. The rest nodded, smiling.

Hattie's hair rose on her neck as Jack's words echoed. *Wanderers kill orex!* "Let's not do that, but pretend like you're going to. Maybe we can scare them away. We can take the stairs..." She remembered with a sinking feeling that the stairs were closed off. She would have to climb.

Outside, the wind blustered. Ragged clouds drifted in front of the moon like specters. It had rained and the rooftops gleamed. Hattie found the ladder and climbed with the fengul hovering beside her. A pair flew ahead and whispered advice, "Go this way. It's drier. Go that way. The rungs are more steady."

They passed the fourth, fifth, and sixth floors without trouble. On the seventh—

"Hide!" Hattie whispered as the window opened. The fengul fled under the many roofs like fish scattering to coral, but there was nowhere she could hide. She pressed herself close to the ladder and squeezed her eyes shut, hoping whoever it was wouldn't see her. Whoever had opened the window was doing their best to be quiet, too. It was a marvel Hattie had heard the movement at all. The only sounds she could identify were the soft brush of fabric against the sill, the dragging of something heavy against the shingles, and the creak of the window closing, each of which were nearly obliterated by the wind's moan.

A whiplash-lean figure dressed in black leather and wool stood near her on the other roof with an enormous sack lifted over its shoulder. In the moonlight, long furry feet stuck over the edge of the roof like a diver's over a diving board. Whoever it was had long ears tied back to an almond-shaped skull covered with black and blue scarves. The orex shifted and checked the bag. A slice of grey moonlight illuminated the face. A rabbit-orex, but not the one from the cave. Pale gold fur gleamed in the small ray of light.

The rabbit-orex leaped from the roof as if from a spring-board, falling, falling, and melting into the night. Silent and swift as a bird shadow, the orex bounded across the grounds and disappeared into the forest.

Her foot squeaked loose on a tile, but Hattie clung to the roof. When she was sure she wouldn't fall, she took a deep breath and continued. Hattie kept climbing until the ground was so far away that looking down made her dizzy. Her muscles quivered and ached. She pulled herself onto the seventh-floor roof with a gasp of pain and relief. The shingles were slick and cold; she didn't dare stand. She pulled herself along with the fengul close behind. She thought that this was the second party that had gone wrong in recent memory and prayed it wouldn't be a pattern.

The roof encircled Baba's round wall like a skirt, with walls as blue as robins' eggs dotted with round windows. To Hattie's left, a feathery fold swallowed the roof and wall, ruffling in the breeze: Baba's wing. Hattie climbed beneath it. Her head brushed against its underside where it was silky and smelled of sweet must and oily warmth. Wan light glimmered from the window. She pushed the window experimentally and it swung open. Lowering herself, she crawled inside, held the window open for the fengul, and let it gently close after they entered.

The abandoned eighth floor was eerie. Blue shadows collected in corners and hardened the faces of the portraits. One door was ajar. A slice of light flickered outside, and unfamiliar voices murmured.

"Is it our fault we are forced to dirty our hands?" said a familiar passionate voice.

Hattie crept to the door and peeked through the crack. The room had been ransacked. Ink splattered the walls and carpet, pages were ripped out of books and crumpled along the floor, and the cabinets had been smashed so that glass glittered amid splinters. Candles lay everywhere like small naked bodies, and where their flames had not been snuffed out, fires chewed paper to ash. The blue scarfed orex from the cave stood with princely dignity amongst the other bird-headed orex, who shuffled and muttered uneasily. She could still not see his face but could tell it was Ven.

"Bastard Jack," said Ven, his voice heavy with distaste. "Answer me." At first, she couldn't see where he was looking, but as Ven reached out to a figure gagged and tied to a pole, her breath caught. Jack's hair was craggy with dried blood. His left eye swelled blue-black, and bruises mottled the skin she could see. Tied beside him was Jane, who was hollow-eyed, huddled, and still.

"Do you deny your crimes? And what about this young ossifel?" He gestured at Jane. "Surely you don't want her to die? Though she is a resident of the land of the dead, reentry would be exceedingly painful."

Jack tightened his jaw and didn't answer.

"Where is Dr. Creon?" Ven's hand closed over Jack's skull and squeezed. There were small gasps of pain. A fengul whispered in Hattie's ear, "Going to other window."

"What do I do with these tags?" she whispered.

"Throw them."

The soft catch of the window latch made her flinch, but the Alate didn't notice.

Ven said in a ringing voice, "Where is the human?"

Something passed over the window across the room. Ven paused. Puzzled, the Alate followed his frowning gaze. While they were looking elsewhere, Hattie softly pulled open the door and ran toward them as she ripped a tag free.

Ven was barely able to block Hattie's thrown tag. The balled-up tag hit his whip handle with a startling *clang* and the weapon spun out of his hand. Orex yelled as fengul swarmed, biting and howling. But Ven recovered in an instant. He vaulted after his whip and snatched it up. She cringed, but he beamed.

"No antlers! You are human!"

Her hand flew to her head. The antlers were gone; they must have fallen off in the stampede. Jack let out a strangled yell. "Hattie, run!"

"Hattie," Ven said in a serious, controlled voice. "Though I promised to leave you alone, I cannot. You are new to this rude world and have been misinformed. We of the Alate are not as ineffective as you think."

In her hysteria, she had forgotten one crucial thing: her knowledge of fights was limited to kicking other kids in the nuts on the soccer pitch. But Ven fought like he knew what he was doing. Her rage gave her strength. She didn't care if she got hurt, but she knew, somehow, that he would not hurt her. She ripped out a handful of tags and flung them at him. Though it was as effective as throwing a handful of confetti, Ven backed away, and the fengul swarmed him. Ven shrieked and recoiled through the window, toppling out onto the roof in a heap with fengul chewing on his arms and legs. One had his scarf in its mouth and yanked, causing him to gurgle and clutch his neck.

Hattie ran to Jack and Jane and pulled the ropes tying them over their heads. "Are you okay? You're bleeding!"

"Jane's worse." Jack gestured at her. Jane was pressing one hand to her back as if preventing it from giving out, and her head was bowed. "If she has cracked vertebrae..."

"How can we move her without the elevator?"

"We can't until we can get the Alate out."

The fengul had cornered the goldfinch and the kestrel pair of Alate members. The fengul's eye sockets had expanded, and their mouths opened so far that they looked ready to swallow them whole.

Hattie stuttered and shuffled to the pair. "Stay where you are or the fengul will eat your faces." A fengul flipped around with a scowl as if to correct her, but the rest hissed and it flipped huffily back to the Alate.

The fengul shrieked. A moment later they crashed into the

walls and clattered to the ground with the sound of breaking dishes. Ven and two other Alate members stood on the roof with their swords held ready. Ven's scarf had unraveled in the wind from the fighting. He tore it away and it snaked off beyond the roof. He had the face of a hero in a fairy tale. Black mask-like markings of a cardinal feathered across his brow and cheekbones. His eye sockets were blackened, and his eyes were the violet-blue of a mountain lake. His nose was over-large and beaky, and his scarlet hair peaked in a cardinal's crest.

His voice softened again as he smiled and said, "Hattie, I am not your enemy. I and my commanders only meant to show the lunaries a little bit of our might. Look, if you come with me now, they will believe I kidnapped you, and you can escape to Earth."

Fengul darted in front of her, hissing. Using the distraction, Jack threw a tag at Ven that exploded, making him stagger away. She ripped out a handful of tags, balled them up, and pitched them straight for his head. How could he wreck Baba and invite her to join the force opposing Ran Corp and this stupid world when she couldn't leave, not without her parents? It was dumb, insane, even cruel for him to ask when he should have known she couldn't go.

Ven blocked her tags with the flat of his blade, but when he blocked, the paper balls fell apart and the tags stuck like burrs to his clothing. *Slap!* One pasted to his right shoulder whiplashed around his arm and bound it tightly. Before he could tear it away, *slap!* Another stuck on the other arm and activated. *Slap!* The legs. *Slap! Slap!* The torso and both hands, binding them together as tight as a mummy's bandages.

Ven teetered, completely wrapped, before falling with a thud on the shingles. Jack pulled back his arm to throw more tags, but something long and black struck him in the shoulder. He cried out and cringed away. The fengul darted behind Hattie just as she heard a nasty crack. When she screamed, the fengul scattered to the roofs and did not rise. The two orex the fengul had cornered descended next to Ven and cut the wrappings with long pulls of their blades.

Hattie grabbed the last of the tags in the coupon book Jack had given her. Jack raised a dagger as the three Alate took fighting stances.

The three-bell chime of Baba's speaker sounded. "I have an important message for the Alate," said a polished female voice. Ven glanced at Hattie, but she was as baffled as he was. "The Monarchy's guards in New Sprout are on their way. Get out or get dead."

Ven's lip curled. The kestrel spoke. "There isn't anything more we can do. We haven't seen the other cells breaking through Baba's barrier. We should pull back."

Ven's jaw worked for a moment. To Hattie, he said with a hint of a plea, "They aren't going to keep their promises to you, whatever they are."

"Better the devil you know than the devil you don't," she replied. "My dad said that once."

He shot her a blistering, sorrowful look. Then the three leapt into the howling night. She watched them soar, black against the stars, silhouettes in front of the moon.

The speaker clicked. "Back inside, kids. I'm going to seal the windows."

The fengul who had been knocked aside rose groggily and descended off the roof. *Back to the queen*, Hattie thought. Jack helped her over the jagged edges of the broken window as they climbed back inside. He knelt beside Jane.

"How are you doing?" he asked.

"My back is killing me, but I don't think it's broken." He helped her stand. Each of them trembled.

Jack's voice had a tremor. "Do you think you can walk to the elevator?" he asked.

"No. I think you'll have to carry me," she said piteously.

"I can't, with my shoulder."

The speaker clicked. "Hattie, go to the ground floor, *now*."

The urgency in the speaker's voice made her breath catch. She opened the window again, ignoring the deep scratches from the glass, and climbed down. Her feet slipped on the ladder rungs and dropped the last few yards. She hit the grass and fell, scraping her hands and knees, but got up and ran for the front doors. Jack hit the ground next to her and ran with her. Even before she had gone through the doors, the keening seeped through the cracks, making her skin crawl.

In the ballroom, the carpet was smoking, scarred, and strewn with bent machine parts and pieces of bodies, some still struggling to move. Most orex clustered together in the center of the ballroom. They were bent over something in the middle. Fengul levitated in the air around them, their faces stretched with wailing.

En Law waited for them outside the group with a closed, guarded expression. He called to the orex, "She's here." The whispering grew and the orex turned their gazes on her, moving out of the way, revealing something moving feebly in a nest of flossy white hair: the queen. Half of her face had been crushed.

"Go on," En Law said, his eyes hooded. "She asked for you."

Hattie knelt next to her. The queen seemed to pull herself together enough to set her empty eyes on Hattie. When she spoke, the sound scarcely disturbed the dust particles floating through the smoky air.

"...I wanted...to ask first...if you wanted this. I don't have any more time...I'm sorry."

"What are you talking about?" Hattie whispered.

"I'm sorry," she repeated hoarsely. "My children told me... your bravery...in the motaspace...in battle...I thought I would have...more time to watch you...to know if you're the right one. I pray you are. Put on the antlers."

A brief, hurried search. The found antlers were passed along the hands of the watching orex, over wings, claws, tentacles, many-fingered hands, and insubstantial flesh, before they were jammed onto Hattie's head. Quivering, she straightened the antlers and tied them under her hair.

"I...grant you sanctuary beyond the physical...standing with the wanderers...and the perception and expression of telos."

Her antlers pressed down with terrible weight. Her skull cracked open. Roots drilled through the bone as pain spiked through her brain. She screamed and thrashed as words sunk her deeper into unconsciousness.

"I describe you...Perceiver."

12

BECOMING NEVER ENDS

Hattie woke with a start. Sunlight streamed through her window in a long golden bar. Judging by the angle and the color of the light, it was past noon. She couldn't remember getting into bed. Her head felt unbalanced; tilting it one way or the other made it bob.

She ran her fingers through her hair to braid it, and her fingers bumped into her antlers still on her head. It was a miracle they had stayed on after...and then she remembered. She tugged at them, but they were stuck fast. She fumbled under her chin for the strings, along her jaw, behind her ears; maybe they were tangled in her hair. But as she failed to find the strings, a terrible, vibrating feeling rose inside her.

The antlers were growing directly out of her skull.

She tried to scream, but it was strangled. She yanked at the antlers hard but only wrenched her neck.

"Come on!" She pulled at one with both hands until tears started from her eyes. "Come off already! Come on! Please!" A tine dug its point into her hand and scratched it. She cursed, nearly crying with frustration, and held her wounded hand tightly until she could stand the pain. What did the queen do to her?

Footsteps outside her door.

"Hattie?" Jack opened the door to her room. Bruises colored his face with purple, blue, yellow, and green. He whistled as he saw Hattie's antlers. "They really are stuck to your head!"

"They won't come off! How do I get them off? Why are they there?" An unpleasant thought came to mind. "Did the queen turn me into an orex?"

"You're still human," Jack replied. "Probably."

"*Probably?*"

"En Law and Creon have been trying to figure that out since yesterday. That's probably why she wanted to talk to you. The queen died right after she gave you a description and stuck the antlers to your head."

"Description...the Perceiver?" The word struck an odd note in her mind. "What is it?"

"Honestly, I don't know. The name itself sounds like the descriptive of a wanderer, but not a wanderer I've heard of. Nobody could ask her before she died last night, and nobody can find a fengul to say."

Maybe it was selfish, but she wished the queen had lived just a while longer and told her what she meant to do when she rooted the antlers to her skull. Now that she thought about it, there were so many other mysteries. Why were fengul following her? Why was she able to cross the motaspace? Why could she see orex at all? And most of all...

"Why me?"

His face was drawn and haunted. "I don't know. I'm sorry."

He sat next to her, and his weight on the bed made her lean into him. He put his arm around her shoulders and hugged her. Being held again drained away the wound she'd carried since the night everything had gone wrong.

After a time, Hattie pulled away from him and mopped around her eyes. Jack was flushed and wouldn't meet her gaze. They sat for a while until she broke the silence. "I'm sorry I told you I hated you. I don't hate you."

He smiled wanly. "I deserved it. I've done horrible things over and over again." His face cracked. "I'm sorry."

"I know." Hattie touched his arm, filled with pity. They sat together without saying anything. Forgiving him seemed to make her lighter, though she wasn't done being angry. And there was one thing she needed to know if she was to be his friend.

"Why are you working for En Law?"

"I don't want to talk about it," he said curtly.

"Please."

For a moment, she thought he might yell at her or cry. "Remember the stroilmen?" he asked. Hattie snorted. "The orex who sent them is probably the Monarch, my mom. We think she's been sending the stroilmen after me to capture me. To bring me home." He picked at a loose thread on his pants. "It's happened for a while, but the last few times...the stroilmen have been trying to...kill me." His face cracked again. "I don't know why. I think one of the royals has been giving them kill orders, and she hasn't realized it. She *wouldn't* realize it. She's not very bright. She's the queen of the Monarchy, but she's like a kid. She wouldn't hurt anyone."

"Do you think someone has been trying to kill you because they want the throne?" she asked.

"I'm a bastard. My dad's not royal. I don't even know who he is. Though I'm technically the first-born, nobody in the royal court will acknowledge me as heir to the throne. Which is fine. I don't want to rule a trash can." His voice sounded bitter. "I didn't want to deal with the royal court anymore, so I asked Ran Corp for a job. Creon likes someone who knows important people. He hired me because he thought that I would make connections with the Royal Court on behalf of Ran Corp. More business deals, funding. That sort of thing. But they don't want anything to do with me. He kept me on, just in case. And now I'm here. I'm not like you. I don't think I'd even try to save my mom if she was taken."

"If I went back in time, I don't know if I would," Hattie said after a pause. She flushed saying it out loud, though Sonorra and Matilda had told her to stay on Earth. "Everything just happened. Sometimes I don't think I'll ever get them back. I think they're dead."

"They aren't dead," said Jack. "Their selves are in the closet somewhere. So are your neighbors."

"But if I don't get them back..."

"You will."

A knock. Jane opened the door. "En Law wants to—" When she saw them sitting together on the bed, her eyelights flashed and voice turned wintry. "Hattie, En Law wants to talk to you."

Jack stayed behind. As Hattie got in the elevator, she heard Jane say, "Her?"

En Law's office had been tidied up, but evidence of the assault was everywhere, like a bandage over a wound. Books only slightly burned had been slotted back into their places in the bookshelf. The charred remains of others spilled out of the trashcan. The broken candles had been replaced with new, tall, smooth ones and there was an odor of new plaster from the damp patched holes in the walls. The broken, burned furniture had yet to be removed. En Law stood at his desk sorting documents. When Hattie closed the door behind her, he stopped and examined her.

He asked, "Can you take off the antlers?"

"No."

"Are you an orex?"

"I don't think so."

"You don't think so." She fought the urge to squirm under his gaze. His eyes picked out every slight movement. "Do you feel different?"

"No."

After a tense moment, En Law said, "May I remind you, Hattie, that your contract with Ran Corp comes before all else.

If you do not repay your debt in full, and if you break your contract, you will never have your parents." She hadn't expected any different, and he seemed to read it in her face. "I wish to clarify your situation. You are more valuable to Ran Corp now. Who knows? Perhaps your contract will be shortened to three years if you do well." What did he mean? How was she more valuable now? His answer made her stomach twist. "Dr. Creon will be returning soon. He is most eager to begin studying you."

Satisfied she wasn't going to leave, he said more briskly, "Now, as I'm sure you're aware, employees typically get one day per month off for freedom in the town of New Sprout, or to visit their family, or whatever it is they do. Your day off was supposed to be the day after the banquet. You will have it soon, but first I need you and Jack to go to the convenience store and pick up some items which will be on..." There was a flash of fire and a charred length of paper floated in the air before her. "...this list. Your money." En Law tossed a bag to her. It jangled as it hit her palm. "Do not spend it all, if you can. You have until the sun slips below the horizon. Remember, you represent Ran Corp in every action you take. Do not tarnish our reputation. Dismissed."

Hattie started back to her room. The meeting raised more questions than answers. What had the queen said to him? Why was she more valuable now? Why had he asked if she felt different? The queen had done something to her. She tugged at the antlers again. She knew antlers could shed. *Maybe*, she thought hopelessly, *they'll shed eventually*.

When she arrived at her room, Jack and Jane were still there. They looked like they had just finished having a monstrous argument. Jane had her face in her hands and Jack breathed as if he'd just run a race.

"En Law said we need to get stuff at the store for him," she mumbled, anxious that she was intruding.

"Great! Let's go!" Jack shouted, scaring her, before he

stormed off. Hattie ran after him, shivering with the feel of Jane's glare on her back.

Hattie's spirits couldn't help but lift when they stepped out of the secret entry onto the lawn. The sky was seamless. The wind whisked the scents of sun-warmed green things from the wood and lawn. Jack took overlong strides as he fumed. It was only when she called for him to slow down that he slowed down and let her catch up.

"Should we go back and visit the Room of Succor?" he asked after a pause. "You look... bad."

"I feel like I survived a few explosions," she replied.

"Want me to carry you?"

"Well, I think I'll be okay, since I can walk and all. I don't want En Law to think I can't work. I'll have my day off soon. I'll just stay in bed and sleep then." Jack twisted his mouth. To ward off an argument, she asked, "So what's at the convenience store?"

"Blanks, snacks, supplies...little things you need but don't want to go into town for. There's a professional scribbler there who we have a contract with. Did you bring any of your money?"

Hattie pulled a handful of coins from her pocket. "This is all I got from tips, and I don't know how much it is."

Jack pointed at the coins. "This white one is a pon. It takes ten of them to make one of the red ones, a mark, and about a hundred to make the blue ones called petals. So, you probably have enough to buy something for yourself while you're there, like a book or something. They have a juice bar, too."

As he talked, a strange whine built in her head, like a radio being tuned. Irritated, Hattie looked for the source of the noise, but the forest seemed empty.

She interrupted, "Do you hear that?"

He stopped talking, offended. "No."

"I hear something. It's like—" Even as she spoke it happened again. "There! Hear it?"

He gazed around the wood before looking back to her,

puzzled. Dismayed, she asked, "Can't you hear it?" Jack shook his head. Then she saw it: a fengul smiled from a knot in a tree. Hattie flinched back.

"There's a fengul!" she hissed to Jack. The smile blew out like a light bulb. The fengul retreated into the knothole. It had grey cracks all over its body, like an egg.

"Oops," it whispered.

"I hope you're here to tell me what the Perceiver is and why I have antlers on my head." Jack glanced at her. She remembered him saying something about how wanderers kill people, but Hattie had lost the ability to care sometime in the night.

"Frank will...at the store." Its voice was halting and rough. "Follow me."

A low whistling moved through the forest. The whine built in Hattie's head in a fever pitch. A dry wind coursed through the trees, making them billow, tearing leaves and unbraiding Hattie's hair, roaring and rushing. The fengul tumbled from the knothole and sailed down the road.

Hattie shouted and started to run, but Jack caught her. "It'll be at the store. We don't need to run."

"Why can't they just tell me themselves?" she said roughly. "Who is Frank?"

"That's what they're like," Jack said simply.

The wind's mighty exhale subsided, and the trees sighed in relief. The whine faded. The closer she got to finding out the truth, the faster it would escape from her and the more carefully it would hide.

The forest road widened and smoothed further down the road. Signs spouted along the edge, saying strange things like, *Only fools ignore the sweet taste of Chooka-brand chewing gum!* in neon or pastel colors. The first orex Jack and Hattie ran into was a pair of women with demon faces and fangs jutting from their puffed lips. One noticed Hattie and elbowed the second, pointing. Hattie could feel their stares prickling her back unpleasantly as she hurried after Jack. The road grew busier. Some eyes would roam over Hattie and Jack and not comprehend who or what she was. Others would see Hattie, stop dead in their tracks to stare, or direct someone next to them to stare, too. The thicker the crowd, the more nervous she became.

The forest thinned to a grove of trees whose branches swayed low with fuzzy-skinned and pinkish-red fruit. There was something familiar about them. Jack plucked one of the fruits, bit into it, pulled off two more, and offered her one. "Want a peach?" He said in a voice thick with juice.

"Tsava has peaches?"

"Funny. I said that when I went to Earth."

Beyond the orchard was a two-story building like a partially twisted Rubick's Cube. The floors were out of sync with each other and rimmed with neon lights. Antennae bristled from the roof and an eerie, thin whistle emitted from them like an alien wind. Orex passed through a wide set of automatic doors that played a recording of a bell. A sign in curling neon over the doors read: *Peach Bit.*

The inside of the Peach Bit looked like the inside of an ordinary supermarket but far more bizarre and interesting. Shelves stretched to the pitch-black ceiling on a floor of the same black-glass material. They held objects with as much variety as the orex themselves, who acted as any shopper would by comparing different products, slowly pushing floating carts down the aisles, or telling children, "No!" *No* to disturbing toys or candies, and *no* to food that didn't look like food but rather gunpowder or bundles of candlesticks. A chemical soup plopped quietly with large bubbles in what looked like a produce barrel. Loud bangs and whirs came from a corner where three little orex laughed at a spinning and flashing toy that blasted apart and flew back together. Why would the fengul meet her here?

Dazed, Hattie picked up the product nearest to her. It was a test tube filled with pale, rose-colored cubes of gelatin. A sales tag read: *mork jelly, two for a mark.*

"What's it do?" asked Hattie, putting it back.

"It changes your voice. Makes it as high or as low as you want. Some orex speak or hear in really high or low registers that are impossible to understand without a tag or a jelly infusion altering your hearing or their voice. The jelly helps you understand them. En Law uses it sometimes for guests, but they don't come often. We can look at everything while they get En Law's order ready," Jack added, sounding business-like. "He wants more tags. He's going to raise security. If the Alate come back, he can blast them back to wherever they came from. And apparently, they stole some valuable stuff from the closet, so he's going to get another gunterphisch to guard everything."

Hattie's mind flashed to the rabbit on the roof. What had she stolen? But she had forgotten to tell En Law and didn't care if he knew. In the back along the escalator, open-air refrigerators hummed with power as they wisped cold, pearly vapor over bright cans and bottles of liquids. Jack grabbed a can and led her to the escalator.

"Something to drink while we wait," he explained.

The second floor was more subdued than the first. There were fewer orex here, and they moved with purpose. Racks of fluttering paper lined the floor and walls like extra-long receipts. The tags were made of rough handmade paper and were covered in geometric symbols, numbers, and letters. At the other end was a counter where an orex painted ink on receipts and manned the register. Jack approached him and placed a slip of paper on the counter.

"Everything on this list, plus a book of blanks for my personal purchase," said Jack, sliding the paper to the orex. "And this soda."

The clerk took up the list and bowed. "I will have your orders ready in a moment."

Jack cracked open the soda and sipped. "Want to try?" Hattie sipped. It tasted like fruit sodas on Earth, though not of any fruit she ever tasted. The clerk reappeared with several boxes teetering in his arms.

"This order will be one hundred petals, two marks, and a pon," he grunted as he set down the boxes.

Hattie heard Jack say, "Is there a discount for the casino, or has Mr. En Law not renewed his membership yet?" But the rest of his words were lost once she spotted the fengul.

It nestled in a pile of discarded, crumpled tags beneath one of the racks. Up close, she could see how fragile it was, like crystal. Its mask pulsed delicately. A fine web of cloudy veins branched beneath the shell, as if filled with milk, and the eye hollows had narrowed until they were almost shut as if tight with pain. Shallow bursts of breath were the only indication it was still alive.

"Hattie." It mewled, and her stomach twisted in revulsion and pity. "Motaspace...through the computers, there...over there." Its eye hollows widened, and its mouth opened horribly, like a baby's trying to scream. "Quick...please...hurry."

At the end of the row in a corner, covered in dust, was an ordinary desk computer. She gathered the tag nest in her arms. Careful not to touch the fengul, she walked as quickly and smoothly as she could to the computer. Thankfully it looked the same as the computers back home. The keyboard had a few extra buttons with symbols she couldn't fathom, but otherwise, she was confident she could operate it. Its screen was simple: a box for a password against a plain black background. Hattie switched the fengul to the crook of her arm while she got ready to type in the password.

The fengul drew a rattling breath. It made little choking noises as if trying to talk.

"What do I do?" she whispered to it.

"Password...*Becoming never ends*."

"All one word, no capitals?"

A light wheeze.

"Guess that'll work," she said as she pressed enter.

The computer dinged. A simple face appeared on-screen, two pixelated eyes and a smiling-line mouth, like a spirit's.

"Hello," it said in a pleasant voice. "Are you wanting to enter the—holy shitake mushrooms, what happened to him?" The mannerly act disappeared. It *was* a spirit. "Stick it through the screen, quick!"

Hattie tipped the fengul against the screen clumsily. It passed through with a static crackle and drifted through the concerned face.

"Jeez," said the spirit, worried and annoyed at once. "You'd think they'd remember to come back to the motaspace once in a while so they can rest, but no. They love the physical. Anyway," it added. "You're the human the fengul are so buzzed about, right? I'm going to print a tag design for you. Do you know how to use tags?"

"I can't. I tried."

"Try again. The queen was supposed to connect you to the motaspace with the antlers." Hattie sputtered. "I know you have questions, and I'll answer them, but for now I need you to be like a pasture and hold your horses." The screen's face vanished and was replaced by a picture of a red book. "See this book? It's called the Song-jim, Book of Tags. Buy it from the store if you can, or borrow it, and buy a book of blanks, too. I'm going to print you a scribble—a bunch of lines that you draw on the tag to make it do stuff. Don't share the scribble with anyone else!"

"Song-jim and book of blanks," she repeated, bewildered.

"Good. Now my printer's all set, just remember to keep the scrawl somewhere you know others will never find it, or memorize it and destroy the paper. I recommend the latter. Good luck."

The screen blanked. Hattie cried out, "Wait!"

The face returned. "Hmm?"

"Good luck with what?" Hattie asked desperately.

A bulky box with a wide slit hummed. "I can't tell you here. This place is public, and we don't have time. Copy the scribble and stick it on a big mirror. Go through the mirror. I'll be on the other side. I'll explain as much as I know to you. I promise. I got lots to tell you."

The screen blanked again. A tongue of paper curled through the slot, and the paper whispered to the floor.

13

STRANGE FREQUENCIES

"Hattie!"

Hattie jumped. Jack and the clerk stood over her, livid.

"What are you doing with our computer?" the clerk demanded. "That's not for customer use!" Hattie crumpled the scribble into her pocket so that they wouldn't notice it.

"I'm sorry," Jack said in a formal, sorrowful voice, bowing to the clerk. "If you'll please excuse us, we'll be on our way."

Jack whisked her to the escalator. "What were you doing? You almost got us kicked out of the store!"

"Sorry. The fengul..." In a fast whisper, she told Jack about finding the fengul and the computer spirit's instructions. The computer spirit had said not to tell anyone, but if it was Jack, she thought it would be all right.

"There's a scribble for getting into the motaspace? Interesting. The Song-jim...I just bought a book of blanks for myself, so we should be all right with this, but I don't know how much the book costs."

They walked off the escalator and edged between shoppers to the newsstand. The magazines looked more sinister and lurid than the ones back home. Jack plucked a book from the shelves and held it out. It was clothbound in scarlet with a stamped, gilt pinecone adorning the front cover. The edges of the pages were stained black. Hattie wanted to tear off her ears as they waited to reach the register. The line was miserably long, and those orex who weren't shrieking for the queue to move along stared at her until her face steamed. Even reaching the register gave no relief.

"May I help you?" the cashier asked them irritably.

Jack held out the book. "Price check, please."

The phone-like orex focused her tiny camera lens eyes on the book. "Three petals, five marks, and five pon. You gonna buy it?"

"Yes, please." Hattie set the coins on the counter. The coins disappeared one by one with a *ping, ping, ping.* A receipt rolled out of a slit on the counter. Hattie took it and the book with a thank you. The cellphone gazed at Hattie with a perplexed look. Was she supposed to get a bag for the book? No, this was something else. The spirit lit up.

"You're that girl! You're on the news and mags and stuff! You're that human!"

"No," Hattie lied.

The orex pointed to the magazines. Hattie was sprawled across the covers, unconscious, surrounded in the rubble of the casino. *The Fengul Queen Describes a Human!* blazed the headlines.

"We don't look anything alike!" Hattie said in a ringing voice. Before the cashier could argue, she snapped, "Get your eyes checked."

She marched out and kept marching all the way down the road. Jack jogged to her side.

"I'll have to tell En Law about this," he said. "If this happens while you're doing a job for him..."

Hattie stopped. "No! He'll lock me in Baba!"

Jack kicked at the road moodily. "I have a job to do. I can't cherry-pick everything I say to En Law."

"What'll he do? Fire you?"

"Yes." There was such flatness in his voice that Hattie believed him. "I'm not going to tell him about the fengul and the tag stuff, but I'll tell him about the magazines, all right? That's the best offer I can make. Otherwise, he'll get suspicious, force feed us tags that will keep us from lying to him, and then neither of us will be safe anymore."

Hattie considered his offer. "Thanks." As they walked, she asked, "Who do you think that was? The computer spirit?"

"I barely know what a computer is." Hattie gasped. Jack pinched her antler and gently pushed her off course.

"Stop it! I didn't know. Computers are big on Earth. My dad fixes them."

His eyebrows jumped. "In Tsava, computers are only used by quanta. They're experimental machines. I've never heard of a computer spirit. There are more kinds of spirits than an orex can count."

"I don't get it." She booted a pebble, and it hit a tree trunk with a smack. "Why not just tell me what they want? What's the point of keeping secrets like this?"

"Maybe they don't want Ran Corp to find out."

It was the only explanation that fit. They talked until they exhausted every possible explanation, from the silly to the bizarre, but uncovered nothing new.

* * *

"You will not be allowed out again until this dies down," En Law said to her after Jack recounted their narrow escape from the store. "And don't talk to anyone about it."

Hattie had leafed through the book on the walk back but was forced to keep it in her room as she was put to work again fixing the roof with the longhouse girls. Jane announced Hattie's return with a giggling warning not to talk to her at all. But threats didn't stop Doro. The ladybug-orex snuck a purple flower and a badly misspelled note onto Hattie's roof. *Aye mis u!* it said. Hattie tried to sneak a note back but was caught by Jane and was forced to read it out loud to everyone.

She lay awake at night, alone. Her thoughts were unstoppable and circled the question of whether she was causing En Law too much trouble for him to keep her. Maybe he would take away her self and be done with it. Fired. She kept her head down and refused to answer questions when she helped clean.

She was sweeping the casino room when Lirk, the crystalline orex who had met her the first night at the casino and was also working, nonchalantly swept closer to her. Hattie tensed and focused on a patch of floor, sweeping it over and over.

"Hey, Hattie," they whispered, also sweeping an already-clean patch.

"What?" she whispered back.

"Are you really human?"

Other orex casually swept closer.

"I can't say," she whispered.

"How'd you get here?"

"Can't say."

"Why'd you come to Tsava?"

"Can't say. I'm sorry."

Softly, scarcely louder than their sweeping, they asked, "What did Ran Corp take from you?"

She froze. The other orex swept noiselessly, the bristles of their brooms just above the floor. Every ear turned to her like satellites. "My neighbors and parents."

They bowed their head. Under their breath, they said, "Good luck." As a group, they moved away and continued swiping at the floor. Later in her mailbox, she found a small drawing of Hattie with two larger, antlered people and one sentence.

To member yer Mom and Dad—Doro.

She kept the drawing next to her mirror. It didn't matter that Hattie's drawn parents had six arms and black and red spots. Did Ran Corp take Doro's parents too?

Things like that helped fight Hattie's instinct to sleep after work. Safe in her room, she took out the tag design that the computer had given her. It was complex; all lines, circles, and squiggles crossing over and linking up. She was a fast reader, and the Song-jim was so engrossing that in a few hours Hattie had read straight through it.

The book was divided into three parts: the Bob-jim, which detailed the history of the spirit's interaction with zenzen and discoveries, the Sam-jim, which explained what zenzen was thought to be (this part hurt Hattie's head. *The matter of the idea-realm? Atoms of thought?*), and an extra section in the back with worksheets for practice and helpful advice for drawing.

To make a tag, also known as a blank, you needed something to write with and meta-paper. Meta-paper was special paper cut into rectangles the size of a receipt and infused with zenzen. Luckily, the book came with booklets of meta-paper, and Jack had given her some blank tags. The tag designs, known as scribbles, were used to take an idea and manifest it into something concrete using a series of lines, squares, circles, parabolas, and triangles. The lines mimicked natural patterns, such as electromagnetic waves in the brain, waves in the ocean, fractal growth, etc. It got so tedious that Hattie skipped the rest.

There were forty worksheets in all. They started on a beginner's level and gradually increased in complexity and difficulty. The first worksheet said, *Draw a square on a tag. Don't let the lines overlap and keep them straight. Use a ruler if necessary. If done correctly, a box shall appear.*

Encouraged by the easiness, Hattie tore a blank from the booklet and bent over it with her pen. Her square was neat enough. She read from the book again.

To activate a tag, think of what its purpose is. In this case, to be a standard cardboard box. This is more difficult than it sounds, so please do not be discouraged by your first attempt. Imagine the tag transforming into a cardboard box.

She mustered her imagination and visualized the tag poofing into a cardboard box with a cloud of white smoke, just like the elevator.

Bang!

Hattie ducked as singed paper whizzed around the room and stuck, smoldering, on the furniture. In the epicenter of the blast, surrounded by burnt carpet and still smoking gently, was a tiny cardboard elevator. Hattie was too thrilled by her summoning to be put off by her failure to summon the right object. She tried afresh. This time the tag crumpled into a lopsided box, but it was not cardboard. Five fruitless tags later prompted her to change tactics. Instead of imagining the box poofing into existence, she imagined the box constructing itself, folding into a cube from the paper and the paper swelling and roughening to become cardboard. Hattie doodled, positioned the tag, and thought. The tag expanded and turned dull brown and folded flaps and corners and at last became a perfect cardboard box. She cheered privately, and she immediately set upon the next worksheet.

She managed to complete the next ten worksheets with few do-overs, but on the eleventh, she paused. Maybe she should try doodling the design the computer spirit gave her. She was getting good at doodling. The scribble didn't seem that hard to copy. But there was the matter of not knowing what happened after. Stick it on a mirror and go through it? She would be in the motaspace afterward, but then what?

Hattie checked the Song-jim for answers. Yes, she could use a tag without knowing what it did, but it was difficult, and the worksheet that dealt with the technique was next-to-last. Her eyes ached from concentrating. She slid the Song-jim and the book of blanks under the bed with the rest of her things, wondering what she should do.

* * *

The next few days were spent rebuilding damaged corridors and furniture, and at night, studying. En Law ordered the casino closed for the time being, so the meadow was disturbingly empty during the night. Hattie was used to the ghostly foxfire-like lanterns of the customers trickling from the road and funneling through Baba's door, or seeing amorphous shapes part the grass in the daytime. Instead, neatly lined chairs waited in the halls to be moved upstairs. Dust settled on alcohol bottles. What was cleaned stayed clean. For the first time, Hattie could hear the soft throb of Baba's heart, the gurgling of her stomach, the bellows of her lungs, and the sluicing of some thick liquid in the pipes. The sonic undercurrents helped her concentrate.

She tried to finish a worksheet per night at least, but got stuck on the twentieth. Jack usually helped, but En Law kept him busier than her, and she didn't have the heart to ask questions when he slouched out of the elevator, mussed, sallow, and dour. And she still hadn't found time to tell him that the whine she'd heard in the forest returned more and more often, and that the sound intensified and slipped away like a specter passing by.

About a week after the queen's death, Hattie was called into En Law's office. En Law, barely visible behind stacks of paper, wrote at his desk. Creon loomed beside him, flexing his ugly hands.

En Law said, "Dr. Creon will run tests on you to understand the queen's blessing. I, unfortunately, must be going. Dr. Creon, please let me know when you finish."

"Of course," Creon croaked. Rather than leave, En Law went inside the closet and shut the door with a snap. The monster sighed. "Alone at last." Hattie's hair rose. Creon took a black leather case from beside the desk and rummaged inside it for a moment before showing her a series of clamps with wires running from them like jumper cables. "Please clip one to each point on your antlers. And when you are finished, let me know."

"What do they do?" she asked, nervously.

"They measure zenzen. Put these on your body." Electrodes,

also wired. "I will administer zenzen to your body in the form of electrical signals. It will not hurt, but it will feel funny. I am, I admit, upset with myself," he added. "I did not test you before you received the queen's blessing. That is, before you were altered. And yes, you were definitely altered. Now I may never know what your original state was and why you could see orex." His voice was wistful, but it changed to hopeful. "Unless you know?" Hattie shook her head. "No? Ah, well. I will start the tests. If it becomes too much, let me know."

With a remote in one hand and something like a handheld TV in the other, he pressed a button. A long, low, resounding noise went on and on, and she could feel it resonating in her sternum. He let the tone last for thirty seconds before changing to another. A tongue of paper ticked out of the briefcase, filled with numbers. The sound climbed in pitch. Soon it grew so high Hattie couldn't stand it and unclipped one of the clamps. The noise stopped at once.

"Please put the clips back on," Creon said calmly. "Why did you remove them?"

"Too loud. One second."

"Too loud?" Creon knelt in front of her and examined the clip she removed. The clip, a shiny, metal, toothed jaw, was only a clip. "I heard nothing. What did you hear?"

"Like a bell, or like a radio between stations. Or dial-up internet." It sounded like what she heard in the forest, but she didn't want to tell him that.

"I know radios, but the internet?"

"Machines for talking to people. The internet is...I don't know exactly how it works. Well, I kind of know radios."

Creon took out another pad of paper and put the tip of his pencil on it. "Please explain."

"Okay. Radios listen to music or words and change sound into radio waves. Other radios can pick up on them and change them back into something people can understand."

"And radios do this on their own?" He scratched notes on a

pad. "Do they agree to speak a language to each other? How do they know what to say?"

"Are there no radio spirits in Tsava? Humans built radios." Hattie wondered what she was missing.

Creon's nostril slits flared. "Humans *built* radios? But they are a new kind of spirit! They appeared twenty years ago! That's a longer time than the last—" He clamped his jaw shut and continued writing, his eyes bulging from their slits.

Spirits had types? And they could just appear? "How do new types of spirits appear?"

"Nobody knows, but if humans invented them first..." He changed tactics. "How long ago were radios invented?"

"Maybe a hundred years ago. Probably more."

Creon asked the question she'd been thinking. "If humans invented radios before radio spirits appeared in Tsava, the implication is that what humans invent can become a spirit."

"But there are peaches here," Hattie added. "We didn't invent those."

Creon tore a few sheets of paper from his pad and gave them to her. "I must ask En Law some questions. While I am gone, please write down everything that you have seen on both Earth and Tsava, and mark whether it is a spirit. Be as thorough as you possibly can." He stepped through the door and left Hattie to write. In the fifteen minutes he was gone, Hattie filled two pages front and back. She didn't want to help him, but she wanted to know the answers, too. What was Tsava? Earth and Tsava were clearly connected, but why, and how? The motaspace obviously, but what was it? And the computer spirit?

Creon returned with En Law, the tall monster gesturing, the small monster, impassive.

"Oh my, that's quite a list. Are you still writing? You can complete it later." He held out his clawed hand and studied it with En Law.

En Law scanned the list. "We knew most of these already."

"Not everything. And we certainly didn't know that humans

built radios, and that some technology crosses the motaspace, but not others. Why does human technology become spirits? And..." He checked the list. "What are rabbits, cactus, and skeleton?"

"I don't know the orex name for rabbit. Rabbits here are bigger and they talk. A cactus...I can draw one. Earth has different names for everything."

"Interesting. En Law, perhaps she might help your—"

En Law cut him off. "No."

"But what if she could save them?"

The air in the room seemed to vanish. En Law radiated rage from every rigid line of his body. Hattie felt like she had witnessed something blasphemous. En Law, saying no to Creon?

Then, En Law said in a soft, caustic voice unlike any she had heard from him before, "Hattie, do not tell anyone what we will show you."

En Law led them to the closet door. Hattie tucked her body so as not to touch him when he held the door open. Creon took a luminous balloon, reading her list as they walked into the musty darkness.

"English?" he asked, pointing at the list.

"One of Earth's languages. I always wondered why you guys could understand me."

"Convenient," En Law said derisively.

Creon and En Law led her deep into the closet, where the shelves ended and broad dark spaces opened up. Bird cages and lockers faced all directions, only visible in the light, which crept over them and slid away like a veil. Her antlers chimed and whined, as if tuning. Sometimes the sounds grew loud, sometimes they changed tone or rhythm. Once there was a beat, a *ping...ping...ping...*like water dripping into a metal bowl. Behind all sounds was a deep drone that felt oppressive and sinking in her chest.

Creon noticed her turning her head. "Do you hear something? From the shelves, the lockers?"

"Everywhere," she said, amazed. "What is all this stuff?"

"Priceless zenzen relics. Is it possible that you can hear zenzen?"

Hattie wished she'd hid it better from him. "Probably."

They passed a cart filled with glass jars, each with one slip of paper inside. Her antlers rang with voices:

"Mom! The horses are out again!"

"I need to get ready for work."

"Hush, baby, shh, shh, shh..."

"I'm...finally!"

"The trip to Canada is going to be cheaper than I expected. Do you think..."

Hattie stepped closer to hear. Creon swept her away from the cart, and the chattering chorus faded to nothing. Her whole being strived to touch the jars like a lodestone to the north. She tried to memorize the shelves, their arrangement, and their artifacts, so she could find her way back.

En Law and Creon led her to a room built of folding screens with painted silk landscapes. Pearl lights floated over the top, and their illumination bloomed onto the ceiling. The powerful drone was loudest here. She craned her head to see where the sound might be coming from and saw nothing but more shelves and piles of junk against the walls.

En Law grabbed her upper arm in a tight, inflexible grip, making her gasp. "Do not tell Ann May you are a contract worker. If she asks, you are simply working for money for school. Make no mention of your family." His face was cinched. "Is that clear?"

"Yes, sir," Hattie replied uneasily.

En Law opened one of the folded screens. Inside, a lush blue carpet with scarlet and emerald designs spread over the floor and pillows were heaped along the sides, surrounded by books and board games. In the midst of them, a young woman sat with a toy pinwheel in her hand. Her large liquid eyes roved over Hattie. Her hair flowed sleek and black down to her embroidered slippers. She looked like a sweet-faced doll, made large and brought to life, wearing a plum-colored dress with gold flowers and birds on the sleeves.

"Dear, what is it?" she asked En Law.

Creon answered, "I am testing a marvelous new skill in our employee. Hattie, please listen, and tell us if you hear any discrepancies." Creon took a small microphone from his pocket.

"Okay." Hattie held her breath and listened carefully. Beneath the droning, from the woman, a weak heartbeat. From elsewhere in the room, another heartbeat.

"I can hear your heart," she told Ann May. The woman's face opened, radiant.

En Law asked her urgently, "What does it sound like?"

Hattie listened. It flickered out of time with a normal heart in fits and starts. "Not...in time," she said at last. His face closed. The woman, sorrowful.

"We always knew," she said to En Law, taking his hand.

"Yes," said Creon to En Law in satisfaction. "Now Hattie, can you do anything with your antlers?"

"I don't know. Just hearing."

"Do some objects sound louder or have different sounds?"

"Yes. I don't know why."

En Law murmured to Ann May and she pointed to the pile of pillows where the second heartbeat emitted.

"I have a hypothesis. You have heard it, but I must test it. Wait while I gather materials." He stepped through the screens. "En Law, would you come with me?" En Law gave Hattie a piercing look, touched Ann May's shoulder, and followed Creon.

Ann May smiled at Hattie. "I'm Ann May, En's wife. He has told me all about you! The human!"

"Yep, that's me," she said, trying to sound upbeat. "Hattie the Human. What did he say about me?"

"That you were in trouble. I'm sorry to hear about your parents' deaths. It must be so hard to work at such a young age." Her eyes sparkled with tears. "I don't know if I could stand it if I knew our son would be left alone in Tsava. Did you come far to work for En?"

"Um, yes, pretty far. I'd rather not talk about it, if you don't mind." Ann May nodded, wiping her eyes. "You have a son?"

She brightened. "Oh, yes. Ko! Come here! He likes to hide," she added apologetically.

Something moved in the corner of Hattie's eye; the second heartbeat shifted to a different pile.

"He thinks he's going to be a warrior like his father, but he's only six. And he isn't going to be one, for his own good," she said in a clear voice to the pile.

Hattie knew how to deal with little kids. Her best friend back at her old home had two little brothers and a little sister.

"That's okay. He probably sucks anyway," Hattie said in a slightly louder voice. While Ann May looked shocked, a pillow winged at Hattie from the pile. She caught it and hurled it back at the heartbeat, which moved. A tiny boy dove into a second pile, popped out, and began throwing more pillows. She swatted them away. She caught the last and flung it at the sound the instant it moved. The pillow hit the boy just as he darted away. He toppled into the pile and flailed upright. He had his mother's enormous black eyes and his father's round, babyish face, but also arched and dark eyebrows and a tuft of black hair; he resembled an outraged owl.

"Aw, you're so cute!" Hattie said mockingly.

His face puckered. "No, I'm not!" He charged Hattie with a pillow over his head. She battled against him gently with her own pillow, though it was hard not to fight seriously. What he lacked in size and strength, he made up for in enthusiasm and tenacity. His red face made her laugh even as he hit her so hard feathers flurried. She heard Ann May's soft laugh, and then En Law's chuckle.

Her excitement extinguished. En Law and Creon had returned and were watching her play. Her muscles locked. She did not want him happy, or to feel anything close to happiness.

She caught his eye. His expression flickered. Shame? It hardened again.

Ann May said worriedly, "Hattie?"

Creon set down a large leather box.

"Now that all of us are acquainted," said Creon, opening the box. "I will test my hypothesis." Ko threw feathers at her, trying to get her attention. Creon smiled a nightmarish smile full of grimy, spiky teeth and told him sweetly, "Behave now." Ko dove into his mother's lap and watched from a safe distance.

"Hattie," Creon continued. "Your antlers seem to have become highly-sensitive external sensory organs. They are not really antlers. More like satellite antenna. You can hear the sound of their zenzen processing discrepancies. The heartbeats." Creon took one object out of the box: a humming red orb. "This box blocks zenzen emissions. Do you hear a loud sound? That sound comes from...well, I can't say. But the sound suppresses their strange frequencies and lowers the risk of them having a fit, which could kill them."

Creon went on. "Ann May and Ko both have a disease known as Heartbreak Syndrome. Their spiritual hearts are out of sync with their physical ones due to difficulty processing environmental zenzen. If there is no zenzen to process, the disease's progress slows. The key to understanding their disease lies in knowing what frequency Ann and Ko can't process. I want you to pick which object most closely matches their sound."

Hattie teetered on telling a lie or saying that she wouldn't do it unless En Law released her parents. A tiny hand closed on her fingers. Ko gazed at her with his owlish eyes and jammed his other hand into his mouth. Her resolve wavered and fell away.

"This one?" Creon held out the orb.

"No."

He lifted out one thing after another.

"No. No. No."

The seventh was a maybe. Creon examined it cryptically and

set it aside. To En Law he said, "If she is right you will need to carry out the original treatment after all."

"Original treatment?" asked Ann May.

En touched her cheek. "Later," he murmured, rising. "Come, Hattie."

Ko took his fingers out his mouth, frowning, not letting go of her hand.

"I have to go," Hattie said gently as she pulled away.

"She'll play with you again." Ann May reached and pulled him into her lap.

His face puckered again. "No, stay!" he whined, wriggling away. "It's boring here! Stay and play with me!"

Hattie's throat clogged. "I can't. I have to work."

En Law's head turned slightly, and he seemed about to speak when Creon replied. "Yes. And I must run as many tests as possible today. I will not have another chance for a long time. Hattie, let's return to the office."

"I'll see you again soon," En Law told Ko. While he and Ann May bent over their son, as Hattie slipped out, Ko began to cry. Hattie bit the insides of her lips as she tried not to cry herself on the walk back.

❧ 14 ☙

TESTING

During the following week, Creon ran more tests, hmm-ing and ahh-ing over every result.

"What is the highest tone you can you hear? Tell me when you can hear the sound. Now low frequency. Hmm. What about softness? How far away can you hear? Can you emit zenzen?"

Hattie thought about lying to him, but with his instruments around, he might be able to tell if she was. She answered as vaguely as she could and left at once when it was over. The tests stopped after a week, the same night as the reopening of the casino.

En Law sent invitations to every patron, asking them to return to the casino and promising extra security and perks. When Hattie heard that the casino was reopening, a curious wave of relief washed through her. If it stayed closed forever, she might not be able to work to get her parents back, though she wondered whether she had become valuable enough that they would simply take her for their experiments. She daydreamed about breaking into the closet and grabbing her parents' jars.

When Hattie went down to work that night, Jack and Jane, who had been whispering near the lobby desk, looked up.

Jack's face appeared strained and angry. "I don't think we'll need to work tonight. En Law's about to cancel the reopening." Hattie's bewilderment curdled to dread as Jane handed her a sheet of paper.

To the lunaries:
Many of you have participated in the stifling of the sub-lunaries, who you now enslave with your wealth and heredity. As of today, we declare that whosoever visits the Red Hen Casino will be killed.
The Alate

"One of the workers found this on the door a few minutes ago," said Jane.

"Did anybody come?" Hattie asked. Jack and Jane shook their heads. "What did En Law say?"

"He's so angry," said Jack in a low voice. "He's recalling the invitations. He just bought stroilmen, too, and they are stupidly expensive. And I found out from Creon why the Alate attacked Baba when they knew the Fengul Queen would be there. They were just trying to scare people so they wouldn't come back. Our customer base was cut in half that night. There was another note that came just a few minutes ago, but En Law's not telling us everything it says."

En Law's voice made them jump. "Come to the casino. I need to speak with all of you."

In the entryway of the casino, En Law paced between a row of slot machines. Creon stood a little to the side, unperturbed.

En Law stopped pacing and massaged his forehead. "We are going to do nothing. We can only wait for Ran Corp to petition the Monarch to send forces and clear them out." Jack twitched when he heard him mention the Monarch, but En Law disregarded him.

"You three, inform the workers in the longhouses that the casino is closed. I'll make an announcement on the PA."

Creon bowed and the pearl lights extinguished as if hands had closed around them. Nobody made a sound in the dark, not a word was spoken, but Hattie could sense the departure of En Law through the lobby and the insect clicking of Creon's feet as he shambled after him. The curves of Jane's skull glimmered in the black like a specter.

"Let's go," Jane whispered. "It's creepy in here."

"A skeleton afraid of the dark?" Hattie whispered back, and something like a bony finger flicked her hard on the back of the head. "Ow!"

"Stop it," said Jack. "Jane's right, we need to leave. The stroilmen are being kept here."

She could feel it then: an oozing, warm dark made oily and humid. Sloshing echoed from the cracks and corners. They went to the slit of light marking the lobby, and blinked at the change in brightness.

They had just reached the lobby when Chiros bolted through the front doors. "Move!" They jumped out of her way and she disappeared into elevator.

"What's her hurry?" Jane complained. The front doors swung in the breeze. The guards were running to something out on the pathway.

"Did someone try to come?" Hattie asked.

"Let's stay out of the way," Jack replied as the elevator returned.

They had just stepped off the elevator on the fourth floor when an alarm howled from the speakers in the hall corners.

Jack yanked her and Jane back inside the elevator. "En Law's calling all the workers downstairs!"

"You don't think the Alate—"

Jack's face paled and his veins stood out beneath his skin. In the lobby, the guards slicked long tags over the doors in an X pattern. In the casino, a crowd of murmuring, whimpering orex bent over something in their midst. Chiros ran through the doors with En Law. The crowd parted to let them by, and that was when Hattie saw the smashed, tiny body of Limn, his bright coal cooling to a fragile ball of ash.

🜲 15 🜲

FIRED, KIDNAPPED, OR DEAD

En Law stood over Limn's body with a grim expression. He turned on his heel, plunged his hand into the sleeve of his robe, and produced a small jar, which he thrust into Hattie's hands.

"Pick up what's left of your friend. He'll survive if you hurry." He strode past her to the lobby. Hattie's hands spasmed as she tried to pick up Limn. Merely brushing the jar's edge sent ash feathering to the floor, and she sobbed. Jack plucked the jar out of her hands and knelt before the mess of paper and wood. With little sweeping motions, he maneuvered the spirit's body into the jar without leaving any of it on the floor. He stood and pushed the jar into her hands.

In a low voice, he said, "Go feed blanks to him until the coal reignites. If it goes out completely, he'll die. I'll tell you if anything happens."

Hattie ran to the elevator with the precious jar against her chest. The ride seemed as slow as pouring molasses. The jar was warm, though cooling fast, and the glow was fading before her eyes. When the elevator stopped and the doors cracked open, she squeezed through and ran to her room. She dug her blanks out from under her bed, ripped out a handful, and shoved them all inside.

The paper squashed the coal. For a terrible moment Hattie thought she had ruined everything. Then, a penny-sized flame ventured from the coal to nibble at the paper. This fire grew steadily until the coal was cupped in flames. Two smudges of soot, like fingerprints, appeared on the inside of the jar, blinking woozily.

A moan echoed in the jar. "Ugh...I feel terrible. Wa'z happening?"

"Eat this." She stuffed more blanks in the jar. That seemed to revive him a bit, and the soot eyes stayed open longer.

Jack walked into the room. A bee-like orex as tall as Jack with yellow and black striped skin, four cellophane wings, and antennae curling out of her hair appeared a beat behind him.

"Is he—" Jack began, and Hattie held up the jar.

"Not so fast! Urgh..."

"Sorry," she said, placing him on the nightstand.

The orex plucked small vials and spindly copper tools out of her satchel. "You're a tough little spirit, aren't you? The Alate destroyed his body as a warning to En Law," she said to Hattie. "They meant to kill him. Give Limn one of these vials every day while he's in the jar as we look for a suitable container for his spirit. Put the fireball candy in his jar with these tweezers."

Hattie nodded and said yes and tried to listen as the bee-type orex demonstrated how to treat Limn. When she finally left, Jack closed the door.

"Do you remember anything?" he asked Limn.

"Yeah." Limn slurred, "I waz comin' back from the store...an' someone hit me as I waz going through Baba's front door. Didn't see him."

"You came through the front door?" Jack persisted. "Not the servant's entrance?"

"I couldn't remember which shingle to open." Hattie and

Jack crowded around Limn to hear better. "Never saw anything...just on the steps and something hard comes down on me, and now I'm here."

Hattie caught Jack's eye, and his expression told her he was thinking the exact same thing she was. The Alate must have thought he was a customer. Since Limn was running errands when the message arrived, he wouldn't have known. The smudges faded from the glass, though the coal was still burning bright. Limn must have gone to sleep. Hattie marveled how his entire being could fit neatly inside a single ember.

"Keep him on your nightstand," Jack said. "I don't think he or En Law will care that he's in your room. And En Law didn't say anything important, just vowed revenge, but he already said after the first incident that he was going to do something. Nothing we didn't already know or wouldn't have guessed. Also, I brought you more blanks."

Hattie took the blanks gratefully. "What will En Law do? Send out the stroilmen?"

"I don't know. I don't know what to think about En Law anymore." He straightened. "Good night. Keep your windows shut, or bird-boy might come flying in."

"Thanks," she called as he left. Too anxious to sleep, she read the Song-jim again and had another whack at lesson twenty. She managed to succeed, but lesson twenty-one was even worse. The night sky hung more stars and polished them as she struggled. Sometimes she would stop and stare blankly at the page as a heavy feeling rose and threatened to engulf her. Avenues to getting her parents back had closed and she could not trust the Alate. It was looking like she couldn't work to get them back, either. Stealing them was a last resort, though her cynical mind countered that Ran Corp would simply follow her home and take them back. Maybe through zenzen there was a way? Maybe through the unknown of the queen's gift she could save them?

Moonlight glided across the open curtains onto the floor. She was too tense to sleep but too exhausted to stay awake. Near midnight, the elevator banged and gave her a start. Was it Jack? Maybe there was news. She left her room, closing the door carefully in case of a draft, and ran to Jack's room. He didn't answer her knocks; he might still be downstairs. Music thudded from Jane's room. Was she there or had she left her radio on? But radios didn't exist in Tsava. Or maybe they did, if Jane had one. Hattie didn't want to talk to her, but she wanted to know if anything was happening.

She knocked on Jane's door. She could hear Jane singing to wild and complex music, something like gypsy melodies and electronic instruments. Maybe she couldn't hear her?

"Jane?" Nothing. "Jane!" Finally, Hattie knocked one last time, and opened the door.

Jane danced in the center of her room, wielding mallets, drumming on her bones, kicking and turning and singing. It—she, the instrument—sounded like a low-pitched marimba, and her voice was cool and smoky. Mesmerized, Hattie stood in the doorway and listened for far too long. Jane turned once more, locked eyes with Hattie, and screamed so suddenly that Hattie screamed too.

"What are you doing in my room!" Jane shrieked and hurled a mallet at her. It missed. Behind Hattie, glass shattered.

"I wanted to ask you a question! I was only here for ten seconds! Ah!" Jane had thrown the other mallet and it thudded into her shoulder. "I thought it was really good!"

Jane snatched up a third mallet that was on her bed and stalked forward with it raised over her skull. Her eyelights flashed erratically. "What is your problem?"

"My problem?" Hattie realized that it wasn't about coming into the room. "*My* problem?"

"Yeah. Your problem." The mallet was still high, to strike like an axe.

Hattie's fright burned away. So it was her fault? "You tell me," she said icily. "I only wanted to ask you something. I knocked."

"You come here, and now everyone wants to talk to you. The queen of fengul describes you, the Alate want you, and Jack—" She raised the mallet higher. "Jack was my friend before we went to Earth," she hissed. "We had plans. Then there was you. It's like he hates me now." Her voice wobbled.

Hattie glared. "Talk to him."

"How can I talk to him when he's always with you!" Jane screamed.

"Ask!"

Jane snarled and hurled the mallet. Hattie ducked. "That's it! That's it, that's it, that's it! The answer is always obvious to you. Ask! Go there. Do something. And you get away with it! You're just there, and orex look at you, and you have no idea—" She passed her hand in front of her face in agony. "—it's not fair."

"They look at me because they know I'm not an orex and can't explain why," Hattie said in exasperation. "I just want to do my work so I can get my parents and go home."

"You're lying. You always say or do something, and if anyone else did it they'd be fired."

"Do you think I'm trying to get fired? You were there when En...you helped him!" Her voice rose. All the bitterness she held under her tongue spewed out. "Are you stupid? Do you think I would do anything to risk getting fired? My parents—"

"Your parents," Jane sneered. "That's how you get sympathy. You have a real-life sob story."

"*Sob story?*" Repeating Jane was the only thing Hattie could do. Her voice quivered.

"You tell everyone your backstory to gain sympathy, but you haven't done anything to earn your position other than crying to the right orex. You admitted you got a lot of help. If En Law hadn't told Jack and I to watch you, you'd be fired, kidnapped, or dead."

"I know! I know I can't do anything on my own!"

"Don't you even care about doing anything on your own instead of piggybacking on other orex?"

"No, because I can't," Hattie said coldly. "At least I know I need a lot of help instead of pretending I'm above it."

Jane raised a fourth mallet. Hattie tensed, ready to dodge, when a pair of red wings draped across her shoulders like a warm cape.

"Hattie," said a familiar voice. She looked up and saw the scarf-swathed face and violet eyes of Ven. "I've come to rescue you."

Jane screamed enough for both of them. Hattie struggled as Ven dragged her toward the window. "No! No!" She stomped and kicked his legs and grabbed the doorknob, her wrists and shoulders jarring as Ven tried to yank her over the windowsill. "Let go! Jane, help!"

But Jane could only gape. Ven gasped between yanks, "Why —are—you—helping—them?"

"You know why!" Hattie shrieked. She bit the wing under her chin and tore out feathers. "Jane!"

"Argh! Stop struggling!"

She headbutted him. The antler tines dug deep red holes above his cheekbones, under his eyes, and he jerked back. She lunged to break his grip, but with a roar he wrenched her back and hoisted her over his shoulder.

"*Jane!*"

Jane only raised the mallet higher. Ven hefted Hattie back to the broken window, and she grabbed the edges of the sill. "Jane!" She sobbed. Glass bit into her fingers, and her grip slipped on blood. "Please!"

A bang! The elevator!

"We'll have to tighten security again—" En Law, Jack, and Chiros walked out and froze. Hattie, her arms and legs braced against the window, Ven's wings around her waist, Jane and the silly mallet. The trio bolted forward and grabbed Hattie, dragging her back inside. En Law seized Ven's wing and screamed, "Not this time!" Ven released Hattie to retaliate, and she fell on Jack and Chiros, who staggered under her. Meanwhile, En Law threw tag after tag out the window as Ven winged into the night.

The hallway became quiet except for their panting. En Law backed away from the window, wrote on a blank tag, and smoothed it over the sill. A new window popped into place.

"Are you all right?" Chiros asked in a low voice. "Your hands are cut up." Blood slicked her fingers and trickled down her wrist. Her stomach knotted. The slashes were deeper than any cut she'd had before. Chiros took tags from her pocket, wrote briefly, and wrapped Hattie's hands with them.

"What happened?" En Law's glare snapped from Jane to Hattie. "How did he get in?"

Jane dropped the mallet. "He...the window was broken. He must have seen..."

"Why was the window broken?" En Law couldn't seem to speak normally. His voice hissed out like a gas leak, and his eyes were dilated and black. "You know it breaks security. How this overlooked?"

"It was smashed a minute before he came in," Jane rasped. "He must have been watching her."

"How did the window break?"

"An accident," Hattie said quickly, "I—"

En Law kicked open the door to her room.

"Sir!" Chiros began to warn, but En Law seized Hattie's arm and flung her back into her room. The door slammed behind her as she bounced off her bed onto the floor.

His furious voice rang through the door. "I have been far too nice! She is at the center of too many accidents and problems. Creon will study her, and that will be the end of it. We should have done that from the beginning."

"None of this is her fault!" Jack pleaded. Chiros' low, urgent reply was interrupted by the bang of the elevator. Their voices were muffled, then snipped silent. The room seemed to pulse. With each throb of her hands, scarlet spots bloomed in her palms until she held all red.

"Hello...Guys?" No answer. She tried the door. The instant her fingers made contact with the knob, the metal slicked with an invisible oily substance and her antlers *gonged*. Try as she might, she couldn't get a decent grip to turn the knob. She pushed on the wood of the door next, but that turned into a chilling unpleasant sensation under her skin. Would she be let out? But he had said no more. Did he mean her contract was over? Could he do that? *Someone would let her out when he calmed down,* she told herself, trying to quell her galloping heart. It wasn't her fault. He hadn't listened at all! Jane had broken the window, not her! En Law wasn't stupid. The Fengul Queen had named her. She was human. She was valuable.

Yet, the brutal, truthful part of her responded. She had caused more trouble than she was worth, even if it wasn't her fault. She was a child who had to save her parents, a human in a world that treated humans like delicacies. She was the Perceiver and Hattie, but she did not own herself. What was she going to do? What was? What? Why? Her thoughts darted ceaselessly, uselessly, and she sobbed until she slept.

* * *

Hattie woke to rain tapping on her window. She had used the Song-jim as a pillow, and she discovered in the mirror that the pinecone symbol was imprinted on her cheek. Daring to hope that the effect would be gone, Hattie tried to open the door. Nothing. The invisible oil made her bandaged hands squeak and slip uselessly. For the next ten minutes, she tried the most creative ways she could think of to leave the room, including throwing the Song-jim at the window hoping it would break, but in the end, she was sweaty and still in the room. She opened the Song-jim for another crack at countering the tags when an *ahem* came from her nightstand. The jar that held Limn's burning coal-soul was filled with ash from the charred blanks. Two eye-shaped patches of soot pressed to the glass and blinked at her.

"Lock yourself in your room?" he asked with interest. "I didn't know you could do that here. Are the doors on Earth different from the ones in Tsava?"

"No," said Hattie, snapping the book shut. "En Law put something on the door so I can't get out."

"Why?"

She told him about Ven and her fight with Jane.

Limn's flame burned higher. "Jane! I don't hate many orex, but I hate her. Not surprised. Not surprised at all." He simmered for a minute before he continued, "Are you going to stay?"

"I'm locked in this stupid room."

"I mean with Ran Corp."

"No." Saying it out loud lifted a weight in her chest she hadn't realized was there. There was a sense of rightness in the word. Strongly, she said it again. "No. I need to get out of here."

"Good." Limn paused. "Take me with you."

"Sure," she said. "But why?"

"If Ran Corp doesn't honor its agreements, I have no reason to hold up my end." At her puzzled look, he added, "I'm like you. I came from a remote place few people know about to get back something Ran Corp stole, and I can't go home without it." He paused. "We both crossed vast distances to be here. We can handle a door, right? If you don't know the doodle you're trying to counter, you should try to find a spirit. Most can tell what a scribble does just by looking at it and some can remove them by force; I can't do either. You could also find an anti-zenzen object and touch the tag to it."

Hattie's hand jumped to the pouch. She had forgotten she wore the bullet. "I think I have one. Is an anti-wanderer bullet good?"

He flared. "How do you have one of those?" She told him. "Anti-wanderer bullets are the most anti of all of the anti-zenzen things. And they're illegal." Hattie teased open the bag. His expression puckered. "Ugh, it reeks. Don't touch it! Roll it up in the bag and use that to hold it. Don't let it get too near your fingers. There...be careful..." With the bullet held inches from the doorknob, the tags became visible and peeled off like snakeskin. "Okay, now try."

Wary as an alley cat, Hattie opened the door and stepped out. Nothing. No alarm or no reaction at all. She withdrew and closed the door.

"What are you doing? Wasn't the whole point of this to get you out of here?"

"If I leave now, En Law will know I'm gone, and he'll come after me. I know my parents are in the closet." The jars with the voices could only be them. And the neighbors. She could save them, too. But if En Law and Creon could go back to Earth and recapture them, then all her hard work would vanish. She couldn't just sneak into the closet, grab the jars, and run for the blackwater pool. She had to make sure they couldn't follow her home. But how? "Let me think."

It was as if the gears in her head were stuck. So many unanswered questions. She wished she could call a fengul and ask for help. But there was someone she hadn't tried yet...

She asked, "Can you copy a scribble just by looking at the original tag?"

"Depends on the scribble. Some are harder to copy than others because they are more complicated or use more zenzen. I could if I wasn't in the jar, but..." he trailed off. Hattie understood. He was too weak right now.

She pulled the Song-jim into her lap. "You know a lot about zenzen, don't you?"

Limn snorted. "Duh."

"I need you to help me doodle this." Hattie uncrumpled the design and held it up to the jar.

Limn's eyes widened. "Where did you get this?"

"A computer spirit gave it to me. I can't tell you what it does or why he gave it to me. And don't tell anyone I showed this to you."

"I've never even seen this tag before, and I've seen *a lot*," he said, troubled. "The lines are so complicated. It looks like something a quanta would use for an experiment."

"We have to try it." Hattie cleared the floor and spread out the book, the blanks, and the tag.

✣ 16 ✣

USED TO BE HUMAN

L imn and Hattie stared hard at a blank piece of paper. They had been staring for over five minutes, and Hattie's face showed her strain. Finally there was a *ding,* and the metatag arched and rolled up to become a handle. Hattie pulled the handle, and a section of the floor opened, revealing a square hole large enough to fit inside.

They sighed, relaxing. They had stayed up until dawn greyed the sky working through the rest of the lessons in the Song-jim. Hattie thought they could shave off time simply by having Limn copy the tag and activate it himself, but he insisted she finish the remaining lessons.

"Having pre-made tags to activate isn't the same as scribbling and activating your own tags," he explained as she laboriously copied the computer spirit's scribble. "There's something in doing it yourself that makes the scribble yours. *You* put the energy into doodling, so the scribble becomes a channel for your own zenzen. With something as complicated as this, it's best to do it right."

"I'll believe it when it works," Hattie said. She stood and stretched, aching from hunching over the blanks and squinting at the tiny print in the book. Dots and lines throbbed in her vision. "The computer spirit told me to stick it on a mirror after scribbling."

"Oh, so it's a portal tag," said Limn. "Stick it on the mirror before you activate it. You have to put the tag at head-height so when you activate it, you aren't looking at your face in the mirror. It's an old superstition. Orex used to believe that fengul lived in portals. If the fengul latch onto your face, you're done for, so they stick tags at face height, so there's a layer of something preventing fengul from glomming onto you."

"And if they glue antlers to my head?"

He laughed. Sarcasm helped her breathe a little easier. *You've done harder things, and you've come out fine. You can do this too. You're not alone.* Holding her breath, she smoothed the tag over the mirror, stepped back, and activated it. The tag gently sank into the mirror's surface and fluttered, flipping and looping like a leaf caught in a breeze. It sailed around Hattie's reflection and soared back to the mirror face where it slapped onto the upper right corner. It stretched elastically to the opposite corners until the entire mirror was obscured by the now enormous tag.

Limn gasped so hard he sucked in soot, and the glass blackened as he wheezed and choked.

"Take it easy," she cautioned.

"No! Not that! This is a motaspace portal!"

"Well, I knew that."

Limn gaped at her. "It's theoretically impossible to travel through the motaspace. This is a big deal!"

"But that's how I got here! And that's how Jack and En Law and everyone else got to Earth."

"Wow." He frowned at the tagged mirror. "I wonder how they figured it out. Try breaking the seal and seeing where it goes —you can see your destination, usually, when you use a portal tag."

Hattie poked a hole in the tag experimentally. Nothing. She

made the hole wider and tore the paper away to reveal a glutinous, smoky darkness like black gelatin. It was icy and quivering
when she touched it. Like before, the motaspace didn't seem to
have any floor, and the light dissolved a few feet from the
surface.

"Yep, motaspace," she said. Limn's coal had become stark
white. He looked aghast. "This is deep space! There's nothing to
orient yourself with, so you can't leave by relying on sight, or
magnetism, or gravity. Don't go in!"

"I've gone through it before, on the way over." She remembered the goldfish glittering in empty space. "Someone helped
me though."

"Are you kidding me? There's a fine line—"

"You know why I did it."

"—between bravery and stupidity and you like to play
hopscotch on that line," he finished. "You had a good reason last
time. But this time? This is wrong. Why didn't the spirit explain
anything in the store? What was he doing there, anyway?"

"I'll ask."

She eased her foot into the gel. It was like stepping into a
pool of ice water, and her blood icicled immediately.

"Argh, fine! Good luck!" cried Limn as Hattie took a deep
breath and plunged completely into the dark.

Instantly a strong current carried her away from the open
mirror. She thrashed toward it to the surface, but the current
bore her deep into the abyss.

"Kometa!" she screamed. "*Kometa!*" But even her voice tore
away.

She screamed again as the screen of the computer spirit
floated leisurely past her head.

"How's Tsava working for you?" asked the spirit.

"It isn't! How do I stop?" The computer seemed to move like
an octopus with cables instead of legs that opened and closed,
umbrella-like. Meanwhile, Hattie pinwheeled. He caught her
with a cable and wrapped it around her. She still felt the flow of

the motaspace like wind, but the spirit didn't seem to be as affected.

"Now, Perceiver Hattie, I bet you're wondering what it is you're doing in Tsava, and what the antlers on your head are supposed to do."

"Hey, I'm quitting Ran Corp, taking back my parents, and going home."

The screen flickered. "Now?"

"Yes!"

"Then I'll make this quick." Her face must have appeared mutinous. He added, "I'm sure you're probably angry with me and with everything that's happened to you, and you're confused." She snorted. "And I'm real sorry about all this secrecy, but if you relax and get comfortable, I'll explain everything I know." The screen flashed and his face was replaced by a green handprint on a white background. "Put your hand on my face. Don't slap."

Hattie did. The antlers chimed with a clear sound, and the vibrations rolled out invisibly, dissipating.

"How long have your antlers been ringing?"

"You can tell?"

"I can hear. But only in the motaspace. In the physical, I would hear zip."

"They started making sounds the day I met you."

"Neato. Not a moment too late."

"What?"

"Get your hand off my face and I'll tell you." When Hattie took her hand away, the screen changed back to the spirit's friendly face. "When the queen gave you those antlers, she tied you to the motaspace and the nature of zenzen."

"Why?"

"Do you mean, why are you tied, or why did she tie you?"

"Both."

"Save your questions for the end."

Hattie boiled with impatience. The computer spirit watched her with sympathy.

"I know it sucks," he said. "But this is the moment where you finally get some answers. Keep in mind one thing, if you please. I don't know everything. Because the Perceiver is a new descriptive, recently evolved and bestowed upon you, I only know of one power you have, the power to hear zenzen. That's the whining or bell-chime sounds you've been hearing. Think of your antlers as a radio antenna for zenzen. They receive and transmit at the same time. I don't know why the queen stuck them on your head, but I do know that she thought the motaspace and the physical is in danger."

"From what?"

His face disappeared. She thought he might have crashed. Just as she was about to call his name, his face reappeared. He seemed to wince as his screen flickered, and he spoke with a glitch in his voice. "I...don't know. Sorry." His screen returned to normal. "Personally, I don't think the Perceiver is a prophesied chosen one. Wanderers are chosen by fengul, but there's no fate. Perceiver, as a word, is just nine letters, three syllables. A sound." He raised a pixelated eyebrow. "If I were to choose someone to make the word mean something, I'd choose somebody who I know is a good person. She chose you, not because you're human, but because you're someone who chose to do something incredible and difficult out of love. It could have been an orex, but it happened to be you." He lowered his eyebrow. "You look lost."

"I'm sorry, but I think I need to sit down and process everything. I still don't understand *why*. I can't be the Perceiver. I'm going home!"

"What, you thought you could take off your antlers and leave?" She felt like he'd hit her. He studied her expression and his own softened. "I'm sorry. That was rude."

"I'm going home," she said through tears. "Get a different orex to do it. Whatever it is. I don't want it."

He hesitated. "I don't know if...Well, to recap..." The screen showed a pixelated number one. "You're the Perceiver. Not really sure what that is, probably something special. You probably will be able to do something with it in the future." The screen showed a number two. "You're the Perceiver possibly because the queen sensed imminent danger in Tsava." His face returned. "Too much is happening right now. Go get your parents. If you ever need advice, just use the scribble I gave you to pop in anytime. I'll be here."

Hattie's head throbbed. Everything she'd seen and learned was incredible, but she was exhausted. Questions still rose in her brain. She picked the most important ones, and asked, "How do you know all this? Who are you? And why are you helping me?"

"Well, my name is Frank. I used to be human, like you. I'm friends with fengul. And it's everyone's job to save the world, not just yours. But it's more my job and your job than, say, the average orex." Though light, his tone indicated he wasn't going to say anymore. "You should get back in case En Law returns. To get back to the door, you can either imagine yourself going to the door, or the door coming to you. Personally, I like to imagine rocket boosters on myself and blast off, but whatever floats your boat is okay with me."

"Wait! Can you help me get my parents?" she asked desperately. "I know where they are, but if I take them and run, En Law and Creon can still follow me back and kidnap them all over again. I need to stop them *forever*."

Frank looked thoughtful. "You know, the Alate have also been trying to stop them since forever." She grimaced. "I can't leave the motaspace for the time being, but I can give you a tip. Ran Corp has lots of enemies. And you know what they say, *the enemy of your enemy is your friend*. And maybe you don't know how to find the Alate right now, but do you know who they've enslaved for the longest time, who they're absolutely dependent on for shelter, their most powerful servant, and who has nothing to lose?"

Hattie stared at him, nonplussed.

The spirit grinned. "Her head is on the balcony. Now get outta here!"

The door's light rushed at her like the headlights of a car. Hattie toppled over the dresser and Limn screamed.

Hattie winced as she stood. A plan began to take shape in her head.

17

MEMORIES

S moke filtered from Limn's jar by the end of Hattie's story.

"You're like a spirit now!" Embers puffed out of the jar. "You can probably do all kinds of stuff with zenzen!"

Everything she'd just learned swirled in her head. Frank said she wasn't chosen but whether she was or not, she didn't care at the moment. Would it help her get her parents back? The computer spirit said she had power. Hattie had been locked in her room, spent hours learning how to doodle the computer's tag, and met with the computer. *What a long night*, she thought. Yet she was awake, restless, even exhilarated.

"I'm not going to wait for him to do something first. The computer spirit told me I should be friends with Ran Corp's enemies. And he told me to be friends with his most powerful servant, and that her head is on the balcony. The only orex who that could be is Baba."

"She can probably help," said Limn. "I heard she won't let En Law go on certain floors in her body. That's big. You normally can't stop En Law from doing anything he wants to do. Also, she knows everything that goes on in her body. Which means she can hear us right now."

They both looked at the ceiling. If Baba could hear every-thing, why hadn't she reported Hattie for sneaking around? *Maybe she wanted En Law gone, too,* Hattie thought.

"Hey, Baba," Hattie said to the ceiling. "We're coming to see you, okay?"

"I'm not," said Limn loudly. "I feel like I'm going to snuff out each time I move, so I'll stay here."

She pulled on her shoes and peeked out the door. The hallway was empty.

"Good luck," he whispered as the door closed.

Hattie was on the fourth floor, with six floors between her and Baba's head. Should she risk the elevator? Or would it stop on the third floor, stranding her with En Law? Deciding it was far riskier to climb six floors, Hattie stole to the end of the hall.

Before she could even touch the bell, there was an explosion of steam, and the elevator materialized in front of her. Hattie made a strangled sound as the doors opened. She raced behind the elevator and waited there, biting her fingers.

"—expect that you stay out of the way during the fight, and that goes for Jane as well, so tell her when you see her."

"Yes, sir." Jack's voice. He was moving out of the elevator.

"And check on our human. Remember, do not approach the ground floor for anything."

The elevator vanished with a snap. Hattie fell on her face. She'd been leaning on the elevator while listening. Her face fell level with Jack's shoes. His dour expression almost made her laugh.

"And you're out. Of course." He was holding a plate of food and a can of water, which he held out to her. She scarfed down the fried vegetables, meatish cubes, and the quivering aspic. "How did you get out? Are you finally running away?"

"Yep. Everything is preventing me from doing my job and getting my parents back, so I'm just going to take them." Saying it aloud felt like more like a confession, which made her angry. It wasn't a confession because she was only taking back what was hers. "I should have done it earlier and saved time." She rang the bell.

"You don't sound very confident."

"I'm not. But I'm tired of things happening to me. Now, I'm going to make them happen." Jack smirked. "What?"

"Nice confidence. But what will stop him from retaking everyone? What happens if you get caught? And how are you going to leave?"

"I'm going to talk to Baba," she said. "Can you make sure En Law doesn't go to the balcony?" The elevator re-exploded, empty. She held the door open with one foot.

Jack hesitated. "En Law shouldn't bother us. He's preparing stroilmen to go after the Alate in the forest. But Baba probably won't let you up."

"How can I get there, then?"

He chewed his lip while staring into the distance. Then, he moved past her into the elevator and punched the button for the sixth floor. As the elevator shuddered and rose, he said, "We'll take the spine, the master staircase. Her memories put up a defense starting on the seventh floor, where the stairs start, so if you aren't expecting them, you'll be overwhelmed. I can take care of them."

"But what if En Law looks for you?"

He gave her a look equal parts exasperated and terrified. "I'll tell him that I quit. I should have done it after Earth." Hattie felt like the sun was rising inside her. He gave her a quick grin.

Hattie wondered what kind of memories a wanderer had. What were the earliest memories? Did Baba grow? Was Baba born, or was she always there? And why, in a living building, were the memories the defense? When the elevator doors opened, she leaned out in rash curiosity.

The hall appeared to extend to eternity. Vivid red doors stood against grey shimmering wallpaper. Portholes punctuated the walls between every two doors, and there was no glass to block the balmy breeze that ghosted through the corridor and stirred the pale fine grass sprinkled with bright red poppies growing in place of carpet. Her antlers chimed lightly, like a windchime answering a breeze. Hattie could feel Baba's breathing and the zenzen pressure tingling, though not unpleasantly, on the skin.

They separated to each side of the corridor and tested the doors. Each door had a gleaming brass knob which would not turn and would not respond to Hattie pressing herself against it. The ringing from her antlers increased in sound and pitch like an annoying phone. Absurdly, she wondered if Baba was calling.

"Jack—"A great ocean of wheat billowed out from under her feet. Hot blue sky unrolled from the ceiling.

Jack hissed. "Baba's memories are responding! Don't move!"

Something trundled over a hill. Two scaly feet supporting a square timber body layered in colorful shingles tromped along. On top, a yellow, fuzzy head with oil-drop eyes. It was a giant chick that wore its hen-house like a snail wears its shell. More hen-houses tottered over the hill in a spill of colors. The ground shivered as an enormous salt-and-pepper hen-house, comb and wattles trembling with each step, rose over the hill. It continued to rise, story after story, until the entire hen-house stood on the hill. The mother hen-house loomed like a castle surveying the land while her children played in her shadow. The baby hen-houses dove into the wheat, tearing and snipping heads from stems. Spilled kernels were crushed underfoot as they burbled and nibbled. Dry, pollen-laden wind lashed and threshed the wheat so it scratched Hattie's skin and her lips dried from the heat. The baby hen-houses were so close she could feel their weight pressing the ground when they moved.

The first chick they saw in the memory was acting differently than the others. It teased a male chick whose body timber was pine green. She held a wheat stem in her beak and tickled him with the other end before the male grabbed it. They tugged the stem back and forth until it snapped. Something about the female's shingles looked very familiar.

"Jack," said Hattie slowly. "That chick...is that Baba?"

"Yeah. These are her memories, remember?"

The scene stopped, as if frozen, then faded away and revealed the corridor they were currently standing in.

"It didn't do anything," said Jack uncertainly. "I thought the memories attacked, but this one didn't."

"Maybe Baba's trying to tell us something," she suggested.

They split up again and checked the doors further down. Soon Jack called her over to an open door. Beyond it, a highly-polished ivory staircase whirled above and below the floors. At the top was an unwinking blue and yellow-tiled dome, the distance shrinking it to the size of an eye. Sunlight and fresh air gusted through more portholes lining the sides.

"Why doesn't Baba just let the elevator go to the balcony?" Hattie asked as they climbed. "Why make everyone go through this?"

"Because then they would think again about going to the balcony. There aren't many giant beings like her left, and even though they can see her feet move and her wings stretch, everyone wants to figure out if she's the real thing."

They took a step and fell through air. Their bodies plummeted through cold white vapor as if falling from the belly of a cloud. Tsava's hills and forests unrolled beneath them.

"It's another memory!" His hair flamed wildly with the speed. "Don't let go of me!"

Something huge sailed past them. An older Baba, three stories tall, soared through the air on wings each the length of a football field. Her feathers were salt-and-pepper colored, and her eyes were large, gold, and fierce. Hattie felt a jerk on her chest as they were tugged after her, floating above her back like kites. Green hills stitched with the four-toed footprints of a flock of hen-houses rolled beneath them. Watching the flock ambling over the grass was akin to watching an entire town go for a stroll.

Another hen-house joined Baba in the air. A rooster, green-black and glossy, whose building shell looked like a wooden castle. It crowed, and Baba cackled as if it had just told her a joke.

Hattie's antlers gonged. Streaks of fire shot over mountains, arched high into the blue, and screamed past Baba and the rooster. Both hen-houses squawked as the fireballs exploded into the flock. Shrieks rose with the thick blue smoke.

"No!" Hattie gasped as the missiles rained down. Soon the cries of the birds could no longer be heard.

The scene changed. Craters fissured the rolling hills like open, smoking sores. Fire crawled upon broken houses and mangled bodies, and feathers scattered like ash and snow. Tall malformed shapes stooped over the hen-houses. Baba blasted through the smoke like a cannonball. The creatures skittered as she bit one, shook it like a napkin, and tossed it over a hill. Her roof was cracked, the windows were all broken, and her right wing bled freely, but a frenzied light shone in her eyes.

She screamed, slicing at the forms with her wings and biting. The creatures hung back on the fringes of the flock. Others crawled over the hills, licking their teeth. Choking on her sobs, she called, "Is anyone alive? I'm still here! Is anyone alive?"

The scene vanished. They were back on the stairs.

Chills ran through Hattie's skin. "Why did they die? Whose missiles were those? They weren't spirits, were they?"

"No," said Jack grimly, beginning to climb again. "That memory must have been from the war. All those things were wanderers looking for a free meal. The war destroyed the flock."

"But there were so many. How could orex not think Baba was real?" Like bad math, nothing added up.

"We'll ask her." There was a door at the top of the stairs. As Jack reached for the handle, grass sprouted beneath their feet. Giant trees rocketed upwards and surrounded them. It was the same blackwater pond where Hattie had first arrived. Baba sat at the edge of the pond. She was now twice as tall as the trees. A balcony like a ruff circled her neck, and she wore a square roof on her head like a hat. She bent over the pond, gazing at the goldfish circling in the water.

Jack leaped away like he'd received an electric shock. En Law stood beside them, shoes barely edging over the stones. His face looked almost babyish, and his clothes hung from his tiny frame. He didn't seem to notice them as they scrambled away.

Baba's golden eyes did not leave En Law.

"Who are you and what do you want?" she said in a ringing voice. Birds squawked and rose from the forest in alarm.

"My name is En Law, and I am here on behalf of Ran Corp."

Baba spread wings wide enough to hug a city block. En Law stiffened. Baba brought her wings down like axes and wind blasted through the forest. Trees creaked, rocked, and crashed down. The water dashed out of the pond. Satisfied, the hen-house tucked her wings to her sides once more and surveyed the damage. Something moved feebly in a pile of branches. En Law, bleeding from his mouth, nose, and arms, staggered over a trunk and flopped down. Tags glowed blue on his robe before dissolving to ash. Baba *tched* and raised her wings again.

"I have a deal for you," En Law gasped.

She raised her wings higher.

"I know where other hen-houses are rumored to dwell!"

Baba held her wings up still. "Where?"

"If you let—"

"No," she said clearly. "Tell me, now."

"How do you know...that I won't lie?" En Law tried to stand, but his face twisted every time his injured arm or leg moved.

Baba raised her wings still higher; they blotted out the sky. If she swept them catastrophically down...

"You will wonder if I was right!" Slowly, she lowered her wings. He spoke quickly. "Work for Ran Corp, and they will help you find your family. Only as long as it takes, then they will tell you how to find them."

Baba regarded him as if he was a bug.

"Remember," she said softly. She raised her wings, turned in a great, sweeping rush, and brought them down. The forest roared, cracked, and ripped out of the earth. When the destruction was over, there was a bare, torn-up clearing. She settled into it, as if settling into a nest, and opened her doors.

The memory faded, and the door appeared before their eyes again.

"So En Law knows where other hen-houses are and she wants to know, too," Hattie said. "But why is the casino in Baba? Why do they need her at all?"

"We'll ask," said Jack as he twisted the knob.

The door slammed open as a freezing wind roiled into the stairwell. Hattie's flesh crawled with goose bumps. They fought against the wind to step onto a grassy balcony in the sky. The balcony was a massive circle of wood that had decomposed, softened, and accumulated dirt blown up from the ground. It was springy underfoot, with wisps of bright green grass and lacy white, violet, and yellow flowers clustered at the posts of the railing running along the edge. The sun was closer and brighter; it dazzled her eyes. Beyond, a great green forest spread to the horizon. New Sprout's buildings were the size of thimbles and buttons, and a vast meadowland to the east looked no bigger than a lawn. Clouds raced around the balcony and wet the grass.

In the middle of the terrace was a white-feathered head as large as a house. Wind ruffled thick feathers, and in the feathers were eyes like pools of golden oil and a beak like the prow of a ship. A pleasant oily smell exuded from the feathers. Musky body heat smoothed the goose pimples from Hattie's arms.

The eyes caught them as surely as talons.

"Hello, Hattie. Jack." Hot, moist air stinking of guts and lungs curled across them. The voice was deep and dry. "In the old days, my inhabitants would prepare you something suitable to eat and drink, perhaps prepare something for you to relax with, but as you have seen, En Law isn't so welcoming." The eyes blinked slowly. "I know what you're up to."

"Can you help us, please?" Hattie shouted into the wind.

"Please," said Baba smilingly. "How sweet to hear that word again. I have wanted Ran Corp out of me for a long time. And you, of course, need to make sure they can never follow you home. I have been mulling over several plans, if you would like to hear them."

"Yes, please!"

"Listen. Get Zeya, Creon, and En Law into the casino room. From there, I can expel them."

"Zeya?"

Baba blinked lazily, and her long eyelashes fanned their hair out of their faces. "When you were in the closet, you heard the droning zenzen. That sound is the breathing of a wanderer named Zeya the Brutal. Somehow, Ran Corp captured him. En Law plans to use Zeya to heal his wife and son's disease. Permanently. I don't want him to do it inside me! But it seems my wishes are to be ignored once again." She clacked her beak. "And then there's the problem of the Alate."

"I wonder if they're still open to saving us after what we've done to them," Hattie said.

Baba looked thoughtful. "That's not a bad idea. *If* you can talk to them." She fixed her eyes on the horizon for a moment, thinking. "Excuse me. I'm going to lean." The balcony tilted. Jack wrapped his arms around a post and dug his heels into the lawn. Hattie grabbed the rails within reach as her legs dangled. With the balcony tilted almost vertical, they could see orex swarming the lawn, carrying boxes and weapons. Flying figures looped above the lawn. Orex in green forced others out of the longhouses. With their hands over their heads, workers filed into the trees under the eyes of the Alate.

"The Alate are here?" Hattie asked. "Now? Why?"

"You," Baba replied. "They want to kill En Law and Creon, but they want you especially. Thanks to their failure to kidnap you last night, they realize that Ran Corp knows they want you. They know that Ran Corp is going to move you elsewhere soon. They're here to rescue you."

Hattie never thought she'd be happy to see the Alate. "Can you let them in? Maybe they can help."

Baba straightened. They picked themselves up off the balcony. "I can control who can come to the balcony and who can enter the building, but thanks to Creon, it has to go through him first. The Alate know that thanks to their failed raid."

Jack said, "I can rip up the tags En Law keeps on his desk. I think there's lock and mute tags. I know Creon keeps the rest on his person."

"That changes things." Baba clacked her beak. "Hattie, go get your parents first. You can free them simply by opening their jars. Their selves will find their way home. At least according to what I overheard from Creon. You will have to find their physical containers on your own; I can't move around objects within my own body. Once the lock tag is gone, go tell the Alate what's going on." She squinted at the sun. "It is almost time for Creon to visit me. I'll bring the elevator, but you cannot be seen here. I can hear you talk and know where every living being in my body is. When the tags are gone, I can help you avoid En Law and Creon."

"Thanks a bunch, Baba," said Hattie as the elevator burst into existence.

"Wait," Baba said. Her eyes seemed to grow more golden. Jack stopped with his foot in the door. "Once you free your parents, get out of me. Don't come in until you know for sure En Law and Creon have been captured. If the Alate fail again, run to Earth, and never return to Tsava." Hattie started to protest, but Baba's eyes flashed. "Don't argue with me! You have no idea what Ran Corp has done to the orex within my walls. There are some who Ran Corp is stringing along, trying to squeeze the most work out of while keeping the things most precious to them. One of them is in your room. They were never going to give back Limn's Atlas of Stars."

"Then let's go pick him up," Hattie replied.

❧ 18 ❧

NO CHOICE

The ride back to the fourth floor was short and noisy because Jack and Hattie talked over each other in their excitement.

"So, Baba is on our side," said Jack.

"Why did you think she wasn't?"

"Because I thought she told Creon everything. She did say she was controlled by tags though, so she might still be under his thumb. He might have told her what to tell us."

"It's too late—what's that?"

A klaxon wail rose all around them. The elevator materialized on the fourth floor. Windows were slamming shut and locking on their own; small sirens popped from wall corners and howled, "Attack! Attack! Attack!" Through the window, on the ground far below, orex flashed through the grass in a deadly V formation.

"They're attacking." Jack's face was ashen. A low *boom* rolled through Baba. The walls shook and dust sprinkled from the ceiling. Distantly, they heard Baba curse. They sprinted back to Hattie's room while more explosions sounded and the building rocked.

Limn was yelling and bouncing off the walls of his jar like a fiery tennis ball. "Somebody get me out of here!" Another *boom* rattled and Limn shrieked as he toppled off the nightstand. Hattie caught him just in time.

"Thank Mota, you guys are back!"

"We're leaving." She grabbed the booklet of blanks and the pens and shoved them into Jack's hands. "You're coming." Hattie grabbed the jar and tucked it under her arm.

"Gently! Thanks! But where? If you leave Baba, you'll run into the Alate. If you stay, you get En Law."

"The closet," Jack replied, holding the door open. "Hattie's getting her parents. And you're getting your Atlas."

They ran through the hallway, stumbling as another *boom* shook the floor.

"Jack, I thought you're a paid employee!" Limn yelled over the noise.

"I am!"

"Then why are you helping?"

"Because I'm tired of doing the wrong thing," Jack replied. "If there is anything En Law took from you, tell me now, because we'll need to be quiet once we get to the closet." They crammed into the elevator, and Jack jammed his thumb on the button for the third floor. "And why do you have the Atlas? Aren't you a lantern spirit?"

Limn smirked. "I'm in disguise."

Jack stared at him for many seconds. Then, incredulously, he said, "You're a *star spirit?*"

"Argh, Limn!" Hattie tossed the jar from hand to hand as it sizzled in her palms. Limn ping-ponged inside, yelping.

"I'm sorry! I stopped!" The jar cooled and the elevator doors opened.

"Explain later," Jack whispered to Limn. The corridor was quiet, but Hattie held her breath anyway. "Stay in the elevator and hold the doors open. If he's there, let them go and get back to your room."

She flattened against the elevator wall and listened to Jack knock on the office door.

"En Law? Are you there?" The creak of the opening door. A pause. "Come on, guys."

En Law's normally tidy office was a mess of paper. Plans were tacked to the walls. Memos fluttered from the door like moths. Pens lay scattered across the floor, their cup on its side near the desk. A jar of something heaving, black, and liquid rattled on his desk as they came in. Jack opened a filing cabinet under En Law's desk and riffled through the folders. He dug through one and pulled out a pair of tags, which he ripped in half.

A speaker popped out of the wall. "You did it! Now hurry. The Alate are taping tags to my legs and I don't want to find out what they do. En Law and Creon are in the casino room. I think they'll be there for a while."

They picked around the mess to the closet door. Jack squatted, smeared his thumb with ink from the pen, and pressed it into a paper pad on the door. The thumbprint absorbed, and the door clicked.

"First, Hattie's parents," Jack whispered. "Then, Limn, your Atlas. I'm sure it's in the library section. We might as well steal a lantern for you because I'm going to be fired. I hope you both appreciate what I've done for you."

Limn grinned. Hattie said softly, "Thank you for everything." Jack, looking embarrassed, seemed to pretend he hadn't heard.

Walking as quietly as they could, they stole into the closet. A gaseous odor lingered. Hattie held up Limn and as they moved, his light fell into crevices and corners, holding back shadowy curtains and illuminating looming silhouettes, which, as they drew close, became sad and forgotten junk. Her antlers crackled and whined zenzen static, increasing, decreasing, jumping and falling like a weird symphonic voice.

Something shifted in the dark. As quick as thought, the electric whine rose in her head.

"Hide!" she gasped. "Something's coming!"

"What?" Jack hissed.

"I hear zenzen coming closer!"

There was a gap between the shelves and the wall. Hattie squeezed into it, antlers scraping the plaster. Jack followed her and together, arms kinking to fit in the space, they covered Limn's light with their hands. His jar crushed uncomfortably into her sternum. The whine amplified unbearably as the source moved into the light from the open door.

Its body was all head, all dusky purple skin stretched over a thin skull. Its rag-like fins paddled the air. The monster's mouth opened as if to sift the dust particles for scent, revealing translucent needles of teeth. It could have easily engulfed a car, yet it drifted in the air, maneuvering its bulk with tiny movements of its fins. As it floated soundlessly, the slender antennae that extended from its forehead dangled a single pearl light, which cast a skirt of illumination that puddled on the ground before it. It angled the pearl light over the door. The three stayed perfectly still.

It cast its spotlight along the ground and the shelves. After a time, it propelled itself eerily into the depths. The electric whine eased and faded.

They waited five minutes before tiptoeing out from the crack.

"Gunterphisch," Jack breathed. "That was a big one. And En Law's got two of them." He edged out from the shelf and helped Hattie. "Looks like the antlers are good for something other than decoration. Come on." He led the way to the same open area where Hattie had heard the voices. She walked quicker next to Jack before running ahead of them to a shopping cart full of jars and whispering souls. She knew at once this was her neighborhood.

She picked up a jar. It was light, the weight of the voice, and her shaking fingers slipped as she twisted the lid to open it. The voice trailed away, like an invisible person walking off. She twisted the other lids and dropped them to the ground as soon as they were opened so she could move to the next jar. The voices continued drifting away like a dispersing crowd. She wanted to scream at them, *get away! Hurry!* But she wasn't sure if they would hear her. In the last few jars, she heard her parents' voices. She dug for them, clinking jars, and heard a familiar voice within one at the very bottom: "Hattie, stop that. You're going to change the world. If you'd stop picking at your face, you'd look good doing it."

A different voice came from behind them. "What are you doing?"

Jack jumped and hissed, "Hattie!"

Hattie clutched the jar and slowly turned. Ann May stood a few meters away. She was wrapped in a shawl and was pale and out of breath. Her heartbeat was a hair off-kilter, as if veering from stress. "Those are my husband's. Are you destroying them?"

"Ma'am," Jack began.

But Hattie stopped him. "Hang on, Jack. Mrs. Ann May, do you know what this is?" She held out the jar.

"I do not, but I know they aren't yours," she replied frostily. "Put them back immediately. I will be informing my husband."

"This is my mom!" Hattie's shout shocked the dust from the floor. Ann May covered her mouth with her hand. "Your husband kidnapped my parents and neighbors and said I could work to get them back, but only my parents. He kidnapped *everyone*! How would you feel if I kidnapped you and En Law and made Ko my slave until I thought he worked enough to earn you back?"

Ann May's chin trembled. Her eyes were moist and hard.

"You're lying," she retorted. "En Law wouldn't do that."

Hattie dug through the cart and held up her dad's jar. "This is my dad," she said in an equally rough voice. "If I'm lying, then why am I destroying these tags?"

Jack spoke. "Check documents 131-M.E. for the records of traveling to Earth and the human selves brought back. We can wait."

What was he saying? They couldn't wait! Hattie opened the jars and took out her parents' selves.

Jack shook his head at her and addressed Ann May again. "You've been in the dark. Check all records from 100-150, 172, and 203 too. You should know what he's been up to. Meanwhile..." He held up a jar. "We're going to rip up all these tags. Hattie?"

Hattie ripped her parents' tags in two. Their selves wafted away, talking about the new house, the new job, and her.

"I wonder if we'll be all right here?" she heard her dad say as the selves evaporated.

An enormous pressure removed its hands from her shoulders. She opened the last of the jars and ripped the tags as Ann May shouted, "Enough! Stop, or I will call my husband!"

"Do it." Now that her parents were gone, nobody could threaten her. She ripped more tags to confetti and tossed them in the air. Ann May pulled a necklace from her neck. A red jewel on a gold chain swung, twinkling.

"One..." Ann May threatened. "Two...Three..." Hattie was reminded of her own mom's countdowns and bizarrely felt homesick. She ripped the last of the tags and listened to the voices laugh on their way to another planet. "Four..."

"You need your Atlas of Stars," Jack said to Limn. "Let's go."

"I will call him!" Ann May said furiously.

A rumble rattled the empty jars and a few things fell off the shelves. "Oh, and you should be careful. The Alate is attacking Baba. That's what's causing the shaking."

Ann May's heartbeat jittered. "Why is this happening?"

"Because your husband has been living up to his descriptive and everyone's sick of it," Jack replied, backing into the shelves. "Remember, records 100-150, 172, 203, and 131-M.E. All the proof you need. Guys, time to go."

Hattie jogged after him, listening to hear if Ann May would alert En Law or follow them. Hattie didn't hate Ann May, but she couldn't like her, either. Was she in the dark because she trusted her husband too much, or because she was too afraid of what she would find if she left?

"Keep your voices down," Jack whispered. "There might be lanterns in the armory or relics, but the gunterphisch are more likely to be there because it's between the valuables and the stuff En Law accesses often. What kind of body do you want, Limn?"

"Anything small and easy to carry around. Even a pearl light would be okay, except they're fragile. Anything used to carry really hot fire would be great."

"We'll keep an eye out."

Hattie's boldness disappeared. Hyper-sensitivity made her jump and flatten herself to the walls when a lure-light flickered in the distance, only a will-o'-the-wisp bobbing and vanishing. Each time she spotted the lights, her antlers' whining would amplify, and when the lights vanished, the whining died, too. Occasionally the whining would crest when no lights were visible. When it got so bad that Hattie thought her head would split, she furiously motioned Jack into the crevice of a bookcase. Just as they hid, an enormous gunterphisch, twice the size of one they'd seen before, drifted out of nowhere like a nocturnal blimp.

Jack led them through canyons of junk Hattie wouldn't have believed was valuable except for the insistent, constant chiming of the antlers. She pinched the back of Jack's shirt to keep them from getting separated. His super-black eyes glistened in Limn's light and swept over whole shelves as he navigated the labyrinth. Jack flung out his arm to stop her as he peered around a corner. He lifted a finger to his lips and pointed that same finger into the space he'd been inspecting. There was a gap in the shelves where a crowd of short, white pedestals displayed spiky, nasty-looking weapons that made her antlers toll like a gong. A gunterphisch hovered over the pedestals like a thundercloud. Hattie followed Jack's motion and saw a gleaming metal lantern near the wall. Her antlers rang like wedding bells.

"No!" whispered Limn. "I can settle for less! That big blimpy fish is guarding it!"

"It's the only one we've seen, and time is running out!" Jack whispered back. "We still haven't found the Atlas!"

The gunterphisch hissed like a gas leak. They froze, but it only yawned and snapped its jaws before floating back to the ground.

"I'll get it." Jack seemed to be trying to speak without moving his lips. He looked like he had lockjaw. "Don't move."

Hattie and Limn held their breath as Jack slipped away, skipping across the shelves out of the gunterphisch's sight. The monster lifted its ugly head and sniffed, alert. Hattie's lungs seared from holding her breath. She scanned the shelves, grabbed a harmless-looking jar, and hurled it far in the opposite direction of Jack and their hiding place. At the distant tinkle of breaking glass, the monster drifted toward the spot and disappeared. In the excitement, Hattie had taken her eyes off Jack. His soundless return caused her to jump, but he wore a grin and had the lantern in his hands.

They snuck away to another gap in the shelves and hunkered down. Jack pressed a latch on the top of the lantern with a tiny click, and the top opened like a tea kettle.

"Give him to me," he said. Hattie passed him Limn's jar.

"Be gentle," whined Limn as Jack tipped the jar into his open palm. Hattie winced when the coal rolled into his hand, but he seemed not to notice. The lantern was a metal box the size of Hattie's head and made of dull grey steel with rectangular panes of clear glass. Limn's light played over the metal. Under the once-dull surface were streaks of pine green, cloudy blues, and constellations of purple specks. Jack placed Limn in the lantern as if placing an egg into the bottom of a basket, and shut the lid. The light within flickered when Limn rolled around inside as if exploring a new room. Her antlers tingled. It felt like the spirit was doing much more than poking around in the physical part of his new body. It felt like he was *feeling* every atom and inch and scar in its making.

"Wow, this is the best body I've ever tried on." His voice

echoed like he was at the bottom of a well. "I'm not sure what will happen when I try it on, but...Hattie, did you know spirits can get rejected by a new body? It's really noisy and pretty bright, so if anything happens, run. I wouldn't be surprised. This is a pretty good body. Okay, here we go..."

The glass glowed scarlet. Hattie hugged the lantern, trying to shield the brightening light with her body.

The antlers clamored like a phone call. Jack gasped, gazing at something she couldn't see. The lantern rattled and grew uncomfortably hot in her hands, steaming like a tea kettle. "Hattie, let go of him!"

"Is he being rejected?"

"I don't know, but a gunterphisch is coming!"

The lantern shook violently as if firecrackers exploded within it. The antlers sang out.

"Jack—"

"No! We have to leave him, or we won't make it ourselves!"

"No!"

"Hattie!"

Her arms and hands seared, and she released it with a gasp. The lantern rose into the air, still shaking. Its chain snaked and clinked along after it before the top sprang open. Fire geysered high above the ground, washing the murkiness with red-gold brilliance. A pair of gunterphisch charged at the lantern with their jaws slung open and their teeth glinting.

"Limn!"

"Hattie!"

Jack sprung at the monsters with a small silver dagger. He leapt away before Hattie could register that he was gone. One monster twisted and howled as a slit in its side spewed fumes.

"We have to go!" Jack's typically neatly-parted hair radiated around his face; he looked demented.

"We can't leave Limn!" Hattie grabbed a jar off the shelf, slapped a tag—she didn't see which one—and flung it into the mouth of a gunterphisch. It spat the jar out in disgust, but she threw another one inside. She launched anything and everything she could put her hands on in desperation. An explosion rocked the floor and flung her back. Her eardrums popped from the blast. Heat seared her skin as she and the monsters and Jack screamed. The gunterphischs' baggy skin crinkled and blackened when they caught fire, thrashing and shrieking.

Arms hoisted her around the middle. She bounced against Jack's chest like a doll as he sprinted down a passage in the closet.

"Jack, stop!" He veered around a corner and set her down, gasping. There was a cut under his eye, and blood dribbled down his chin where it was scraped.

"Are you all right?" she asked.

"Peachy," he wheezed, rubbing off the blood. "And Limn's having fun. Listen." Maniacal laughter drowned the howls of the monsters. There was a flash of fire and thunder, and cinders skittered down the aisles. "He got a new body just fine."

Her head whirled, feeling light. She wobbled to her feet. What was it that they needed to do? "We need to get out. Where's the exit?"

"In the same direction as the gunterphisch."

"We'll have to kill them while they're looking at Limn," she said in despair. "Unless we can sneak out."

"Just walk out, guys." Limn floated over the shelves like a small sun, grinning in a punch-drunk sort of way. "This body is great! I got both of them in one shot! I could challenge my dad! Follow me!"

They jogged after him, relieved. The body of a gunterphisch smoldered in a ruin of pedestals and stinking smoke curled from it. They hurriedly checked every bookcase Jack knew of, aware that En Law could have heard the noise, that Ann May was somewhere in the dark, and that the Alate were pounding on the walls. Limn sobered as they scanned the bookcases. Minutes crawled by. Finally, they'd searched the last shelves.

"It's not here," Limn said disbelievingly. "They have it. I saw Creon pick it up. It's in my contract."

Jack had a smear of dirt across his nose. "It could be in another part of Baba. I know there's a library. Do you want to check there?"

An enormous *boom* rattled Baba. Items jumped off the shelves and smashed on the floor. Cabinet doors slung open; drawers slid out and were upended.

"I'll ask the Alate when we help them kick En Law and Creon out!"

They found the door to En Law's office a few minutes later and fell through it. Mercifully, the office was empty. They ran to the elevator.

Baba's speaker popped from the wall. "I've been trying to catch the Alate's attention, but they won't listen to me. Be careful when you go outside."

"What are En Law and Creon doing?"

"I don't know. They put blackout tags in the room."

Jack chewed his lips. "We'll need to know, or the Alate might be in danger."

"Ann May is heading there. And—" Suddenly Baba gasped, and the horror in it made Hattie's blood freeze. "Ko! I was so busy watching—" Her voice cut. They waited, breathless, but Baba was silent.

"Ko?" Limn said.

"Ann May is En Law's wife, and Ko is his son. Ko is six, I think." Jack pressed the button for the second floor. "He likes to escape from the closet and play hide-and-seek in Baba. I hope the Alate don't find him. I don't think they'd hurt a child, but if it's to catch En Law..."

Hattie, Jack, and Limn slipped onto the balcony and peeked over the edge. She barely recognized the casino. The slot machines, card tables, roulette wheels, and bars had vanished, as had the great red velvet carpet. A bare expanse of gleaming wood floor spread from wall to wall. Oil drums studded the floor, fringed with tags. Behind the oil drums was an enclosure of folding screens tall enough to reach the second-floor balcony and big enough to enclose several cars. Something on the other side of the screens paced like a caged bear; each footfall made the ground quiver. En Law and Creon stood before it talking in tense voices.

"They're already here," Jack hissed.

Hattie whispered, "Wait!"

Ann May hurried from a door with a folio of paper. En Law caught her hand.

"What are you doing? It's dangerous here. The Alate are on the first floor! And where's Ko?"

She thrust the folio into his chest. All of its contents slapped to the floor and slid out: pages of reports, charts, graphs, numbers, signatures. "What have you been doing? Kidnapping humans? Hattie's not an orphan. You lied to me!"

For a moment, he appeared speechless. He stiffened. "You will die without the treatment their selves paid for," he said in a harsh, yet pleading voice. "You and Ko."

"I don't want to live if this is the price!"

"Can you say that for Ko?" Ann May sobbed, but En Law continued more insistently, more gently. "After the treatment, he can have a life with all the opportunities we couldn't have. Yes, it isn't the best way, but it was the best chance to seize the best cure. We will *live* together, all three of us." He embraced her. Teeth gritting with anguish, taut with rage, every cell in Hattie's body focused on him. "Here. The treatment is ready. Where is Ko?"

Jack jerked his head toward the door. They crept toward it but stopped when a speaker mushroomed from the wall. Baba's voice rang out. "En Law, Ko is no longer in the building."

Ann May screamed like she was being rent in two and collapsed. Her hair flowed around her body like spilled ink. En Law caught and held her close, stricken. He carried her behind the folding screens in the center of the hall. A few feet away, near the entry, Creon spoke into a device. Hattie nudged Jack and pointed to him.

"I would like you to relay the position of all the Alate within you," Creon said into the radio.

"There are two on the second floor and five in the lobby," crackled Baba's voice. "And I think there are about fifty outside trying to tie explosives to my feet."

"Have the Alate moved yet?"

A pause. "One was on the third floor. Now he is on the fourth. I think he is flying or using the ladder or elevator."

"The human," he murmured to himself. "What if..." He slipped his ugly hand into his pocket and pulled out a tag, which he smoothed on the wall. The tag melted into the wall without leaving a trace. Baba shuddered, a seismic quiver Hattie felt in her bones. The speakers hissed with static.

"Ugh...a truth tag? Why?"

"I will remove it if you answer honestly." Limn flared but quelled the light at once. Hattie backed toward the door.

"I don't have any choice but to answer honestly!"

"Tell me what the Alate orex is doing on the fourth floor."

Jack hissed, "Go without us! We'll distract them!"

Another shudder ran through Baba. "He is...going into Jack's room." Hattie crept toward the exit. "Now Jane's...Now Hattie's."

Hattie's hand was on the handle. Her hair stood on end and her skin prickled. She was ready to spring out the door.

"And now he's leaving...he's going to another floor."

"What did he do when he discovered Jane and Hattie? Are they in their rooms?"

"Jane is not in her room." Another tremor. "And...neither is..."

Hattie slipped out the door and sprinted to the window. She hurtled through it a second before the window snapped closed. There was a distant roar. She scrambled down the ladder, dropped to the long grass, and bent double, using its height to hide her as she stole for the forest. Now she was well and done with En Law. It was a relief that her intentions were out in the open, but Jack and Limn were still inside. Limn might be all right, since they believed he was still recovering in a jar, but it would take a hop, skip, and a tiny step of logic to figure out Jack had helped her. He might be punished, even now...

Voices came from Baba's legs. She halted halfway to the forest. The Alate? They sounded as if they were coming closer. She could see heads bobbing above the grass. Any second now they would find her.

"She wasn't on any of the first five floors," said a scarfed orex as two approached her hiding place. "Perhaps she's already run away."

"Then what? Ven'll slime everyone if we don't find her today." The second orex spotted Hattie. His glass jaw dropped and shattered on a rock.

Hattie stood up and spoke before either of them could. "I need to speak with Ven, please. It's an emergency."

✣ 19 ✣

THE WANDERERS

The two orex stared at her with their shiny, bird-like eyes through slits in their scarf folds. One withdrew a tiny knife the length of her thumb and stepped toward her, not menacingly but gingerly, as if approaching a snake.

"Excuse me? Didn't you hear me?" Hattie snapped, irritated. She realized how much she sounded like her mom and how it flustered the orex. Would pretending to be her mom work twice?

"Uh..."

It worked before. She decided to go with it. "If you haven't noticed, En Law's about to wipe you out, and if you don't take me to Ven, you'll be known as *that guy*." The two looked at each other helplessly. "Where is he?"

"By Baba's legs," the first said, pointing. She marched between them back toward the legs. The pair whispered to each other as they scurried behind her.

Hot wind rose off the lawn and carried the odor of scorched gunpowder. Orex in pine-green scarfs wove beneath Baba, pasting and tying bundles of tags to her titanic legs in a rehearsed, purposeful way. Some hunched over incomplete scribbles and traced wet black lines over blanks. Still more kept watch. Ven directed the activity like a foreman at a construction site, yelling and striding and waving his hands.

"No, no, would you like for us to blow up as well? Put them *here* and *here*, and—oh!" He'd spotted Hattie picking her way through the grass.

"Hello, Ven," she said breezily, as if she'd never fought him on the rooftop. He looked flabbergasted. "I have a deal for you and the Alate."

"A *what?*"

"I know how to defeat En Law. And Baba's helping, so you'd better stop putting tags on her legs and take off the ones you've already put on," she added. His expression grew more pronounced as she continued. "En Law locked me in my room a few days ago and told me he was tired of me. He didn't intend to give me a fighting chance to get my parents back anyway, so now I'm here."

"I—I—what?"

"So, the deal. In exchange for helping the Alate take down En Law and his wanderer, I want everybody freed and everything in the closet returned to their owners. And I want to go home. That's all."

"That's all!" Ven pulled his hair. The orex finished taping tags and watched them uncertainly.

"We should hurry," Hattie said, glancing at the windows of the casino room. Velvet curtains had been drawn over them. "En Law's got a wanderer and a ton of stroilmen in formation to do...something."

"Ven, the tags on Baba are primed," said one of the orex.

Ven scowled. "I am aware!"

"You can't set them off! Baba's innocent!"

Ven pulled his hair again, casting his eyes to heaven. "Oh, Atom's—"

"Sir," said one of the guards severely. "Not in front of the kid."

A small, sticky hand closed around her thumb. Ko, chewing

his other hand, gazed at her. He took his hand out of his mouth to wave at her. "Hi."

Hattie sputtered for a moment. He'd been four floors above the ground trapped in a dark closet crawling with gunterphisch. Was Ko even tall enough to reach the elevator bell? "How did you get down here?"

The guard explained, "We found him climbing out a window."

"I wanted to go outside," Ko added. "Dad doesn't let me out, but it's time for my medicine and they won't let me back in. My chest hurts." Hattie knelt and listened to the zenzen beat. Its rhythm was more off-beat than the first time she'd heard it.

"Oh no," she gasped.

Ven's hand closed around her upper arm. She was well and truly caught. "What does 'oh no' mean?"

"Ko and En's wife have some kind of disease. They can't process zenzen or something. I can hear it getting worse. You need to put him near something that subdues zenzen." When he frowned, she added, "The antlers made me able to hear zenzen."

"En Law is *married?*"

"He's my dad," Ko said. Everyone's head snapped to him, astonished. He shrank and hid behind her.

Ven's face opened with realization. "The purchase of medicine, the transport of a lone wanderer to Baba. It wasn't that it was one wanderer, but that the wanderer was Zeya!" His expression became cunning. He knelt and gently pulled Ko to his side. Ko whined and Hattie warned, "Don't hurt him."

"Ko," said Ven sweetly. "Do you know what your father is doing in the big room?"

"No." Ko's owlish face scrunched and his voice cracked.

"Really? Are you playing a game with me?"

"No!"

"Ven," said Hattie harshly. "En Law didn't even tell Ann May he'd gone to Earth. Ko doesn't know anything."

Ven scowled and straightened. "Do *you* know what he's doing?"

"Sort of," she said, speaking quickly when she saw the orex who'd been attaching the tags to Baba's feet march back toward Ven.

"May I join this conversation?" A new voice, deep and bright like a brass bell, joined them. A second orex waded through the grass in their direction. The Alate thumped their fists to their chests and stepped back smartly. He wore the same pine-green scarf and brown poncho as the rest. His dark brown skin was speckled with cream-colored freckles and he had long-lashed yellow eyes, a beaky nose, and feathery brown hair escaping from his scarf. "Ven, Arni, Jos, Perceiver...and Ko, was it?"

"Yes sir," Ko squeaked.

"Ah, so polite," said the orex warmly. His eyes lifted to Hattie. It was like moving into a sunbeam. "And the Perceiver. I apologize for not greeting you earlier. I am Rostom, second in command of the Alate. I am in charge of this campaign. Ven?" he said calmly.

Ven bristled. "I was deciding whether to deal with her myself before telling you!"

"Ah," replied Rostom. "In the future, please let me know. As for Baba..."

"You heard?" said Ven swiftly.

"I did. I don't yet believe. Please fly to Baba's head and confirm this information."

"But—"

"Ven," said Rostom firmly. Ven bristled still further. Then, he crumpled impossibly small, his whole body becoming scarlet, and took off over Baba's roofs in the form of a cardinal.

Rostom lifted his eyes to the sky where Ven had gone. "What changed? We'd given up on you."

She told him how En Law had taken her parents' and neighbors' selves, and how she'd just released them to return to Earth.

"And you want to make sure he can't take them back,"

Rostom said. "Ah...we may be able to do this. For now, we will leave the tags on Baba's legs. Because it will take more time than we have to remove them," he added meaningfully as she protested. "They are harmless until two separate key tags are activated. If all goes well, we will remove them afterward."

The cardinal fluttered down and expanded into Ven. "She was telling the truth. Baba is under the influence of a truth tag with that doctor's signature. Baba has told me we have five minutes before En attacks. We move now." His melodramatic way of speaking was clipped, and his eyes shone with a strange, excited light. "Rostom, let me take over."

"As you wish," said Rostom at once. "And my role?"

"Stay as general and babysitter."

"I'm not a baby!" Ko informed him. With the severity of the situation, nobody chuckled. Rostom merely said, "You have my permission."

Ven spoke rapidly. "Arni, Jos, fly to Baba's head with zenzen removal tools and universal counter tags, the most powerful ones we have. If the truth tags are unremovable, bring back information about Baba's condition and what she has been forced to tell already. Hattie, is there a way we can observe the casino room without being spotted?"

"Y-yes. The servants' entrance has peepholes." His change threw her off guard. She led him to Baba's side as the other orex leaped into the sky. She pressed the combination of shingles and put her finger to her lips before she motioned him in. The hallway was as cool, shaded, and empty as ever. Pinpricks of light indicated the peepholes. They crept to them and saw a horrific scene.

Jack was sprawled on the floor, bleeding. His already-pale face was lead-white; his color was amplified by the shockingly-red blood dripping from his nose onto his rumpled shirt. At some point, he'd lengthened his body, but it hadn't done him any good because his hands and legs were tied together and pasted with smoking tags.

Limn had been captured as well. He snarled and his new chain strained taut between the nail staking it to the floor and his new body as he fought against it. A tag plastered his left eye shut and may have been what prevented him from spewing fire, because En Law stood a mere three feet away as if taunting him. Creon had disappeared. A horrible, deep droning, the same sound from the closet, penetrated the walls and exuded pressure like a storm.

Hattie's muscles were rigid. *Please groan or move*, she thought-pleaded to Jack. *Please be okay!* She flinched horribly when Ven grasped her arm. She realized she'd been gripping the fabric of her dress so hard it was ripping the hem with short jerky sounds. He took her, slipped out, and shut the door soundlessly. The orex who'd flown to Baba's head had returned, and their brows were furrowed.

"Baba's too injured to expel them," said one, an orex like a small winged cat. "We damaged her when we set off the first round of boom-tags, and Creon's truth tags are parasitic. They drain her energy to operate, not the activator's, and both have made her too weak. En Law, Creon, and Zeya must be dragged out like prey. Peel the tags from Baba's legs gently and go to her western side. Hattie, how much damage will Baba accrue before she is mortally wounded?"

"I don't know. I think the pipes are like her veins and stuff, and somebody told me that her internal organs are on the upper floors, where En Law isn't allowed." Her voice shook. She was running out of bravery.

Ven was unflappable. "Wait until my orex return." Hattie didn't like it, but she guessed he was waiting to tell them all together, instead of repeating his plan. Her mind tussled and writhed, overflowing with what-ifs and definitelys.

"Can you fight?" Ven asked her. She shook her head. "You did at the party."

"The fengul did that," she muttered, not looking at him.

"Look at me." Her antlers felt like they weighed a ton as she lifted her head. He was unsmiling. "You turned away our help three times. The soldiers know. They will wonder why you're helping us now. They will wonder if you're a spy for Ran Corp. As Perceiver, prove to us that you are with us now." He unsheathed a knife from his belt and put it in her hand. "For you. You will be part of the first wave." He might have said something else, but her ears filled with static as she stared at the knife. It had a black blade, curved slightly, with a hook in the back. When the knife was pulled back from being sunk into someone, that hook would bring flesh with it. Her stomach knotted. She'd already come so far, but this was too much.

Ven knelt in front of her and took her hands. "You seem like you were raised to be kind. Did your parents teach you that hitting is wrong?"

"Yes," she said quietly.

"And that's how children in ordinary times should be raised. But these are not ordinary times. Ran Corp will bring you and your family back to Tsava if you don't fight. They will use your parents, since they no longer need to pretend to bargain with you." His voice grew rough. "I know. They killed mine."

The knife seemed to burn her hand. Hattie was saved from speaking when the orex returned, loaded with handfuls of tags. Ven stood and said, "We will attach three tags to the east wall of the hallway spying on the room. When I say the word, you will activate the tags and we will storm the room. I will deal with En Law. My orex, you will destroy the stroilmen. Then, free your friends and run for the forest. We will call to you when the battle is over. Now, all, be silent and follow."

He led the way to the secret entrance. The Alate slipped one-by-one through the door until the hallway was filled with hushed shifting shapes, their eyes shining in the gloom.

"Set the tags on the wall."

Hattie flashed to the wall and pressed her eye to one of the holes. Jack swayed on his legs. His face was starting to swell and blood from his nose oozed over his chin. En Law's clothes didn't have a single loose thread; he sat with his hands folded in his lap, the picture of calm. His eyes were locked on the enormous pen of folding screens. Stifled, choked-off cries came from the pen. Hattie's skin crawled.

En Law spoke again. "Do you remember the first mission I assigned to Hattie and you? To retrieve my order from the Sage of the Fireflies? The concoction I ordered was a powerful medicine made for Ann May. Expensive. Didn't work. I was lucky to get my money back."

Limn was trying to pull out the stake by tugging in different directions. Jack seemed transfixed on En Law. "So, you're putting her out of her misery now?"

"No. Putting her out of misery, yes, but not by dying. By fusing and un-fusing her with Zeya, her disease should be suppressed permanently. And when Ko is strong enough, he will undergo the same treatment."

Limn strained at the stake. It slid two inches out of the ground before catching and stopping. En Law was too enthralled with the screen to notice.

"The tags are in place." An orex breathed in Ven's ear.

"Good. The moment this wall is destroyed, plant three boom tags on the opposite wall and activate them at once. Use the rest to fight the stroilmen and the wanderer. Stand away from the wall." Ven peeled Hattie away from the peepholes and sheltered her with the other orex behind the door. "*Now!*"

The plastered tags glowed white-hot before the wall exploded, and Baba was wracked by tremors. The Alate poured through the hole and through a cloud of dust. Ven flew out with Hattie close behind him, holding the knife close to her chest. En Law was soon enclosed by a circle of scarfed orex. Another explosion and gush of dust. Sunlight beamed through the hole, and more orex clambered over the debris a moment later. The ring of Alate tightened.

A yell and the shriek of steel along with a spark and a gust of wind preceded En Law's snarling face appearing inches from her own. Ven's shoulders brushed her antlers. The cardinal orex had leaped to block En Law's killing blow with his short sword. En Law leapt back and yanked a book of tags from his sleeve. The Alate surrounding him attacked with swords and books of their own, but he was too fast. A finger-snap later, he popped up next to the screen and the orex placing boom tags on it scrambled away.

Ven flung a tag at En Law. It winged through the air at his head, but he ducked. It slapped onto the screen, glowed white-hot, and exploded. En Law's scream of fury cut through the explosion. *"No!"* Another higher-pitched scream overshadowed his in an instant.

The blasted-away screens revealed a swollen, glutinous tower of oil. It rippled and pulsed like a monstrous glistening grub as tall as the ceiling. An avalanche of sludge collapsed from its side and splattered darkly on the ground. Bulbous heads swelled out of the splatters, and stroilmen breathed into the world briefly then melted back into the tower. A powerful chemical odor wafted from its tentacles, which grew and shrank like feelers prodding the air. Bile rose in Hattie's throat.

One of the Alate sprinted to Limn's chain with a staff and leveraged it to pry the stake out of the ground. Limn streaked through the air like a fiery comet, swelled, and blew red-gold flames at the sludge monster. He zoomed over the monster, jetting flames and dodging the tentacles that whipped and snapped at him.

What should she do? What *could* she do? She turned her bag upside down and everything spilled out. She tore out a fistful of blanks from the book and scrawled every doodle she knew on all of them and flung them at the pillar of jelly swaying in the middle of the ruined casino room.

En Law flung Ven away and slashed at him. Blood peppered the floor in an arc. The Alate danced around the burning stroil tower. They screamed as it lashed out and cracked the orex against the ground like a toddler would hurl toys to the floor.

One, two, three, four more were groaning and inching away on broken bones with more lying still amidst the rubble.

Smack! Her thigh stung as bandages sprung around her, whipped faster than the eye could see. In seconds she was mummified. She teetered for a moment on the spot before crashing, paralyzed, to the floor.

A horrific peace fell over the room. Bits of wall crumbled and trickled to the ground. All of the Alate orex were motionless save for Ven. His breathing was shallow, and his sword tip dragged along the floor as he tried to close the edges of a deep wound with blood radiating from it straight down his chest.

Limn had finally been swatted aside by a rogue tentacle and glowed weakly on the ground by the hole. Jack moved weakly, as if trying to stand; his mouth was bloody. She struggled to break free of the bandages. En Law wiped a smear of blood from under his eye with his sleeve. His breathing was only slightly more labored than normal. He watched the gruesome tower. The outer layer of stroilmen melted and sloughed off the monster with sick slopping noises. They exposed coal-red armor and a face so delicate and kind that Hattie couldn't believe it had survived in the pulsing muck.

"Ann May!" En Law called, smiling.

She was taller than two men stacked, and her body was long and lean, though armored and red with a spiky exoskeleton, mantis-like. Her face was nestled at the top of the neck of the armor. Her black hair curled tightly around her cheeks. Her eyes were closed, and the feathery shadows her eyelashes made against her cheeks were disquieting but pretty.

Her eyes opened like a doll's, without energy or deep emotion. En Law cried out, "Ann May! Look to me!"

The head turned as if oiled. "En?"

"Yes! Yes, dear, it's me! Are you cured? Do you feel any pain?"

Emotion flit across the creature's face before being wiped blank. "I am not Ann May." En Law's smile slipped. "I am Zeya-May, Wanderer of the Noh forest. I thank you for giving me the territory in which to take nourishment. I..." Emotion again. "I am...Zeya-May...I need...death...I need death! I need death! I need to die! Please, if you care about me, kill me! Kill me!" Ann May's face screamed. Chills prickled up Hattie's body.

Ann May screamed and screamed, her face stretching like elastic, her words garbled as if each one was fought for and flung out of her mouth. "He's in my head. He wants to kill everything. Please get him out or kill me so that he is gone from me. Just do something. Get it out! Get it out!"

Weakly, En Law tried to soothe her. "His voice will fade. You just have to apply strength of mind."

"Noooooooooo!"

Hattie redoubled her fight on the bandages. They loosened enough for her hand to grope for a nearby piece of glass. It bit her hand and she dropped it. With renewed determination, she caught it between her fingers and sawed at her bandages. Enough fibers sprang loose that she could rip them away.

"I don't want Zeya in my head! He wants to kill everything! I don't want to kill everything!"

Hattie tore at more of the bandages until, with a rip, she broke free and staggered to her feet.

A flash of mindless rage flitted over Ann May's face, then terror, and then sobbing, helpless frustration. "Get out of my head! I don't want you! Get out! Get out!" She clawed at her face, but her claws couldn't cut her skin. Tears streaked over her cheeks and her hair plastered against her skin. Hattie backed to the wall and gaped. What was she supposed to do?

The loudspeaker clicked. "Attention please." Baba's voice. By pure habit, bizarrely, everyone stopped to listen. "Hattie, please direct Ann May to the blackwater pool west of here. Kometa can annihilate Zeya. Thank you."

"NO!" En Law sprinted and slashed at Jack so hard that Hattie could feel the wind from the sword cut her hair. His hair was slick across his furious, agonized face. Sparks scattered on the floor as Ven, Jack, and En Law's swords and daggers crossed and rang.

"Why—ah!" Ann May's face tightened, struggling. "Zeya doesn't—I don't understand!"

Hattie screamed with her breaking voice, "Hey, Ann May!" She understood. She was the only one who knew where the pool was. "Let's go!" Ann May looked at Hattie and her frightened face showed nothing of the monster inside her. "It will be okay! I promise!"

With immense control, Ann May gathered Hattie in her claws and lifted her against her armored chest. Hattie winced and her heart skipped a beat as Ann May's claws tightened. "Ah! Sorry. Hurry, tell me..." From inside Baba, En Law's voice cried out, "NO!" His scream was full of fury and pain. Ann May ducked through the hole in Baba's wall. On the lawn, the Alate gaped at her.

Hattie bellowed at them. "Move!" She shouted up at Ann May, "Go to that path, right there! You'll see it!"

The Alate scattered when Ann May began to run. Being carried by a wanderer was like being carried by an avalanche or a landslide. Her girth broke the gripping roots, she shouldered aside trees, leaves swirled in her wake, and the forest fell under her stride's thunder. With each movement, her face twisted with the strain.

They came upon the blackwater pond too quickly and they both fell with a crash. The cold shock of the water drilled through the fog of pain. Hattie opened her eyes and her vision blurred. The motaspace enveloped her in its ancient, frigid cold. The starless void was all around her. The surface had disappeared. Ann May sunk beside her like a falling submarine, trailing streams of bubbles. Beside her was a little goldfish who kissed her curiously and swam around her. It wriggled to her nose and felt it with quick velvet lips.

The fish darted away and joined others who had started circling her. Copper droplets rained out of the dark as more of

Kometa wiggled closer to swim around the wanderer's limbs. Hattie knew Ann May was behind them, buried deep in the folds of its brain.

Zeya spoke in a voice sharper than the edge of the moon. "I will kill you for doing this to me and I will kill the woman inside of me. I will kill the orex who captured me and wrenched me apart from my soul, and I will kill the Fengul Queen who named you. The war will seem like a playfight compared to the death I will give all orex."

The goldfish liquefied into red-gold droplets and fused together, becoming burnished copper scales, brilliant eyes, flowing sails of fins, and a sleek, muscular body. Kometa streaked forward and collided like a missile with Zeya. The impact sent them spinning round and round, wrestling for control. Blood plumed and Zeya thrashed and screamed as Kometa sank needle teeth into its neck, twisting and tearing.

The giant slashed through Kometa, who split into two fish and lunged again. One fish ripped off the arm that lashed out, and the other tore away a leg. The limbs whorled slowly into the dark.

Zeya snarled, "Why are you helping her? Why recognize her? Kill her! She's—"

Kometa merged into one fish again and flashed forward, gripping Zeya's neck. Zeya recoiled and its roar choked off in a gargle. Like a banner, Kometa snapped its body and a chunk of flesh was torn away. The fish circled Hattie protectively with one eye on the monster who flexed like a skewered bug. But it was over. Zeya looked pitiful and grotesque, a dismembered insect. Its eyes burned on Hattie, but the intensity weakened as its breathing labored.

It spewed at Kometa, "You traitor. You foul thing! And *you*..." This violent aside was to Hattie. Its voice quieted and drifted. "...You'll wish to un-exist for the rest of your life. I'll die happy knowing this."

Zeya's body seized again. When it finally unloosed, the body dissolved like a seltzer tablet away from a small core where a figure was curled up. Mantis legs twitched where hers used to be, and deep wounds glistened. Hattie swam to her. Kometa circled them.

Zeya still lives in her, said a voice which came from inside Hattie, yet wasn't hers. Hattie looked for the source and found only Kometa. *It's good that you can finally hear us,* Kometa burbled. *But at such a sorrowful time.*

Little tremors ran through Hattie. Ann May's eyes opened, vague.

"You okay?" Hattie asked hoarsely. Ann May's lips moved, but nothing came out.

Kometa said, *Do you still have the bullet Sonorra gave you?* Hattie pulled out the pouch around her neck. *Feed it to her. Or else Zeya will return.*

Hattie asked, "What about her?"

She dies.

"No," Hattie said. Ann May's face blurred with tears. "Do you know if the Perceiver has any other powers? Maybe I can save her. Maybe..."

I don't know.

"I can't kill her! Even if Zeya comes back—"

When Zeya comes back, he will consume her body and spirit as well.

"I can't kill her." The scab that had formed when she had to save her parents tore open. "I just wanted my mom and dad back! I didn't want anyone else to die or be hurt."

"Hattie." Ann May spoke. She focused with great effort on Hattie's face. "Did you come all the way from Earth to save them?"

"Yes."

Ann May touched Hattie's cheek with her one remaining hand. Her other arm had been torn off, and from the ragged red edge, blood signed its name into the dark. Her hand was unbearably gentle.

"I'm sorry," Hattie said. She wanted her mom and dad to

hold her and tell her it would be okay, to tell her she was not the one burdened with saving them. Ann May's thumb stroked her cheek, passing over her bruises and cuts. Hattie crumbled, trying to stifle tears.

"Shh." Ann May continued stroking her cheek. "You're leaking." She passed her thumb over her tears and wiped them away.

"Do orex not cry?" Hattie croaked.

"Monmouths like my husband and I can, but I have never seen him do it. I wish..." Her calm broke. "If he'd been more willing to, he wouldn't have taken your parents. He did everything for me and Ko. I didn't think I would live long enough to see Ko walk." A tremor passed over her face. "I think it's time for me to go."

"But..."

"You are so strong to have done what you did," Ann May said hoarsely, but smiling. "I would be proud if you were my daughter. You should not have to be responsible for this. Give me the bullet."

Hattie unlooped the bag from her neck. "It will burn you."

Kometa replied, *It only burns wanderers.*

Her insides knotted. Ann May took the bag and tipped the bullet into her hand.

"Hattie, what is your descriptive? Not Perceiver?"

"Humans don't have descriptives," she said. "We have middle and family names. My full name is Hattie Anne Flores."

"We share a name." Ann May's greying face brightened, wavered, and faded. The lump in Hattie's throat grew. "My description is the Ephemeral. My parents didn't expect me to live long, but En gave me a good life and a wonderful child." She rolled the bullet between her fingers. After a time, she said, "It will be okay."

Her tears floated off her cheeks. Ann May put the bullet in her mouth and swallowed. Her eyes flashed and her face clenched. The moment passed, and she relaxed.

"You should go back to the surface," Ann May whispered.

Hattie shook her head. "Go. It's not your fault." Hattie shook her head again. She knew that if she went, she would regret it, though she was as afraid as the first time she'd ever dropped through the motaspace.

"I'll stay with you."

Ann May started to speak but her heart gave a sick *thud*. Her face clenched, full of pain and fear. Hattie's voice shook as she repeated back, "It will be okay."

Hattie held her hand and passed her thumb over its back, over and over, as Ann May lost consciousness. Her irregular heartbeat slowed. The pauses between beats stretched until the next was a miracle. Hattie strained for sound, knowing that she shouldn't, knowing what she would eventually hear, yet unable to imagine what it would sound like.

Her whole being tuned in as she listened. The quiet had its own voice. Her mind spoke against her disbelief, quieting it, too, until she was as empty as the space around her. Kometa drifted near. After some time, they said, *Hattie*.

She drew Ann May close and let Kometa take them to the surface.

☙ 20 ❧

SHADOWS OF THE CLOUDS

When they crested the surface of the water, a small riot broke out.

"Ann May!" En Law's face blanched, and he attempted to struggle out of his chains. A half-dozen Alate held knives to his throat, which he ignored.

Her limp body was hauled out of the water by two Alate, one of whom called, "We need a medic!" Ven waded into the water to drag out Hattie. He was so pale that the veins in his face were like roots.

Everything seemed slippery, blurred, and colorful, as if she were in a dream.

The orex around Ann May rapidly pasted tags to the ragged stump of her arm and sprinkled a grass-green powder into her mouth. A new orex Hattie hadn't seen before marched to Ven. "Rostom requests that you move everyone to Baba."

Ven roused. "Of course." His voice sharpened and carried over the commotion. "All! To Baba!" The group began to march.

An orex called, "We'll join you when her condition stabilizes."

"No!" En Law dug his heels into the ground. The four Alate orex holding his chains pulled, but neither side budged. Finally, a large orex enveloped him in four muscular wings, picked him up, and moved him. The orex winced as En Law kicked her repeatedly in the gut. The dull impact carried through the forest as they moved away.

"Oh, En Law! We still have your son!" Ven called. After knowing Hattie would be all right, he seemed to have gained extra confidence. En Law kept kicking. The orex carrying him was buckling. "Shall I kick him for every time you kick her?"

"Don't," Hattie croaked.

"You're compassionate," Ven's voice said piteously, then added in a whisper, "En Law can't know that." En Law stopped kicking. His eyes were rimmed in white.

They reached Baba's clearing. In the quickening dusk and the brisk wind, the Alate waded through a golden, dry surf. The Alate had posted soldiers around the meadow, who kept watch with stern faces and long knives. Ven lowered Hattie onto one of the ribboned boulders and put his hand on her back to steady her and keep her from aggravating her injuries. Rostom held Ko in his arms. Tear tracks ran down Ko's round cheeks, but he was asleep with one cheek plumped against Rostom's burly shoulder.

Rostom hailed Ven. "Success here. And you?"

"Success. Zeya is no more." Ven raised his arms and his voice. "The Perceiver has defeated Zeya!" The Alate cheered.

"And injuries?"

"Ann May is faring poorly. The medics stayed behind to stabilize her. When able, she will be moved."

"Hattie?"

Hattie shook her head. Something vital had been poured from her and wasted. Their expressions lost some of the glow of victory.

Rostom said in a low voice, "Tell us. What happened in the pool?"

Ko began to cry, his face flushed, shining with tears and snot. Rostom motioned over a soldier and murmured, "Put him down for a nap. I'll retrieve him personally." They exchanged Ko, and the soldier took him away to a group of other soldiers. His crying faded.

"Will you say now?"

"No."

"Perceiver," said Ven warningly.

"Zeya is dead. That's all you need to know." Something in her voice must have warned away questions.

Rostom and Ven exchanged looks. At last, Rostom said gravely, "It isn't necessary to know now. We should start. Hattie, you must return home as well." Ven stared at Rostom with bewilderment. "Jack told me about your parents' and neighbors' selves, and their release. They are waiting for you on Earth. Samara would like to speak with you before you go. You will return, at the latest, tomorrow evening. Agreed?" Hattie nodded. Rostom spoke to the orex holding En Law. "Neh, set him down."

The many-winged orex dropped En Law with a sigh. Then there was a *snap*, and she shrieked. En Law had broken her wing with a twist of his hands. Chains slung over him. He staggered, wild-eyed and snarling.

"Another crime," said Ven severely. Neh moaned, rocking, holding her wing. "Your death will be a pleasure to many."

The Alate forced En Law to his knees. They put their hands, tentacles, and wings on his shoulders and leaned down. It took four of them, again, to be successful. Hattie had often fantasized about kicking him in the face before taking her parents and running away with their selves. At the time, she had imagined their selves to be like pale ghosts, wavering in her hands as she ran. She hated him, yet she couldn't stand to see him this way. She could hurt him, but didn't want to. She knew righting his wrongs must hurt, or nothing would be solved. Not far away, coming out of the forest, the medic orex bore someone wrapped in a cloth from head to heel. The emptiness she felt pulled her inward as if she was caving in.

"Rostom?" said Hattie. Her own voice sounded unfamiliar, as if something had been added to it. Ven stopped pontificating and Rostom made a polite gesture. "I want to decide En Law's punishment instead. As Perceiver."

The medics waded through the grass, closer and closer. She could hear no zenzen from them.

Rostom caught Ven's eye. Ven nodded. "Yes. I think Samara would understand." He raised his voice. "Hattie the Perceiver will decide En Law the Merciless' punishment."

Every orex turned their alien faces to her. Each was touched by the smoldering sunset, each face painted gold. En Law turned his attention to her, too, with blazing eyes. The shadows of the clouds passed over Tsava as it descended into twilight, and the grass bowed to their weight.

"En Law," Hattie called. Her voice quavered and strengthened as she fought to do the right thing. "You have to answer for what you've done to me, my parents, and my neighborhood."

"So, will you put me to work?" He sneered.

"Yes. For the Alate," she added. Rostom made a noise like a stifled snort. Ven began shaking his head. "The Alate will decide how much debt you have and how you work it off, with extra so they can take care of Ko."

"And that's all?" En Law asked after a pause.

The medics stood at the foot at the rock. She merely pointed to the shrouded orex in their arms. En Law's gaze dropped to them. His expression transfigured into one of dread as he stared. His rigidly controlled expression shattered, and beneath it swelled grief.

Hattie covered her ears, turned away, and cried as En Law screamed.

✤ 21 ✤

UNCANNY

ostom insisted she stay overnight in Baba so they could treat her injuries. Ven took her personally to the Room of Succor. Hattie lay in the Room in her curtained-off bed, meters away from groaning and crying Alate whose injuries were a hundred times worse than hers. Some had lost limbs and lay in a drugged haze on blood-wet sheets. Others groaned and curled in pain. Ven put her in a bed and rested on the bed stand, wincing with his hand over his chest.

"I may be injured, but it's my duty to make sure you're safe," he said, catching her looking.

"Why? And how do you know who I am?"

"That's a secret," he said with a small smile. "Perhaps, I will tell you later when we aren't surrounded by soldiers."

Such a stupid reason for secrets. Everything now seemed pointless. Even going home. After everything that happened, she wasn't sure if any of it was real. Would the Alate let her go home? Maybe she could sneak out to the pool and get away before they noticed she was gone. She was too exhausted to sleep.

A speaker popped out of the wall near her and whispered, "Hattie, if you're awake, come to the balcony."

Hattie rolled out of bed wrapped in her blanket and padded out to the lobby. Another speaker popped out. "Elevator. I removed the locks."

The elevator no longer came with a bang, but with an arthritic sneeze and a fart of steam. It also shuddered while stopping and starting in fits. Its gold leaf and paneling had been badly scraped.

The balcony's flowers and grasses rippled in the night wind. Hattie could see the lights of New Sprout twinkling. Baba's golden eyes gave off a glow, like twin moons watching over her.

"I thought you might need a reason to get away from the hospital," Baba said. "If the Alate need to find you, I'll let them know where you are."

"Thank you."

"Do you want to talk about what happened?"

"No."

"That's fine." The hen-house blinked thoughtfully. "Until En Law, I was empty for twenty-five years. I hated him for being with Ran Corp. They destroyed my flock, but he was so desperate."

Hattie shook her head. "No excuse."

"No." She paused. "Because I agreed to help him and Ran Corp to find any of my flock, I housed their evil and took part in something unjust. I'm sorry, Hattie."

To say, *It's okay*, would be wrong. To say, *Don't worry about it*, was too flippant.

She merely said, "Thank you," and felt a little freer.

Baba reached out with her beak and carefully guided Hattie to her feathers, tucking her into their massed warmth like she was a chick.

Hattie said, "I thought I would do anything to save my parents until I found out what *anything* meant. Now I'm not so sure."

"That's right." Baba's voice hummed in her bones. "That's exactly right."

Hattie fell asleep in Baba's feathers. How quiet the world was. How muffled and so far away.

* * *

She woke the next morning to Baba's voice humming through her.

"Hattie, it's time to wake up."

Hattie blinked awake. She'd fallen asleep with her arm as her pillow, and it ached with pins and needles. Why did she feel so bad? Then she remembered. She always realized the next day.

"Samara wants to meet with you," Baba said.

"Samara?"

"Samara, leader of the Alate."

Hattie sat up. "Can I go to the bathroom first?"

The elevator wheezed into existence. Hattie wrapped the blanket around herself and took the elevator to the second floor. Orex crowded the hallway. They slung sacks over their shoulders, hoisted boxes of personal things, and wheeled suitcases into the elevator as she stepped out. The activity dismayed her. For a moment, she felt sick with the horror that she had come to work in a blanket. Orex called out to her, "Hey Perceiver!"

"Perceiver!"

"Hattie!" Chiros wended through the mess. "Are you going home too?"

"Yeah, but later. Is everyone moving out?"

"No more casino. No more jobs." Chiros sighed. She had a daisy-yellow backpack. "The Alate made an announcement in New Sprout. Back home to Mare."

Hattie's throat tightened. She stepped forward and hugged Chiros, who froze. "Goodbye," Hattie said, close to tears again.

Chiros patted her head. "Goodbye, Hattie the Perceiver." She pulled away, found an open window, and leaped out. Her wings snapped open like an umbrella, and she sailed away over the grounds.

Hattie showered, pulled on a clean dress, and returned to top floor. Ven, Rostom, and a third orex sat on the balcony. Samara looked like a life-sized burlap doll. Yet, there were no holes for eyes, mouth, ears, or nose. Swords and knives stuck out of her.

"Hey, Perceiver," she said in a rough voice. The fabric where her mouth should have been beat with each word. When she stood, Hattie noted she was taller than Ven and gangly like a scarecrow. "How are you feeling?"

"I'm okay. Mostly."

Samara gestured at the grass for Hattie to sit, and they both settled. "My name is Samara, no descriptive, and I'm president of the Alate. Ven has been trying to recruit you on our behalf. Do you know what the Alate is?"

"Sort of. You're a resistance movement against Ran Corp."

"More or less. We resist the Monarchy too, and others like them. The totalitarian type. Ven extracted a promise from you to join the Alate in exchange for helping you escape En Law safely. He shouldn't have done that." Ven did a doubletake. "We don't force orex to help if they don't want to. We don't ask for anything in exchange for our services, which you knew, Ven."

Ven folded his arms. "The Perceiver is meant to save Tsava, and we save Tsava. It wasn't coercion. Just hastening her membership."

"Ven," said Rostom in exasperation.

"Hattie. Perceiver." Ven said to her, "If I hadn't sealed your promise to join the Alate, what would have happened? Do you think the Alate would have believed you weren't still working for Ran Corp? I had you promise in front of other orex because if I hadn't, nobody would have trusted you."

"Is that so?" Samara asked sarcastically.

"And not everyone knows you are human, or your story. This way, you won't be challenged."

Samara said to Hattie, "We have the same mission. To save Tsava."

Do we? Hattie could not help thinking. Her thoughts must have shown in her expression because Samara continued, "'Orex kidnapped my parents and now I have to save their world?' Is that what you think?"

"Yeah," she admitted.

Samara motioned to Rostom, who slapped a newspaper in front of Hattie. The headline blazed. *HUMAN DISCOVERED WORKING FOR RAN CORP, NAMED BY FENGUL QUEEN.*

Samara asked her, "Have you read this?"

"I didn't know about it." She picked it up. The date was the day after the gala. The article itself was a recap of the night.

"Read the very last paragraph," Rostom said.

There are many unanswered questions left behind. How did a human come to be employed by Ran Corp? How did the Fengul Queen know? Why did she personally name her Perceiver? Why not an orex? Why a human? What does the Perceiver mean to Tsava?

Rostom put another newspaper in front of her.

ALATE CAPTURE RED HEN CASINO AND LIBERATE THE PERCEIVER.

"We told the journalists about what Ran Corp had done to your neighborhood. Jack and Limn backed us up as key witnesses." He flipped to the article and read aloud, "'In light of this new information, we must ask why the Fengul Queen described someone who has no stake in Tsava, and who may also hold a grudge for what happened to her.'"

Hattie shook her head. "I don't hate Tsava. Ran Corp, definitely, but not Tsava or all orex."

"I'm glad to hear that." Samara paused. "What are your plans?"

"Why are you asking?"

"Because we'd still like you to join the Alate."

There it was. "Why?"

"You're smart, resourceful, decisive, tenacious. You're a symbol of triumph over Ran Corp. Why *not* join?"

She didn't want to. She'd rather go home and forget about it. Yet, she knew she wouldn't be able to. She would always wonder what it was she was supposed to do, and she had a feeling that Ran Corp could return to Earth at any time to try again. There were questions unanswered, ends unsolved.

"Can I think about it?" she asked. "I don't even know if my parents are okay."

"Yes. Of course." Samara didn't have any facial expressions and Hattie couldn't tell if she was sincere. Samara reminded her of something, but she couldn't put her finger on it.

"What is going to happen to En Law and Ko?" she asked.

"We'll do what you said. We're offering to pay for his son's treatments in exchange for information. As long as he's helpful, we'll pay. Same deal Ran Corp gave him."

It hadn't occurred to Hattie that En Law had made an impossible deal of his own and it made what he'd done to her seem even worse. Knowing what it was like to be backed into a corner, why would he corner someone else?

Again, Samara read her mind. "As leader of the Alate, I often have to weigh the lives I'm responsible for against the lives of others. Ven and Rostom have been ordered to take Creon's head at all costs. He is that dangerous to us. Lives are only important to Creon if they are important to his research or goals. There were two other lives important to En Law. Just like there were to you. If we can offer something to you that helps those you love, we can work with you."

Hattie rushed to reply. "My contract was only for my parents, but I wanted to save everyone. It was really, really lucky that I could."

"Exactly. Why save twenty-four strangers when you have two you know and love?"

"But I didn't kidnap people to save my parents!"

"Imagine if you never got the antlers, the Alate never touched Baba, and En Law and Creon were still in charge. If you were still working for Ran Corp and they ordered you to do what En Law did, but to some other neighborhood, would you?"

"I...don't know. I think I would try to sabotage it somehow. Or call you."

"Why would you wait to call us when someone else's neighborhood was kidnapped? Why not your own neighborhood?" She hesitated. Again, Samara spoke her thoughts. "You thought you could wait it out. As long as you kept your head down and worked, they'd let you have your parents back at the end of five years. Everyone who has ever had something taken from them by Ran Corp thinks that. The Alate is full of ex-Ran Corp employees who thought that. All of them believed they could keep their dignity if they just worked. The Alate's too violent. Who likes hurting people? They don't see us attacking Ran Corp. They see us attacking other Ran Corp employees with contracts like theirs, contracts that include a time limit and someone they love.

"But they never wonder whether us attacking them is really the worst thing that could happen to them. And by the way, we never target employees. Only certain orex who we know, after incredible deliberation, must be stopped. But we're not shy about roughing up regular employees. They quietly, diligently, cleaned the ship they took to Earth, prepared the tags and the jars to put human selves in, set up the equipment to separate self from body, packed it away, escorted you to the office where you signed away five years of your life, balanced the account books of how long you've worked and how long you have left. If all they do is commiserate with other employees who also have contracts like yours, they're missing the point. They never ask themselves if they played a part in kidnapping your neighborhood. They never ask themselves what's worse: enabling Ran Corp's crimes in the name of the few people they love, or spilling the blood of the wrong orex for the sake of stopping Ran Corp permanently. And it's hard to not choose the former, even when you know it's wrong, because Ran Corp has you and your loved ones by the throat. Of course, you'll bleed for those you love. You know that, and so does Ran Corp. Ran Corp will take everything you have. Weren't you the least bit glad when you heard about us? 'The Alate is fighting against Ran Corp!' you thought. 'I hope they win, and I can get my parents back!'" Samara waited as Hattie squirmed. "No? You don't hope somebody can do what you can't?"

"I was mad because you were going to make it hard for me to get them back," she admitted. "Because I thought En Law would blame me and fire me."

"But you didn't think we would help you steal them back and help you get home?"

"Not really...Ven freaked me out."

Rostom covered his smile with his hand.

Ven shot up, bristling. "I admit, I can be headstrong, intense, and demanding, but remember that Ran Corp killed my parents, and I don't have the time to wait for them to kill others. So, excuse me!" His chin wobbled. He bolted for the balcony fence and leaped off it. Hattie screamed just before a cardinal zoomed over their heads, flying for New Sprout.

"Ven was the youngest member who ever joined," said Rostom. "Twelve."

Hattie felt like the blood had left her face. "How did they..." She wanted to ask how close she was to being just like him.

"Perhaps, if you join, one day he'll trust you enough to tell you."

Hattie hesitated. She didn't know if she wanted to join. Her parents were at home, probably wondering where she was. And how would she persuade them to let her return? Why not let this pass from her memory like a bad dream?

Samara, once again, read her mind. "If you still think that

Ran Corp is worth forgetting, I will show you the list of humans they took from Earth. I'll point out that they didn't label the list with names. Just numbers. Did they tell you your parents' numbers?" Hattie trembled. Samara went on ruthlessly. "Did you read your full contract? I did. At the end of five years, you were going to get jar number one and jar number two, no matter who was in them."

She felt too fragile to hold the electricity and violence whirling inside her. Samara pulled a needle out of her body; it was as long and slender as a walking stick. "We have," she said as she pulled another needle out. "Been trying to kill Creon for a long time. Couldn't at the anniversary gala. Bastard ran and hid. Couldn't today. He slipped out using a portal hidden in the closet. But I always wondered...Do you know why En Law hired you instead of just capturing you?"

Hattie remembered. "I asked on Earth if I could work to get my parents back. En Law said that they didn't have room on the ship to take me, and that if I wanted them, I'd have to prove I'm worth something to be hired."

"Why would En Law the Merciless give you that chance?" asked Rostom.

"I don't know."

Baba spoke. "Hattie, do you know how orex are named?" Hattie shook her head. "I was given the name Baba when I hatched, as an everyday name. But my descriptive, Hospitable, was given to me when I came of age. Descriptives are wishes parents give to their children—a wish for who they hope they will become. Life is long, and orex are strange. Sometimes descriptions become misnomers. Though En Law was usually merciless, he strikes me as someone who doesn't know what mercy looks like and had never been given any himself. But he loves his wife and son." The golden eyes seemed to melt away their brittle rage and leave her limp with sadness. It was as if she knew Hattie was thinking of what she had said last night.

Rostom, who had been sitting quietly, said unexpectedly, "In that light, what does it mean that the Fengul Queen named you Perceiver? You were named a wanderer, Baba. How did it happen?"

Baba clacked her beak. She didn't speak for several seconds. "After my flock was destroyed, a fengul found me and told me I would make a good wanderer."

Rostom persisted. "But why?"

"The fengul told me, 'Tsava needs orex like you. Become more than you are.' And it described me."

They all chewed on her words. Samara spoke gravely, "I've always thought wanderers were selected to serve Tsava in some way."

Hattie asked, "Selected?"

"All wanderers were once regular orex," Baba replied. "Fengul pick them, give them a new description, and give them power. Orex think there's a bigger plan behind their selection, but as a wanderer, I don't think so. The fengul gave me a new description, She Who is Home, and gave me special control over my body. Molluska don't usually grow more than four stories tall, but I'm ten stories tall, and I know everything that happens inside me. That's not usual for Molluska. Other than that, I haven't done anything but *wander*. And house Ran Corp's stupid casino," she added acidly. "Fengul don't do anything but mess around."

"Suppose they aren't messing around," Rostom went on. "What does it mean that the most powerful fengul described Hattie? If wanderers are meant to serve Tsava, maybe you have a larger role to play, Hattie."

The computer spirit. She asked, "Do any of you know a computer spirit named Frank?"

Her question was met with blank stares, and possibly some other emotion from Samara that she couldn't identify. She told them about meeting him in the convenience store, meeting him again later, though she glossed over the portal tag to the mota-space, and what he'd said to her both times.

"He said he didn't think I was like, a Chosen One or anything, but someone who was right for the job."

"The job being something incredible," Samara noted.

Hattie said after a pause, "No. I'm going home."

Samara did not reply immediately but considered the grass on the balcony. After a time, she said, "Well, nobody would blame you. I don't think wanderers are ever charged to destroy specific entities, or protect areas, or save orex. They wander. Where they wander and what they do when they wander is loosely defined by their description. If the Fengul Queen tied you to Tsava and zenzen, like all wanderers are, you'll have to think hard about what your description means, because I doubt you'll stay home for long." She lifted her head and looked squarely at her. An irresistible force caught Hattie's attention; she could not look away from the tiny holes in the burlap over her face.

"Whatever it is the Fengul Queen wanted me to do, I can't do it," she blurted. Rostom looked somber, but Baba nodded her support. "It's not my job to deal with them. That's for orex. I don't even know what Ran Corp *is*. What are they doing everything for? They're a company that has a casino, but they kidnapped humans, and now I've been tied to Tsava and zenzen to take them out? But what are they?"

Flinty-eyed, Baba answered, "About fifty years ago there was a war against the wanderers. Ran Corp rose to the top as a weapons manufacturer. When the war was over, they were large enough to buy out other companies and expand. They own nearly every large business in Tsava. The casino is really just a place to meet powerful orex, get money, and hide other activities from authorities. They want money and power."

"I have a question," said Rostom unexpectedly. "What is Ran Corp doing collecting human selves? Did you overhear them, Baba?"

"I don't know. I know selves are used in powerful scribbles, but human selves are so rare and powerful in Tsava that I can't imagine what kind of zenzen would come of such a scribble. Creon was careful not to speak of them inside me. I doubt En Law knew why Creon ordered him to find them."

All Hattie wanted to do was go home, but the more she discovered, the more it looked like she would have to stay. The antlers weighed down her head.

"Thanks for listening to me," Hattie said after a while. "I'd better get ready to go."

Samara nodded. "Sure. But also..." She leaned forward. "It's fair for you to feel like you have no stake in saving Tsava. Ran Corp existed long before you were here, and it's unreasonable to expect you to take responsibility for destroying them. Even though the Fengul Queen clearly had some reason for making you Perceiver, nobody can choose a savior for an entire world. Nobody has more or less responsibility for this plane than anyone else. But if I find out that the Queen *did* intend for you to save Tsava from Ran Corp, I'm going to send someone to pick you up. Savvy?"

The computer spirit's words echoed in her memory: *It's everyone's job to save the world, not just yours. But it's more my job and yours than, say, the average orex.* Hattie hesitated, and then nodded.

"I hope it doesn't come to that," Samara mused. "It's embarrassing to be saved by a child. Can you imagine what people are going to say about En Law? A teenager took him out."

"I'm twelve," Hattie admitted. "I lied on the paper so he wouldn't have an excuse to fire me. You have to be fifteen to work for Ran Corp."

The three orex looked stunned.

"Smart. Sure you don't want to join the Alate? I'll make you a cell leader," said Samara.

At last, she smiled an out-of-use smile. "I'll think about it."

Ven insisted on escorting her to her room. Jack and Limn were talking outside her bedroom as they stepped off the elevator. Jack limped to them and opened his mouth, but Ven cut him off. "What are you doing outside your cell?"

"Rostom said I should go free. You want to complain, go to him." Ven and Jack had ugly expressions as they sized each other up. Limn hovered between them, an angry red light. "Quit fighting! You're worse than worms. Rostom's cool with everything. Why can't you be?"

Ven sniffed. "I don't answer to you. Please move elsewhere."

"We want to talk to Hattie, our *friend*," said Limn. "Are you feeling up to it, Hattie?"

She didn't, but also couldn't stand being alone right then. "Yeah, I'm okay."

Ven's face puckered in disapproval as he leaned against the doorframe. "I want to talk, too," he said stubbornly.

"Fine." Jack slapped a newspaper on the nightstand. The headline read:

Lawless: Prominent Ran Corp Officer Captured by the Alate.

"Talk," Jack said. "Where's Creon, Jane, and Ko?"

"Ko is downstairs, napping in the dungeon," said Ven smugly. "Happy and healthy. Jane vanished, thank Mota, and so has Creon. May Mota bless us again to find him. Why are you interrogating me, when you're the one who should be in prison?"

"We told you why," Limn growled, flaring.

"Ah, but—"

"Ven, shut up already," Hattie snapped. They jumped when she spoke. "You sound like En Law. Can't we talk about something else?"

Limn dimmed and became his normal brightness. "Sure. This is your party."

"This is the worst party I've ever been to." But she smiled.

"All of the parties involving orex are your worst parties." Jack ticked his next words off on his fingers. "Neighborhood welcoming party, everyone captured by En Law. Fengul Queen welcoming party, she dies, you become Perceiver. This party... you're leaving."

Paradoxically, she had accepted returning to Tsava before she accepted she was returning to Earth. "But what are you guys doing? Are you going home?"

"I'm going to dig through Baba's closet until I find the Atlas," Limn replied. "I can't go home without it. My dad is the sun." Irresistibly, Hattie swiveled around to look out the window. The sun shone white in the cloud-brushed sky. Limn floated to the window and looked out as well, wistfully. "One of a thousand sons of the sun, so don't get too excited. Anyway, when I get back the Atlas, I'm going to give it to Dad, tell everyone about my adventures, and go take a nap. And I will never leave Cosmos Country again for anything, ever."

"I can't believe you're not a lantern spirit," said Hattie, looking at him with fresh eyes. "Why are you in a lantern?"

"The terrestrial atmosphere makes me nauseous. It's like a reverse space suit. A Tsava suit. A Tsuit?"

Hattie asked him, "Wait, how did En Law get the Atlas? Where's Cosmos Country? Why can't your dad get it? How did you come to Tsava?"

"Those are excellent questions," Limn said. "And I won't answer them. The end."

Hattie groaned, "What? Come on!"

"Answer the Perceiver!" Ven snapped.

"The Perceiver should bow to the 100th Prince of Stars," said Limn loftily, grinning.

"It's not like you're the only prince in the room," Jack snapped.

"Ven's a prince?" Hattie asked, forgetting.

"Not him, me! Remember?"

"Oh yeah."

"Why are there so many royal figures in Tsava?" Limn asked no one in particular. "Easy. Tons of tiny kingdoms with two-digit populations headed by orex who want to sound fancy. If you're smart about it, you can become royalty easy-cheesy. Are you royalty, Hattie?"

"No, my family is middle-class."

"Then by the power vested in me, I proclaim you Duchess of Asteroid #78013. There. The Perceiver is now royal. I just need to find a piece of paper and sign it."

"Wait!" Ven leapt to his feet. "That may be what we need to make the Perceiver legitimate in the eyes of the people!"

"*No*," they all said together.

"This is not anything you would understand. Perhaps, if we say she is the Queen of Earth..."

"Can I go to Earth through the motaspace portal?" Limn asked, cutting Ven off. "Maybe I can cross and visit you! And I can go to your world and see all the cool stuff you've got! You've got cool stuff, right?"

"Earth's all right," she said, smiling. She realized almost immediately that wasn't true. Earth was amazing, and she missed it. "I can take you to the convenience store. It doesn't look anything like the ones here. And my new house."

"Like Baba?"

"When you return to Tsava," Ven handed her a card with a design on it, "write this on a tag and contact me."

"Oh, metacards!" Limn flared. "Wait, someone give me a blank."

Jack tore a blank neatly in two and dropped it through the lid atop Limn's body. "Have you seen one of these?" he asked. "Get a blank and make like you're trying to activate a design. Make sure your thumb is on the paper. What will happen is..." He held out his half and showed her that his black thumbprint had appeared on the paper. "Write a message on it, and when you activate it, I'll get the message here."

"And mine." Limn's lid flipped and a burning scrap of paper spit out and sizzled on the carpet. "Oops. Do it again."

* * *

That evening, Hattie, Jack, and Limn, along with Rostom and Ven, hiked to the blackwater pool. Her old clothes were slightly dirtier and smaller than she remembered, but they felt good to wear. It seemed unreal to be leaving. What if she woke up and found that none of it had happened? Or woke up and realized she'd always been in Tsava and would need to get to work soon? She clutched the tags in her pockets to reassure herself she had them until Ven gave her a quizzical look.

"I will come back," she said without warning as they hiked.

"Yes, but when?" Ven asked.

"When I know everyone is all right."

"How long will that take?"

"Until I'm sure." But she wasn't sure already, so what did that mean for the future?

The party reached the blackwater pool. A school of Kometa twinkled in the water.

"If you guys need anything," Hattie said, trying to sound cheery. "Jack knows where I live."

Jack's face looked as wet and crumpled as a used tissue. "But I don't have the ship." His voice caught.

"She said she'll be back. Quit being such a baby." Limn's face wobbled with emotion.

Hattie was about to cry, too. Tears pooled at the surface, but she managed to choke out, "Goodbye!" As she jumped into the pool, the same silver crash of bubbles, and the clearing fizz revealed the depths. Kometa melted into one fish and circled around her. They left the light behind. Closing their eyes would have made no difference to what they saw.

"How do you know where to go?" Hattie asked. "In case I need to come back and you're not here."

I am always here, Kometa replied. *But if you would like to know...listen.*

Hattie held her breath and closed her eyes. Faintly, she heard a *ping* followed by an echo. Again-again. Again-again. Closer together by the barest seconds each time.

"Sonar!"

You can do it too, if you practice. On Earth, learn to signal. Your friends will be happy when you return.

"I will." Her vision blurred. Tears traced her temples and brushed along her hair, pearling in the strands.

Far away, the ultra-black lightened. Soon it had an unmistakable grey shaft. It eased further and the bottoms of leaves floated on a circle of light. Her head broke through them into open space. Earth air dove into her lungs, and she breathed out the last of Tsava's atmosphere. She'd surfaced in the same fountain in the same park. The grass crunched as she climbed out of the murky water. The baked air smelled of mowed lawn and dust. It was the end of summer.

"I have to go home," she told Kometa. "How can I call you? Can you tell everyone I got home okay?"

Sonorra knows how to call me if you want to talk, Kometa replied. *The motaspace is so dull without you.*

"Thank you! For everything!"

Hattie ran away from the fountain and down the road. Her feet beat the dust from the path, and dirt rose to her ankles as the water from the fountain dried on her dress—the same dress she'd worn to the party. Would Mom and Dad notice? And she'd freed everyone the day before. Did that mean they'd been waiting for her for a whole day and night?

The neighborhood's lawns gleamed with water from sprinklers. A few yellow windows blinked as their occupants passed in front of them. Hattie ran up the gravel drive and to the front door with its diamond window alight. As her hand touched the knob she heard her mom say, "I don't know where she is. She's been missing for hours now! Does she have friends?"

"Cassie, she has tons of friends."

"I mean ones we can call. Maybe..."

Hattie opened the door. Her parents sat at the dining table but rose as she came in shyly. Her mom's face changed from worry to anger in a breath. "Hattie Anne Flores. Do you know how late it is?"

Hattie burst into tears and ran to her. Her mom was warm and solid, and stiff at first, but softened as her hands lay on Hattie's head. "Hattie, what's wrong?" Hattie let go of her and hugged her dad too, before crying even harder.

"You're all wet!" He exclaimed, and peeled a leaf off her head. "Did you fall in a lake?"

"Got lost," Hattie sobbed. "Forest."

"Aw, you're okay now." His big rough hands rubbed her back. "It's okay. You're safe."

"Are you both okay?" she asked in a muffled voice. "I feel like I haven't seen you in a while."

"You weren't out there that long!" He laughed. "But now that you mention it, I feel like I just woke up. It's been a long day at the office, but I always wake up when I see you."

"It's funny, but I feel like I just woke up, too," her mom admitted. She frowned and tugged Hattie's antlers. "What are these?"

"Her hair?" Dad joked. He ruffled her hair where her antlers were. *But he couldn't have.* Yet Hattie could feel his hands pass through them. "You need a bath, squirt." She saw her mom's stunned face. Her mom reached out to touch her hair once more and ran into the antlers again, solid under her fingers only. How could Mom see them but Dad couldn't? And how could she have touched them?

"Bath and bed." Her dad pushed her toward the bathroom. "And before the summer ends, I'm going to show you how not to get lost in the woods."

"Yes, bath and bed. We'll talk in the morning." Her mom's expression was uncanny.

"Goodnight," Hattie said to them both and climbed the stairs, full of dawning fear.

Thank you for reading!
If you loved *Perceiver*, please consider leaving a review and
signing up for my newsletter to find out about future releases.

Stay tuned for book two in
The Perceiver Trilogy
coming soon!

ACKNOWLEDGEMENTS

I am always surprised by how many people are named on the acknowledgements pages in other books, but it is now my turn to be humbled. To the crowd who shaped *Perceiver* into the work you now hold in your hands: *thank you* expresses an emotion so deep and broad that it's miraculous it only takes two words to say.

To Nevermore Edits: While none of the members of this fine writing group saw *Perceiver* before it was published, your encouragement and comments on my other stories honed my red pen to cut lightly, deeply, surely.

To Three Point Author Services, specifically Bre Lockhart and Andrea Neil: Your candor and insights manifested a *book!*

To Angela Cordova: You were the first person to read *Perceiver* all the way through, and your excitement gave me the courage to keep going.

To Lauren Vogel: You caught things nobody else did and helped the story grow beyond its tame boundaries.

To Joyce Chen: Your comments for the opening chapters refined them to be their best versions. I am grateful you took the time to help me while juggling classes and work.

To the creative writing classes of Augustus Rose, Vu Tran,

and Rachel DeWoskin at the University of Chicago, which helped me polish the first chapters of Perceiver: The ideas and learning I took away from your classes didn't just make Perceiver better, they made all of my stories better. I became a more discriminating writer and a more omnivorous reader, I made life-long friends, and I glimpsed what a professional writing career looks like. Your classes and the young, ambitious writers in them made an impression on me. I wish all of you luck in your own writing!

To the girls from the second floor dorm of the Oklahoma School for Science and Mathematics, especially Mary Sun, Stephanie Lee, Lane Abernathy: You are amazing, and I have no doubt you will go on to do great things. Thank you for reading the earliest pages of the story. I can't imagine they were much fun to read at that point.

To my parents Maria and Gary Fuller: Thank you for taking me to bookstores, to writing classes, to summer camps on poetry, to buying me books, and for the many, many acts of love I didn't recognize or notice that carried me to the finish line

To the authors who inspired me to begin, Ray Bradbury, John Steinbeck, J. K. Rowling, Phillip Pullman, Nancy Farmer, Jonathan Stroud, Daniel Handler, D. M. Cornish, Cynthia Voigt, Jane Yolen, Beverly Cleary, and many, many more: We become people through other people. I don't know who I would be without you.

ABOUT THE AUTHOR

E.C. Fuller, aka Erin Fuller, grew up in small town Oklahoma, not too far from her current home in Tulsa. Along with awards and mentions in multiple local writing contests, Erin's work has also been featured in *The Tulsa Review* and is forthcoming in *Metaphorosis*. Influenced by everything from Russian fairytales and Lemony Snicket to *Adventure Time* and *Legends of Zelda*, Erin aims to create immersive fantasy worlds that grab the reader and keep them guessing until the end.

Want to know when the next book drops?
Sign up for her newsletter on
Erin's blog
www.ecfullersbooks.com

Want to support future books? You can always send Erin a
coffee on
Ko-Fi
ko-fi.com/ecfuller

To find out what else Erin is up to, check her out at the
following online locations.
Amazon Author Page
www.amazon.com/E-C-Fuller/e/B0722NQXDK
Twitter
@birdshapedhat
Reddit

reddit.com/u/orangebird

And as always, reviews are appreciated!
Goodreads
www.goodreads.com/goodreadscomecfuller
Amazon
www.amazon.com/gp/product/B097XM5KVQ

www.ingramcontent.com/pod-product-compliance
Lightning Source LLC
Chambersburg PA
CBHW020556180626
46810CB00007B/2531